THE NEW JEDI ORDER

EDGE OF VICTORY I
CONQUEST

Also by Greg Keyes

THE NEW JEDI ORDER

EDGE OF VICTORY I
CONQUEST

GREG KEYES

ARROW

Published in the United Kingdom in 2001 by
Arrow Books

1 3 5 7 10 8 6 4 2

Copyright © Lucasfilm Ltd. & ™ 2001

The right of Greg Keyes to be identified as the author
of this work has been asserted by him in accordance
with the Copyright, Designs and Patents Act, 1988

First published in the United Kingdom in 2001 by Arrow

Arrow Books
The Random House Group Limited
20 Vauxhall Bridge Road, London, SW1V 2SA

Random House Australia (Pty) Limited
20 Alfred Street, Milsons Point, Sydney,
New South Wales 2061, Australia

Random House New Zealand Limited
18 Poland Road, Glenfield
Auckland 10, New Zealand

Random House (Pty) Limited
Endulini, 5a Jubilee Road,
Parktown 2193, South Africa

The Random House Group Limited Reg. No. 954009

www.starwars.com
www.starwarskids.com
www.randomhouse.co.uk

A CIP catalogue record for this book is available from the British Library

Papers used by Random House are natural,
recyclable products made from wood grown in sustainable
forests. The manufacturing processes conform to
the environmental regulations of the country of origin

Printed and bound in Germany by
Elsnerdruck, Berlin

ISBN 0 09 941028 1

For Charlie Sheffer
And all of my friends at Salle Auriol Seattle

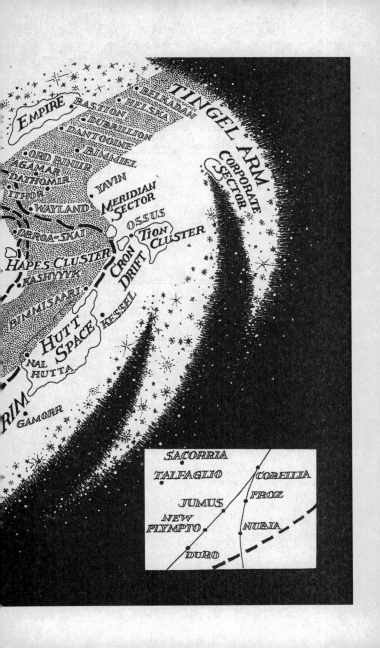

STAR WARS: THE NOVELS

44 YEARS BEFORE
STAR WARS: A New Hope

Jedi Apprentice Series

32 YEARS BEFORE
STAR WARS: A New Hope

Star Wars:
Episode I
The Phantom Menace

22 YEARS BEFORE
STAR WARS: A New Hope

Star Wars:
Episode II

20 YEARS BEFORE
STAR WARS: A New Hope

Star Wars:
Episode III

3 YEARS AFTER
STAR WARS: A New Hope

Star Wars:
Episode V
The Empire Strikes Back
Tales of the Bounty
Hunters

3.5 YEARS AFTER
STAR WARS: A New Hope

Shadows of the Empire

4 YEARS AFTER
STAR WARS: A New Hope

Star Wars: Episode VI
Return of the Jedi
Tales from Jabba's Palace
THE BOUNTY HUNTER WARS:
The Mandalorian Armor
Slave Ship
Hard Merchandise
The Truce at Bakura

6.5–7.5 YEARS AFTER
STAR WARS: A New Hope

X-Wing: Rogue Squadron
X-Wing: Wedge's Gamble
X-Wing: The Krytos Trap
X-Wing: The Bacta War
X-Wing: Wraith Squadron
X-Wing: Iron Fist
X-Wing: Solo Command

14 YEARS AFTER
STAR WARS: A New Hope

The Crystal Star

16–17 YEARS AFTER
STAR WARS: A New Hope

THE BLACK FLEET CRISIS
TRILOGY:
Before the Storm
Shield of Lies
Tyrant's Test

17 YEARS AFTER
STAR WARS: A New Hope

The New Rebellion

18 YEARS AFTER
STAR WARS: A New Hope

THE CORELLIAN TRILOGY:
Ambush at Corellia
Assault at Selonia
Showdown at Centerpoint

— What Happened When?

10–0 YEARS BEFORE
STAR WARS: A New Hope

THE HAN SOLO TRILOGY:
The Paradise Snare
The Hutt Gambit
Rebel Dawn

APPROX. 5–2 YRS. BEFORE
STAR WARS: A New Hope

THE ADVENTURES OF LANDO CALRISSIAN:
Lando Calrissian and the Mind-harp of Sharu
Lando Calrissian and the Flamewind of Oseon
Lando Calrissian and the Star-cave of ThonBoka

THE HAN SOLO ADVENTURES:
Han Solo at Stars' End
Han Solo's Revenge
Han Solo and the Lost Legacy

STAR WARS: Episode IV A New Hope

0–3 YEARS AFTER
STAR WARS: A New Hope

Tales from the
Mos Eisley Cantina
Splinter of the Mind's Eye

8 YEARS AFTER
STAR WARS: A New Hope

The Courtship of Princess Leia

9 YEARS AFTER
STAR WARS: A New Hope

THE THRAWN TRILOGY:
Heir to the Empire
Dark Force Rising
The Last Command
X-Wing: Isard's Revenge

11 YEARS AFTER
STAR WARS: A New Hope

THE JEDI ACADEMY TRILOGY:
Jedi Search
Dark Apprentice
Champions of the Force
I, Jedi

12–13 YEARS AFTER
STAR WARS: A New Hope

Children of the Jedi
Darksaber
Planet of Twilight
X-Wing: Starfighters of Adumar

19 YEARS AFTER
STAR WARS: A New Hope

THE HAND OF THRAWN DUOLOGY:
Specter of the Past
Vision of the Future

22 YEARS AFTER
STAR WARS: A New Hope

JUNIOR JEDI KNIGHTS:
The Golden Globe
Lyric's World
Promises
Anakin's Quest
Vader's Fortress
Kenobi's Blade

23–24 YEARS AFTER
STAR WARS: A New Hope

YOUNG JEDI KNIGHTS:
Heirs of the Force
Shadow Academy
The Lost Ones
Lightsabers
The Darkest Knight
Jedi Under Siege
Shards of Alderaan
Diversity Alliance
Delusions of Grandeur
Jedi Bounty
The Emperor's Plague
Return to Ord Mantell
Trouble on Cloud City
Crisis at Crystal Reef

25 YEARS AFTER
STAR WARS: A New Hope

THE NEW JEDI ORDER:
Vector Prime

Dark Tide I: Onslaught
Dark Tide II: Ruin

Agents of Chaos I: Hero's Trial

Agents of Chaos II: Jedi Eclipse

Balance Point

Edge of Victory I: Conquest

Edge of Victory II: Rebirth

ACKNOWLEDGMENTS

Many thanks to Shelly Shapiro, Sue Rostoni, Jim Luceno, and Troy Denning for their help during the writing of the manuscript. To Mike Stackpole, for his advice and assurance this would be a fun ride, and Kris Boldis who gave that a strong second. Thanks to Chris Cerasi, Leland Chee, Ben Harper, Enrique Guerrero, and Lisa Collins for meticulous fact-checking and editing.

DRAMATIS PERSONAE

Anakin Solo; Jedi Knight (male human)
Ikrit; Jedi Master (male unknown)
Imsatad; Peace Brigade captain (male human)
Jacen Solo; Jedi Knight (male human)
Jaina Solo; Jedi Knight (female human)
Kam Solusar; Jedi Master (male human)
Luke Skywalker; Jedi Master (male human)
Mara Jade Skywalker; Jedi Knight (female human)
Mezhan Kwaad; master shaper (female Yuuzhan Vong)
Nen Yim; shaper adept (female Yuuzhan Vong)
Remis Vehn; Peace Brigade pilot (male human)
Sannah; Jedi student (female Melodie)
Shada D'ukal; Talon Karrde's business associate (female human)
Tahiri Veila; Jedi student (female human)
Talon Karrde; Independent Information Broker (male human)
Tionne; Jedi Knight (female human)
Tsaak Vootuh; commander (male Yuuzhan Vong)
Tsavong Lah; warmaster (male Yuuzhan Vong)
Uunu; Shamed One (female Yuuzhan Vong)
Valin Horn; Jedi student (male human)
Vua Rapuung; warrior (male Yuuzhan Vong)
Yal Phaath; master shaper (male Yuuzhan Vong)

PROLOGUE

Dorsk 82 ducked behind the stone steps of the quay, just in time to dodge a blaster bolt from across the water.

"Hurry on board my ship," he told his charges. "They've found us again."

That was an understatement. Approaching along the tide embankment was a mob of around fifty Aqualish, jostling each other and shouting hoarsely. Most carried makeshift weapons—clubs, knives, rocks—but a few had force pikes and at least one had a blaster, as the smoking score on the quay testified.

"Join us, Master Dorsk," The 3D-4 protocol droid close behind him pleaded.

Dorsk nodded his bald yellow-and-green mottled head. "Soon. I have to slow their progress across the causeway, to give everyone time to board."

"You can't hold them off yourself, sir."

"I think I can. Besides, I need to try to talk to them. This is senseless."

"They've gone mad," the droid said. "They're destroying droids all over the city!"

"They aren't mad," Dorsk averred. "They're just frightened. The Yuuzhan Vong are on Ando, and may well conquer the planet."

"But why destroy droids, Master Dorsk?"

"Because the Yuuzhan Vong hate machines," the Khommite clone answered. "They consider them to be abominations."

"How can that be? Why would they believe that?"

"I don't know," Dorsk replied. "But it is a fact. Go, please. Help the others board. My pilot is already at the controls with the flight instructions, so even if something happens to me, you'll be okay."

Still the droid hesitated. "Why are you helping us, sir?"

"Because I am a Jedi and I can. You don't deserve destruction."

"Neither do you, sir."

"Thank you. I do not intend to be destroyed."

He raised his head up again as the droid finally followed its clattering, whirring comrades to the waiting ship.

The crowd had reached the ancient stone causeway connecting the atoll-city of Imthitill to the abandoned fishing platform Dorsk now crouched on. It seemed they were all on foot, which meant all he had to do was prevent them from crossing the causeway.

With a single bound, Dorsk propelled his thin body up onto the causeway, forsaking the cover of the step down to the fishing platform. Lightsaber held at his side, he watched the mob approach.

I am a Jedi, he thought to himself. *A Jedi knows no fear.*

Almost surprisingly, he didn't. His training with Master Skywalker had been fretted with attacks of panic. Dorsk was the eighty-second clone of the first Khommite to bear his name. He'd grown up on a world well satisfied with its own peculiar kind of perfection, and that hadn't prepared him for danger, or fear, or even the unexpected. There were times when he believed he could never be as brave as the other Jedi students or live up to the standard set by his celebrated predecessor, Dorsk 81.

But watching the large, dark eyes of the crowd that was drawing close, he felt nothing but a gentle sadness that they had been driven to this. They must fear the Yuuzhan Vong terribly.

The destruction of droids had begun small, but in a

few days had become a planetwide epidemic. The government of Ando—such as it was—neither condoned nor condemned the brutality, so long as no nondroids were killed or injured in the mess. Without help from the police, Dorsk 82 was the only chance the droids had, and he didn't plan to fail them. He had already failed too many.

He ignited his lightsaber and for an instant saw everything around him at once. The setting sun had spilled a glorious slick of orange fire into the ocean and lit the high-piled clouds on the horizon into castles of flame. Higher, the sky faded to gold-laced jade and aquamarine and then the pale of night. The lights in the cylindrical white towers of Imthitill were winking on, one by one, and so, too, were the lights of the fishing platforms floating in the deeps, spangling the ocean with lonely constellations.

His own planet hadn't any such untamed spectacles. Khomm's weather was as predictable and homogenous as its people. Likely he, Dorsk 82, was the only person of his entire species who could appreciate this sky, or the iron-dressed waves of the sea.

Salt air buffeted around him. He lifted his chin. Somehow, after all of these years, he felt he was doing the thing he had dreamed about at last.

One of the Aqualish stepped before the rest. He was smaller than many, his tusks incised in the local style. He wore the dappled slicksuit of a tug worker.

"Move, Jedi," he commanded. "These droids are none of your business."

"These droids are under my protection," Dorsk replied calmly.

"They are not yours to protect, Jedi," the Aqualish shouted back. "If their owners do not object, you have no say in the matter."

"I must disagree," Dorsk replied. "I also plead with you to see reason. Destroying the droids will not appease the Yuuzhan Vong. They are beyond appeasing."

"That's our business," the self-appointed spokesman of the group shouted. "This isn't your planet, Jedi. It's ours. Didn't you hear? The Yuuzhan Vong just took Duro."

"I had not heard," Dorsk replied. "Nor does it matter. Go back to your homes in peace. I don't want to hurt any of you. I'm taking these droids with me. You will not see them on Ando again. I swear it."

This time he saw the blaster lift—held by an Aqualish deep in the crowd. Dorsk grasped it with the Force and whisked it through the air until it came to rest in his left hand.

"Please," he said.

For a long moment, neither side moved. Dorsk felt them wavering, but the Aqualish were a stubborn and violent lot. It was easier to stop a nova once it had started than to calm a whole mob of Aqualish.

He heard a sudden hum and saw a security speeder approaching. He stepped back and allowed it to settle between him and the crowd. He did not relax his guard, even when eight Aqualish troopers in bright yellow body armor piled out and started motioning the crowd back.

The officer stepped forward. "What's going on here?" he asked.

Dorsk motioned slightly with his head. "These people are intent on destroying a group of droids. I am protecting them."

"I see," the officer said. "That's your ship?"

"Yes."

"Are there any other Jedi on board?"

"No."

"Very well." The officer spoke into a small comlink, too low for Dorsk to hear, but the clone suddenly sensed what was about to happen.

"No!" he shouted. He spun on his heel and ran toward the ship, but even as he did so, several flares of light too bright to look upon struck it. A column of white flame leapt toward the sky, carrying with it the fragments and ions that had once been his ship, his pilot Hhen, and thirty-eight droids.

Dorsk was still watching, mouth working soundlessly at the pointless destruction, when the stun baton hit him.

He fell, turning that same uncomprehending stare on his attackers. The officer he'd been speaking to stood there, holding the baton.

"Stay down, Jedi, and you'll live."

"What? Why? . . ."

"I suppose you haven't heard. The Yuuzhan Vong have proposed a peace. They will stop their conquest with Duro, and leave Ando, so long as we turn you Jedi over to them. They will take you dead, but they would rather have you alive."

Dorsk 82 summoned the Force, washed away the pain and paralysis of the blast, and stood.

"Drop your lightsaber, Jedi," the officer said.

Dorsk straightened himself and looked into the muzzles of the blasters. He dropped the one he had taken from the crowd. He hooked his lightsaber onto his belt.

"I will not fight you," he said.

"Fine. Then you won't mind surrendering your weapon."

"The Yuuzhan Vong will not keep their word. Their only desire is that *you* rid them of their worst enemies for them. With the Jedi out of the way, they will come for you. If you betray me, you betray yourselves."

"We'll take that chance," the officer said.

"I'm walking away from here," Dorsk said with a slight wave of his hand. "You will not stop me."

"No," the officer said. "I won't stop you."

"Nor will any of the rest of you."

Dorsk 82 started forward. One of the troopers, more strong willed than the others, lifted his blaster in a shaking hand.

"Don't," Dorsk pleaded. He held out his hand.

The blaster bolt grazed Dorsk in the palm, and he stepped back, but the action shook the other troopers from the suggestion he had placed in their minds. The next shot seared a hole through his thigh. He dropped to his knees.

"Stop," the officer said. "No more mind tricks."

Dorsk torturously pushed himself back to his feet. He took another step forward.

I am a Jedi. A Jedi knows no fear.

The dusk lit with blasterfire.

Help.

The automated signal was weak but faint.

"Got 'em," Uldir said. "I told you, didn't I?"

Dacholder, his copilot, clapped him on the back. "No doubt about it, lad. You're the best rescue flier in the unit."

"I have good hunches, that's all," Uldir replied. "See if you can contact them."

"Sure thing." Dacholder activated the comm unit. "*Pride of Thela* to injured vessel. Injured vessel, can you hear me?"

The answer was static—but modulated static.

"They're trying to answer," Uldir said. "Their comm unit must be damaged. Maybe when we get closer. Hey, there they are now."

Long-range sensors showed a craft dead in space, medium transport–sized. It ought to be the *Winning Hand*, a pleasure craft that had made a jump from the Corellian sector and vanished somewhere en route. The *Hand*'s jump had taken her dangerously near Obroa-skai, which was now in Yuuzhan Vong space. Though they hadn't moved overtly on any planets since the fall of Duro, the Yuuzhan Vong had been setting up occasional dovin basal interdictors near their space, yanking from hyperspace ships bold or careless enough to approach their somewhat fuzzy borders. Most were never found again, but the *Winning Hand* had managed to get off a garbled transmission placing them along the Perlemian Trade Route not far from the Meridian sector. That was still a lot of space, but search and rescue had been Uldir's business for the past six years. At the ripe old age of twenty-two, he was one of the best fliers in the corps.

"Dead-on," Dacholder said. "Congratulations. Again."

"Thanks, Doc."

Dacholder was a little older than Uldir, his hair prematurely shot with gray and receding from his forehead so fast Uldir could almost see it redshifting. He wasn't a great pilot, but he was competent enough, and Uldir liked him.

"Say, Uldir," Dacholder began, in an inquisitive tone, "I never asked you—when the Vong came along, why didn't you request transfer to a military unit? The way you fly, you could be an ace."

"Too hot for me," Uldir replied.

"Carbon flush. Rescue is twice the danger with a tenth of the firepower. During the fall of Duro I heard you picked up three stranded pilots under fire from four coralskippers with no backup at all."

"I was pretty lucky," Uldir demurred.

"You sure it's not something else?"

"What do you mean?"

"Well, I heard you attended that Jedi academy of Skywalker's."

Uldir could only laugh at that. "*Attended* isn't the right word. I was there, caused a systemful of trouble in a real short time, and had no talent for the Jedi thing at all. Still, maybe you're right. I guess I figured if I couldn't be a Jedi, I could at least emulate 'em. Search and rescue seemed like the best way. And we're needed in wartime just as much as the flyboys."

"And you don't have to kill."

Uldir shrugged. "That sounds about right. When did you start thinking about me so much, Doc?" He flipped the magnification up on the visual. "Look there," he said, as the derelict ship came on-screen. "She doesn't look half bad. Maybe they didn't have any casualties."

"We can only hope," Dacholder said.

"See anything else out there?"

"Not a thing," Dacholder replied.

"That's good. We're outside of Yuuzhan Vong space, but not *that* far outside. Even with all the tinkering I've done on this baby, I don't want to run up against one of their interdictors."

"I noticed you coaxed another twenty percent from the inertial dampeners. Good work."

"Shows what you can do when you've got no life but the service, I guess," Uldir replied. He adjusted their trajectory a bit. "Looks like they're limping, but life support seems to be okay."

"Yeah."

Uldir gave his copilot a sidewise glance. Doc seemed a little nervous, which was odd. Not that he had the steadiest nerves in the unit, but he was no coward. Maybe it was because they were out so far without backup. The war had forced everyone to spread resources thin.

"Uldir," Dacholder asked suddenly.

"Uh-huh?"

"Do you think we can beat them? The Vong?"

"That's a crazy question," Uldir replied. "Of course we can. They just got a jump on us, that's all. You'll see. Once the military gets its act together and brings the Jedi into the equation, the Yuuzhan Vong will be on the run soon enough."

Dacholder was silent for a moment, watching the ship grow larger.

"I don't think we can beat them," he said softly. "I don't think we ought to be fighting them in the first place."

"What do you mean?"

"Look, they've kicked our butts right from the start. If

they make another push, they'll have Coruscant before you can blink."

"That's pretty defeatist."

"It's pretty realistic."

"Then what?" Uldir asked, a little heatedly. "You think we ought to surrender?"

"We don't have to do that, either. Look, there aren't that many Vong. They already have as many planets as they need, they've said so themselves. They haven't made a move since Duro, and they won't—"

The console got Uldir's attention, so he didn't hear the rest of what Dacholder was saying. "Hold that thought," he snapped, "and hail that ship."

"Why?"

"Because she's playing dead, that's why. All her systems just came on, and she's trying for a tractor lock." He quickly began evasive maneuvers.

"Let her have us, Uldir," Dacholder said. "Don't make me use this."

To Uldir's astonishment, *this* was a blaster his copilot had pointed at his head.

"Doc? What are you doing?"

"Sorry, lad. I like you, I really do. I hate doing this like drinking acid, but it has to be done."

"What has to be done?"

"The Yuuzhan Vong warmaster was very specific. He wants *all* of the Jedi."

"Doc, you fool, I'm *not* a Jedi."

"There's a list, Uldir, and you're on it."

"List? What list? Whose list? Not a Yuuzhan Vong list, because they couldn't possibly know who went to the academy and who didn't."

"That's right. Some of us are in high places."

Uldir narrowed his eyes. "*Us?* You're Peace Brigade, Doc?"

"Yes."

"Of all the—" Uldir stopped. "And that ship. That's what's going to take me to the Yuuzhan Vong, isn't it?"

"It wasn't my idea, lad. I'm just following orders. Now, slow her down like a good boy, and let them have their lock."

"I'm not a Jedi," Uldir repeated.

"No? I always thought your hunches were a little too good. You seem to see things before they come."

"Right. Like *this*, you mean?"

"Doesn't matter anyway. What matters is *they* think you're Jedi. And I'll bet you know things they would be interested in."

"Don't do this, Doc, I'm begging you. You know what the Yuuzhan Vong do to their victims. How can you even think of making deals with them? They destroyed Ithor, for space's sake!"

"The way I hear it, a Jedi named Corran Horn was responsible for that."

"Bantha fodder."

Dacholder sighed. "I'm giving you a three-count, Uldir."

"Don't, Doc."

"One."

"I won't go with them."

"Two."

"Please."

"Thr—"

He never got it out. By the time he got to the end of the word, Dacholder was in vacuum, twenty meters away and still accelerating. Uldir sealed the cockpit back up, ears popping and face tingling from his brief brush with nothingness. He glanced at the missing acceleration couch.

"I'm sorry, Doc," he said. "You didn't leave me much of a choice. I guess it's just as well I never told you about *all* of my modifications."

He opened the throttle, gaining quick ground on the

yacht. By the time they overcame their inertia and started to gain, Uldir had punched into lightspeed and was gone.

To where, he didn't know. If he survived the hyperspace jump, would he be safe?

And if *he* wasn't safe, what about the real Jedi? His friends from the academy?

He couldn't hide from this. Master Skywalker had to know what was happening. He could think about himself after that was done.

Swilja Fenn tried to stay on her feet. Such a basic thing, standing. One rarely gave it a thought. But the long pursuit on Cujicor, copious blood loss, and a foul, cramped incarceration on a Peace Brigade ship rendered even such basic things a struggle. She drew on the Force for her strength and lashed her lekku in helplessness.

The Peace Brigade goons had dumped her, bound and half senseless, on some nameless moon and hauled gravity out of there. Not much later, the Yuuzhan Vong had shown up. They had cut away her bonds and then replaced them with a living, jellylike substance, all the while spitting at her in a language that seemed made entirely of curses.

After that, more travel in dark places and finally here, barely able to keep her feet under her, in a vast chamber that looked as if it had been carved inside of a chunk of raw meat. Smelled that way, too.

Swilja squinted at someone approaching from the murk and shadows at the far end of the room.

"What do you lylek-dung-grubbers want with me?" she snarled, momentarily forgetting her Jedi training.

The lapse got her a cuff in the face hard enough to knock her off her feet.

When she rose, *he* was standing over her.

The Yuuzhan Vong liked to scar themselves. They liked cut-up faces and tattoos, severed fingers and toes. The higher up the food chain they were, it seemed the less there was of them. Or at least, what had *started* as them, because they liked implants, too.

The Yuuzhan Vong standing above her must have been *way* up the food chain, because he looked like he had fallen into a bin of vibroblades. Scales the color of dried blood covered most of his body, and some sort of cloak hung from his shoulders. The latter twitched, slowly.

And like the other Yuuzhan Vong, he wasn't *there*. If he had been Twi'lek or human or Rodian, she might have stopped his heart with the Force or snapped his neck against the ceiling. Dark side or not, she would have done it and rid the galaxy of him forever.

She tried to do the next best thing—hurl herself at him and claw his eyes out. He was only a meter away; surely she could take just one of these gravel-maggots with her.

Unfortunately, the next best thing was exponentially less effective than the best. The same guard who had struck her a moment before lashed out faster than lightning, grabbing her by the lekku and yanking her back. He held her up to the monster confronting her.

"I know you," Swilja said, spitting out teeth and blood. "You're the one who called for our heads. Tsavong Lah."

"I am Warmaster Tsavong Lah," the monster confirmed.

She spat at him. The spittle struck his hand, but he ignored it, denying her even the minor victory of irritating him.

"I congratulate you on proving yourself worthy of honored sacrifice," Tsavong Lah said. "You are far more admirable than the cowering scum who delivered you to us. They will merely perish, when their time comes. We will not mock the gods by offering *them* in sacrifice." He suddenly showed more of the inside of his mouth than Swilja ever wanted to see. It might have been a grin or a sneer.

"If you know who I am," Tsavong Lah said, "you know what I want. You know *who* I want."

"I have no idea what you want. Given what I know of you it would probably make even a Hutt sick."

Tsavong Lah licked his lip and twisted his neck slightly. His eyes drilled at her.

"Help me find Jacen Solo," he said. "With your help, I will find him."

"Eat poodoo."

Tsavong Lah shredded a laugh through his teeth.

"It is not my job to convince you," he said. "I have specialists for that. And if you still cannot be convinced, there are others, many others. One day you will all embrace the truth—or death." With that he seemed to forget she existed. His eyes emptied of any sign that he saw her or had ever seen her, and he walked slowly away.

"You're wrong!" she screamed, as they dragged her from the chamber. "The Force is stronger than you. The Jedi will be your end, Tsavong Lah!"

But the warmaster didn't turn. His stride never broke.

An hour later, even Swilja didn't believe her brave words. She didn't even remember them. Nothing existed for her but pain, and eventually, not even that.

PART ONE

PRAXEUM

CHAPTER ONE

Luke Skywalker stood steady and straight before the gathered Jedi, his face composed and stronger than durasteel. The set of his shoulders, his precise gestures, the weight and timbre of each word he spoke all confirmed his confidence and control.

But Anakin Solo knew it was a lie. Anger and fear filled the chamber like a hundred atmospheres of pressure, and beneath that weight something in Master Skywalker crumpled. It felt like hope breaking. Anakin thought it was the worst thing he had ever felt, and he had felt some very bad things in his sixteen years.

The perception didn't last long. Nothing was broken, only bent, and whatever it was straightened, and Master Skywalker was again as strong and confident in the Force as to the eye. Anakin didn't think anyone else had noticed it.

But *he* had. The unshakable had shaken. It was something Anakin would never forget, another of the many things that had seemed eternal to him suddenly gone, another speeder zooming out from underneath his feet, leaving him flat on his back wondering what had happened. Hadn't he learned yet?

He forced himself to focus his ice-blue eyes on Master Skywalker, on that familiar age- and scar-roughened face. Beyond him, through a huge transparisteel window, flowed the never-ending light and life of Coruscant.

Against those cyclopean buildings and streaming trails of light, the Master seemed somehow frail or distracted.

Anakin distanced himself from his heartsickness by concentrating on his uncle's words.

"Kyp," Master Skywalker was saying, "I understand how you feel."

Kyp Durron was more honest than Master Skywalker, in some ways. The anger in his heart was no stranger to the expression on his face. If the Jedi were a planet, Master Skywalker stood at one pole, radiating calm. Kyp Durron stood at the other, fists clenched in fury.

Somewhere near the equator the planet was starting to pull apart.

Kyp took a step forward, running his hand through dark hair shot with silver. "Master Skywalker," he said, "I submit that you do *not* know how I feel. If you did, I would sense it in the Force. We all could. Instead, you hide your feelings from us."

"I never said I *felt* as you do," Luke said gently, "only that I understand."

"Ah." Kyp nodded, raising one finger and shaking it at Skywalker as if suddenly comprehending his point. "You mean you understand *intellectually*, but not with your heart! The Jedi you trained and inspired are hunted and killed throughout the galaxy, and you 'understand' it the way you might an equation? Your blood doesn't burn to *do* something about it?"

"Of course I want to do something about it," Luke said. "That's why I've called this meeting. But anger is not the answer. Attack is not the answer, and retribution most certainly is not. We are Jedi. We defend, we support."

"Defend who? Support what? Defend those beings you rescued from the atrocities of Palpatine? Support the New Republic and its good people? Shield the ones we have all shed blood for, time and again in the cause of peace and the greater good? These same cowardly beings who now defame us, deride us, and sacrifice us to their new Yuuzhan Vong masters? No one *wants* our help. They want us dead and forgotten. I say it's time we defend ourselves. Jedi for the Jedi!"

Applause smacked around the chamber—not deafening, but not trivial either. Anakin had to admit, Kyp made a certain amount of sense. Who could the Jedi trust now? Only other Jedi, it seemed.

"What would you have us do, then, Kyp?" Luke asked mildly.

"I told you. Defend ourselves. Fight evil, in whatever guise it takes. And we don't let the fight come to us, to catch us in our homes, asleep, with our children. We go out and find the enemy. Offense against evil *is* defense."

"In other words, you would have us all emulate what you and your dozen have been doing."

"I would have us emulate *you*, Master Skywalker—when you were battling the Empire."

Luke sighed. "I was young, then," he pointed out. "There was much I did not understand. Aggression is the way of the dark side."

Kyp rubbed his jaw, then smiled briefly. "And who should know better, Master Skywalker, than one who *did* turn to the dark side."

"Exactly," Luke replied. "I fell, though I knew better. Like you, Kyp. We both, in our own way, thought we were wise enough and nimble enough to walk on the laser beam and not get burned. We were both wrong."

"And yet we returned."

"Barely. With much help and love."

"Granted. But there were others. Kam Solusar, for instance, not to forget your own father—"

"What are you saying, Kyp? That it is easy to return from the dark side, and that justifies the risk?"

Kyp shrugged. "I'm saying the line between dark and light isn't as sharp as you're trying to make it, or exactly where you want to put it." He steepled his fingers beneath his chin, then shook them with an air of contemplation. "Master Skywalker, if a man attacks me with a lightsaber, may I defend with my own blade, that he not take my head off? Is that too aggressive?"

"Of course you may."

"And after I defend, may I press my attack? May I return the blow? If not, why are we Jedi *taught* lightsaber battle techniques? Why don't we learn only how to defend, and back off until the enemy has us in a corner and our arms grow tired, until an attack finally slips through our guard? Master Skywalker, sometimes the only defense *is* an attack. You know this as well as anyone."

"That's true, Kyp. I do."

"But you back down from the fight, Master Skywalker. You block and defend and never return the blow. Meanwhile the blades directed against you multiply. And you have begun to lose, Master Skywalker. One opportunity lost! And there lies Daeshara'cor, dead. Another slip in your defense, and Corran Horn is slandered as the destroyer of Ithor and driven to seclusion. Again an attack is neglected, and Wurth Skidder joins Daeshara'cor in death. And now a flurry of failures as a million blades swing at you, and there go Dorsk 82, and Seyyerin Itoklo, and Swilja Fenn, and who can count those we do not know of yet, or who will die tomorrow? *When* will you attack, Master Skywalker?"

"This is ridiculous!" a female voice exploded half a meter from Anakin's ear. It was his sister, Jaina, her face gone red with internal heat. "Maybe you don't hear all the news, running around playing hero with your squadron, Kyp. Maybe you've started feeling so self-important that you think your way is the only way. While you've been out there blazing your guns, Master Skywalker has been working quietly and hard to make sure things don't fall apart."

"Yes, and see how well that's gone," Kyp said. "Duro,

for instance. How many Jedi were involved there? Five? Six? And yet not one of you—Master Skywalker included—smelled the rank treachery of the situation until it was too late. Why didn't the Force guide you?" He paused and then smacked a fist into his palm for emphasis. "Because you were acting like *nursemaids*, not Jedi warriors! I've heard one of you even refused to use the Force." He looked significantly at Jaina's twin, who sat stone-faced halfway around the hall.

"You leave Jacen out of this," Jaina snarled.

"At least your brother was honest in his refusal to use his power," Kyp said. "Wrong, but honest, and in the end when he had to use it, he did. The rest of this group has no excuse for its ambivalence. If saving our galaxy from the Yuuzhan Vong is not a good enough cause to flex our true might, let self-preservation be!"

"Jedi for Jedi!" Octa Ramis shouted, still in the clutches of renewed grief over losing Daeshara'cor.

"It's both ourselves and the galaxy I'm trying to preserve," Luke said. "If we win the fight against the Yuuzhan Vong at the price of using dark-side powers, it will be no victory."

Kyp rolled his eyes and crossed his arms. "I knew it was a mistake to come here," he said. "Every second I waste talking with you is a torpedo I might be firing at the Yuuzhan Vong."

"If you knew that, why did you come?"

"Because I thought even you must see the pattern on the Huj mat by now, Master Skywalker. After months of doing nothing, of watching our numbers dwindle, of listening to the lies circulating about the Jedi from the Rim to the Core, I thought now, at last, you had decided it was time to act. I came, Master Skywalker, to hear you say enough is enough, to lead the Jedi, united, in a just cause. Instead I hear only the same vacillating I've grown tired of."

"On the contrary, Kyp. I called this meeting to make

some real decisions about how we should face this crisis."

"This isn't a crisis," Kyp sputtered. "It's a massacre. And I already know what to do. I've been doing it."

"The people are frightened, Kyp. They're living in a nightmare, just as we are. They only want to wake up."

"Yes. And in hopes of waking up, they feed the dream monsters whatever they ask for. Droids. Cities. Planets. Refugees. Now Jedi. By refusing to act against this treachery, Master Skywalker, you come dangerously near condoning it."

"Bantha fodder!" Jacen snapped, finally breaking his silence. "Master Skywalker hasn't been complacent. None of us has. But the sort of naked aggression you condone is—"

"Effective?" Kyp sneered.

"Is it?" Jacen challenged. "What have you and your squadron really accomplished? Harried a few Yuuzhan Vong supply ships? Meanwhile we've saved tens of thousands—"

"Saved them for what? So they can flee from planet to planet until there's nowhere else to go? Jacen Solo, who denied the Force, are you lecturing *me* on what is and isn't effective?"

"What isn't effective is this argument," Luke interjected. "We need calm. We need to think rationally."

"I'm not sure that's what we need at all," Kyp shot back. "Look where your *rational* policies have gotten us. We're alone, now, don't you all see that? Everyone has turned against us."

"You're overstating."

Anakin switched his gaze to the new speaker, Cilghal. The Mon Calamari's fishlike head bobbed as her bulbous eyes searched around the chamber.

"We still have many allies," Cilghal said, "in the senate and among the peoples of the New Republic."

"If by allies you mean people without the guts to actually turn us in, yes," Kyp said. "But wait a bit. More Jedi will be killed or captured. Stay here, meditate, and wait for them. I won't. I know what the fight is and where it is." With that he turned on his heel and started from the chamber.

"No!" Jaina whispered to Anakin. "If Kyp leaves, he'll take too many with him."

"So?" Anakin said. "Are you so sure he's wrong?"

"Of course I—" She stopped, paused, started again. "It won't help any of us if the Jedi split. We have to try to help Uncle Luke. Come on."

Jaina followed Kyp from the chamber. After a second or two, Anakin followed. The debate began again behind them, in much more muted terms.

Kyp turned as they approached. "Anakin, Jaina. What do you want?"

"To talk some sense into you," Jaina said.

"I have plenty of sense," Kyp said. "You two ought to know better. When did either of you flinch from battle? It's not like you two to sit while others fight."

"I haven't been," Jaina flared. "Neither has Anakin, or Uncle Luke, or—"

"Spare me. Jaina, I have the greatest respect for Master Skywalker. But he is *wrong*. I can't see the Yuuzhan Vong in the Force any more than he can, but I don't need that to know they're evil. To know they have to be stopped."

"Couldn't you just hear Uncle Luke out?"

"I did. He didn't say anything I was interested in, and he wasn't going to." Kyp shook his head. "Your uncle has changed. Something happens to Jedi Masters as they grow older in the Force. Something that isn't going to happen to me. They become so concerned with light and dark they can't *act*, but can only be acted upon. Like Obi-Wan Kenobi—rather than act himself, he allowed himself to be struck down, become one with the Force, so Luke could then take all of the moral risks."

"That's not how Uncle Luke tells it."

"Your uncle is too close to it. And now he's *become* Kenobi."

"What are you saying, exactly?" Jaina said. "That Uncle Luke is a coward?"

Kyp shrugged and flashed a little smile. "When it comes to his life, no. But when it comes to the Force . . ." He gestured with the back of his hand. "Ask your brother Jacen—seems to me he's going gray early, in that respect. The whole galaxy is falling apart around him, and he's dithering over theoretical philosophy."

"He did use the Force, though, as you pointed out," Jaina retorted.

"To save his mother's life, from what I heard, and almost not then. How long was she in a bacta tank?"

"But he *did* save her, and me, too."

"Of course. But would he have called on the Force to save some Duros he didn't know? Given the fact that he had ample opportunity to do so before that, the answer is self-evidently no. So it wasn't some universal respect for preserving life or anything of that sort that led him to break his self-imposed ban, was it?"

"No," Anakin murmured.

"Anakin!" Jaina snapped.

"It's true," Anakin replied. "I'm glad he did it, and I'm glad he hurt the warmaster, even if he did call for the heads of all the Jedi, but Kyp's right. If you and Mom hadn't been there . . ."

"Jacen was going through a hard time," Jaina said.

"Like the rest of us aren't," Anakin returned.

"I've got to go," Kyp told them. "Any time either of you wants to fly with me, find me. Other than that, I sincerely hope Master Skywalker comes around. I just can't wait for it. May the Force be with you."

They watched him go.

"I wish I didn't more than half think he was right,"

Jaina whispered. "I feel like I'm somehow betraying Uncle Luke."

Anakin nodded. "I know what you mean. But Kyp *is* right, about one thing anyway. Whatever else we do, we're going to have to look out for our own."

"Jedi for Jedi?" Jaina snorted. "Uncle Luke knows that. I'm not sure where he sent Mom, Dad, Threepio, and Artoo, but it's got something to do with setting up a network to help Jedi escape before being turned over to the Yuuzhan Vong."

Anakin shook his head. "Fine, but that's what Kyp meant by only defending. We'll never win this war by being reactive. We have to be proactive. We need intelligence. We need to know which Jedi are at risk *before* they come for us."

"How can we know that?"

"Think logically. Any planet already taken by the Yuuzhan Vong is obviously dangerous. The planets near occupied space are the next most dangerous, because they're desperate to strike a deal."

"The warmaster said he would spare the rest of the galaxy, but only if they turn *all* of us over to them. That sort of spreads the desperation out, at least for people dumb enough to believe him. We saw what Yuuzhan Vong promises meant on Duro. Don't cooperate with them and they mow you down. If you do cooperate with them, they mow you down, laughing about how stupid you've been."

Anakin shrugged. "Obviously a lot of people would rather believe Yuuzhan Vong lies than take their chances. The point is—"

"The point is, what are you two doing out here rather than in the meeting?" Jacen Solo asked from the end of the corridor.

"We were trying to talk Kyp into staying," Anakin told his older brother.

"It'd be easier talking a siringana into a box."

"True," Jaina said, "but we had to try. I guess we ought to go back in now."

"Don't bother. A few minutes after Kyp walked out, Uncle Luke called a recess. Too much angst and confusion."

"It's not going well," Jaina said.

"No. Too many people think Kyp is right."

"What do you think?" Anakin asked.

"He's wrong," Jacen said without hesitation. "Answering naked aggression with naked aggression can't be the solution."

"No? If you hadn't used that particular solution, you, Mom, and Jaina would be dead right now. Would the universe be better off?"

"Anakin, I'm not proud of—" Jacen began.

Jaina cut him off. "Don't you two start again. Anakin and I were talking about something constructive when you joined us. Let's not degenerate into bickering, like the others. We're siblings, after all. If we can't talk through this without losing it, how can we expect anyone else to?"

Jacen held his gaze on Anakin for another few heartbeats, waiting to see who would flinch first.

It was Jacen.

"What *were* you discussing?" he asked softly.

Jaina looked relieved. "How to figure out where the worst hot spots are, which Jedi are in the most immediate danger," she said.

Jacen quirked his mouth as if tasting a Hutt appetizer. "With the Peace Brigade out there, that's an open question. They aren't tied to the interests of a single system. They'll hunt us from the Rim to the Core if they think it'll appease the Yuuzhan Vong."

"The Peace Brigade can't be everywhere at once. They can't follow every rumor they've heard about Jedi."

"The Peace Brigade has plenty of allies, and good intelligence," Jacen countered. "Given what they've managed already, they must have more than a few insiders, maybe even in the senate. They don't have to chase rumors. More often than not, from what I can tell, they don't even make half the captures they boast about. They're just the flesh merchants who turn Jedi over to the Yuuzhan Vong."

"I still have a bad feeling about the senator from Kuat, Viqi Shesh," Jaina muttered.

"My point is this," Anakin said. "It's hard to predict which single Jedi might be next on their list. But if they could get a package deal, wouldn't they jump at it?"

Jaina's eyes widened. "You think they'll move against us while we're gathered here?"

Anakin drew a negative arc with his chin. "Things aren't that bad yet, and who would want to face all of the most powerful Jedi in the galaxy at once? That would be crazy—*us* they'll pick off one at a time. But—"

"The praxeum!" Jacen interrupted.

"Yes," Anakin agreed. "The Jedi academy!"

"But they're just kids!" Jaina said.

"Have you noticed that makes any difference to the Yuuzhan Vong, or to the Peace Brigade, for that matter?" Jacen asked. "Besides, Anakin's only sixteen, and he's killed more Yuuzhan Vong in hand-to-hand combat than any of us. The Yuuzhan Vong know that."

"What about the illusion the Jedi have been maintaining around Yavin Four? That's been keeping strangers away."

"Not since almost all of the Jedi Knights have left," Anakin said. "They've either come to Coruscant to this meeting, or gone off to try to help comrades who've disappeared. Last I heard, only the students Kam and Tionne are left, with maybe Streen, and Master Ikrit. They might not be strong enough. Where did Uncle Luke go? We should talk to him about this, right away. It may already be too late."

"That's a good call, Anakin," Jacen admitted.

"Thanks."

What Anakin didn't mention to his siblings was how

he had awakened in the night, heart thrumming, gripped by a nameless dread. And though he couldn't remember the dream that had torn him from sleep, one image had remained with him: the blond hair and green eyes of Tahiri, his best friend.

And Tahiri was at the academy.

CHAPTER TWO

Luke Skywalker sank into a chair in his study, ran his hand across his brow, and stared out at the night, or what passed for it on Coruscant, the hundred shades of nightglow, shimmering lanes of aircars and transports, bright-studded skyhook tethers lancing toward the unseeable stars. How many thousands of years had passed since anyone had seen a star in the night sky of this city world?

On Tatooine the stars had been hard, glittering promises to a boy who wanted more from life than to be a moisture farmer. They had been everything, and yearning toward them was the seed of everything Luke had become. Now, at the heart of the galaxy he had fought so long to save, he couldn't even see them.

Something drifted in the Force, an embrace waiting to happen. Waiting for permission to happen.

"Come in, Mara," he said, rising.

"Stay there," his wife answered. "I'll join you."

She settled into the chair next to him and took his hand. He felt her touch move closer, and found himself flinching away.

"Hey, Skywalker," she said. "It's not like I'm here to kill you."

"That's a comforting thing to say."

"Yeah?" Her voice took on an edge. "Don't think it hasn't occurred to me. Like when I couldn't hold down breakfast, or when I take one of these twenty-minute lightspeed tours of every emotion I've ever had plus a few that I never knew really existed—and then start over. When my ankles start ballooning up like a Gamorrean boar's and I'm well on my way to Hutthood, I'd advise any responsible parties to start watching their backs."

"Hey, wait a minute. I don't recall the two of us conspiring in this matter. I was just as surprised as you. Besides, your last plan to kill me started this whole thing, pregnancy included. Keep it up, and we'll be ahead of Han and Leia in no time."

Mara clucked. "Darling," she said in disingenuous tones. "I love you, you are my life and my light. If you ever do this to me again, I will vape you where you stand." She squeezed his hand fondly.

"As I was saying," Luke said. "How can I please you, sweetheart?"

"Tell me what's wrong."

He shrugged and turned his face back to the cityscape. "The Jedi, of course. We're breaking apart. First the galaxy turns against us, then we turn against each other."

"It's too bad I didn't take care of Kyp years ago," Mara said.

"Don't even joke about that. And it isn't Kyp's fault—ultimately it's mine. You explained as much to me once, remember?"

"I remember setting you straight about a few things. That doesn't make Kyp right now."

"No, he isn't right. But when children stray, doesn't that say something about the parents?"

"This is a fine time to tell me you're going to be a lousy father. Or maybe you don't think I'll be a good mother?"

She was joking, but he felt a sudden wave of fear, depression, and anger from his wife.

"Mara?" he asked. "It was just a metaphor."

"I know. It's nothing. Just go on."

"It's not nothing."

"It is nothing. Hormones. Mood swings. Very annoying, being jerked around by chemicals, and not your problem, Skywalker. Go on with what you were saying. Sans the parenthood metaphor."

"Fine. What I mean is, my teachings weren't durable enough, or strong enough, or satisfying enough, if the others look to Kyp for their answers."

"We've been betrayed and we're being slaughtered," Mara said. "Kyp's given them an answer to that. You haven't."

"Wait. Now *you* agree with Kyp?"

"I agree we can't just sit and wait. I know you don't want to do that either, but you aren't expressing it well enough. Kyp has given the Jedi a vision, as clear and simple as it is wrong. All we've done is give a muddy jumble of assurances and prohibitions. We need to tell them what to *do*, not what not to do."

"We?"

"Of course *we*, Skywalker. You and me. Where you go I go."

Her Force presence kissed lightly against his again, and for an instant he trembled. It felt good, a warmth against the cold hard nest of his doubts and pain. How could he afford to doubt? How could he let anyone else see it, when it might mean the end of everything?

The touch eased, as if retreating, and he relaxed, and it came again, stealthier and stronger. He gave up, opening himself to her so they mingled in a bright stream. He took her in his arms and let her stroke away the worst of his doubts with her hand and the radiance within her.

"I love you, Mara," he breathed, after a time.

"I love you, too," she replied.

"It's hard to watch it all fall apart."

"It's not falling apart, Luke. You have to believe that."

"I have to be strong for them. I have to be an example. But today—"

"Yes, I saw it. You had a moment of weakness. I think I'm the only one who noticed."

"No. Anakin noticed. It upset him, a lot."

"You're worried about Anakin?" she asked, picking up on the subtext of his spoken word. "He adores you. If there is someone he's always wanted to be, it's you. He wouldn't side with Kyp."

"That's not my worry. He's more like Kyp than he thinks, but he doesn't see it. He's been through so much, Mara, and he's too young to easily absorb what he's had to deal with. He still carries the blame for Chewbacca's death with him, and in the back of his mind part of him still thinks Han blames him, too. He watched Daeshara'cor die. He blames himself for the destruction of the Hapan fleet at Fondor. He's carrying around all that pain, and some day that's bound to add up to something he's not experienced enough to handle. Grief and guilt are only a micron away from anger and hatred. And he's still reckless, still thinks he's immortal despite all of the death he's seen."

"That's what upset him about your weakness today," Mara guessed. "He thinks you're immortal, too."

"He *did* believe that. But now he knows if he can lose Chewie, he can lose anyone. That's not making things better. He's losing faith in everything he's counted on his whole life."

"I didn't have exactly a normal childhood," Mara said, "but doesn't that happen to most children at a certain point?"

"Yes. But most children aren't Jedi adepts. Most children aren't as strong in the Force as Anakin, or as inclined to use it. Did you know when he was a boy, he once killed a giant snake by stopping its heart with the Force?"

Mara blinked. "No."

"Yes. He was defending himself and his friends. It probably seemed like the only thing to do at the time."

"Anakin is a pragmatic lad."

"That's the problem," Luke sighed. "He grew up

around Jedi. Using the Force is like breathing for him, and for Anakin there is nothing very mystical about it. It's a tool he can do things with."

"Jacen on the other hand—"

"Jacen is older, but he grew up like Anakin. It's two different reactions to the same situation. What they have in common is that neither of them thinks I really have it right. And what's worse, I think at least one of them is correct. I've seen—" He broke off.

"What?" Mara gently urged.

"I don't know. I've seen a future. Several futures. However this ends with the Yuuzhan Vong, it won't be me that ends it, or Kyp, or any of the older Jedi. It will be someone new."

"Anakin?"

"I don't know. I'm afraid to even talk about it. Every word spreads, puts ripples in the Force for every person who hears it, changes things. I'm starting to know how Yoda and Ben felt. Watching, trying to guide, hoping I'm not wrong, that I'm seeing clearly, that there is such a thing as wisdom and that I'm not just fooling myself."

She laughed softly and kissed his cheek. "You worry too much."

"Sometimes I don't think I worry enough."

"Worry?" Mara said softly. She took his hand and placed it against her belly. "You want worry? Listen."

Once more she enfolded him in the Force, and once more they merged toward one another and the third life in the room, the one growing inside of Mara. Tentatively, hesitantly, Luke reached in to touch his son.

The heart was beating, a simple beautiful rhythm, and around it drifted something like a melody, an awareness both alien and familiar, sensations like taste and smell and sight but not like them at all, a universe with no light but with all of the warmth and security in the world.

"Amazing," he murmured. "That you can give him that. That you can be that for him."

"It's humbling," she said. "It's worrisome. What if I make a mistake? What if my sickness comes back? And worst of all—" She paused, and he waited, knowing she would get to it in time. "It's easy, in a way. To protect him now, all I have to do is protect myself, and I've been doing that my whole life. Right now, my life is his life. But after he's born, it will never be like that again. That's the part that worries me."

Luke wrapped his arm around her and hugged. "You'll do fine," he said. "I promise you."

"You can't promise that, any more than you can hold the young Jedi inside of you or keep them safe. It's the same. It's the same fear, Luke."

"Of course," he replied. "Of course it is."

They sat and watched the skies of Coruscant, and spoke no more until someone came to their door.

"Speak and they will come," Luke murmured. "It's the Solo children."

"I can send them away."

"No. They need to talk to me." He raised his voice. "Come on in."

He stood and brightened the lights. Anakin, Jaina, and Jacen entered.

"Sorry we left the meeting," Jaina said.

"I knew what you were doing, and I thank you for trying. Kyp—Kyp must walk his own path for a while. But that's not why you came, is it?"

"No," Jacen said. "We're worried about the Jedi academy."

"Right," Anakin joined in. "It occurred to me that if I were Peace Brigade, and wanted to catch a bunch of Jedi all at once—"

"You'd go to Yavin Four. Good thinking."

Anakin's face fell visibly. "You already thought of it."

Luke nodded. "Don't feel bad. It was only a few days ago that we had enough reports to spot the trend and realize just how seriously the warmaster's promise has been taken. Trying to deal with all the local fires, trying to find government support to put a *stop* to this or at least slow it down, I didn't realize that there are no longer enough mature Jedi in the system to maintain the illusion we were projecting."

"So what do we do?" Jacen asked.

"I requested the New Republic send a ship to evacuate them, but they're dragging their heels. They might continue to for weeks."

"We can't wait that long!" Jaina said.

"No," Luke agreed. "I've been trying to find Booster Terrik. I think the best thing for the moment would be to not only evacuate the academy but keep the kids on the move, in the *Errant Venture*. If we just move them to another planet, we don't really solve the problem."

"So they're with Booster?" Anakin said.

"I can't locate him, unfortunately. I'm still working on it."

"Talon Karrde," Mara said softly.

"Perfect," Luke said. "You know where to find him?"

"What do *you* think?" Mara said, smirking.

"But what if the Peace Brigade is already at Yavin Four, or on the way?" Anakin asked.

"It's the best we can do, for the moment," Luke told him. "Besides, the danger is still hypothetical. The Peace Brigade might not even know about Yavin Four. And even if they did, Kam and Tionne and Master Ikrit are there. They aren't exactly defenseless."

"It's not the best-kept secret in the galaxy," Jacen said. "And with the illusion gone, what could Kam do against a warship? Let *us* go."

"Out of the question," Luke replied. "I need you all here, and with the bounty on our heads—especially *your* head, Jacen—it's too dangerous for you to go off alone. Your parents would never forgive me if I sent you into that with them away."

"Ask them, then," Jaina said.

"I can't. They're out of contact now, and could be for some time."

"Shouldn't we at least go check on the praxeum?" Jaina persisted. "We could just hide at the edge of the system until Karrde shows up, keep an eye on things, run back here to report if things go wrong."

Luke shook his head. "I know you're all restless, especially you, Jaina. But your eyes still haven't fully healed—"

"Not to Rogue Squadron specs, maybe," Jaina protested, "but I can see well enough to fly."

"Even if your vision were fully restored," Luke went on, "I still don't think sending any or all of you to Yavin Four is the most productive course. There's important work to do here. Weren't you just telling Kyp that, Jaina, Jacen?"

"Yes, Uncle Luke," Jacen said. "We were."

"Anakin? You haven't said much."

Anakin shrugged. "There isn't much to say, is there?"

Luke detected something a bit dangerous in that, but it quickly passed.

"I'm glad the three of you are thinking about the situation. We agree that the academy is one of our most vulnerable spots. Help me find the rest. Don't think for a second I've thought of everything, because obviously I haven't. And don't forget, we'll reconvene the meeting tomorrow morning."

The three of them nodded and left.

When they were gone, Mara clucked. "They might be right."

Luke sighed again. "They might be. But I have a feeling that whoever goes to Yavin Four must go in force, or they won't be leaving it again. I've learned to trust feelings like this."

"You should have told them that, then," Mara said.

He flashed her a sardonic smile. "Then they would have gone for sure."

Mara took his hand. "No rest for the weary. I'll contact Karrde." She touched her belly again. "Meanwhile,

Skywalker, find me something to eat. Something big and still bleeding."

Anakin checked over the systems indicators.

"How do we look, Fiver?" he asked quietly, studying the cockpit readout display.

SYSTEMS WITHIN OPTIMUM VARIANTS, the R7 unit assured him.

"Good. Just hang on while I get clearance. Meanwhile calculate the first jump in the series to get me to the Yavin system."

That took a certain amount of finagling, including forging a code that would allow him to fly without a check that might alert Uncle Luke or anyone else who would try to stop him.

Because Uncle Luke was wrong, this time. Anakin could feel it in his very center. The Jedi trainees were in grave danger; Talon Karrde would not get there in time. It might already be too late.

It was strange that Uncle Luke still insisted on thinking of Anakin as a child. Anakin had killed Yuuzhan Vong. He had seen friends die and caused the deaths of others. He was responsible for the destruction of countless ships and the beings who crewed them, and that only scratched the most recent skin of the matter.

It was a blind spot the adults in his life had, an ambivalence and a denial. They didn't understand who he really was, only what he appeared to be. Even his mother and Uncle Luke, who had the Force to help them.

Aunt Mara probably understood—she had never really been a child, either—but even she was blinkered by her relationship with Uncle Luke; she had to take his feelings into account, as well as her own.

Well, there would be anger. He could explain to Uncle Luke about the feeling he had in the Force, but that might only alert the Master to Anakin's certainty in this matter. Even if Uncle Luke could be convinced to send someone *now*, it might be someone else, someone older. But Anakin knew it had to be *him*, he had to go. If he didn't, his best friend was doomed to a fate much worse than death.

It was the only thing in his life he was really sure of right now.

"Cleared for takeoff," the port control said.

"Power it up, Fiver," Anakin murmured. "We've got someplace to be."

CHAPTER THREE

When the stars rushed back into existence, Anakin put his XJ X-wing into a lazy tumble and cut power to everything but sensors and minimal life support. Ordinarily he wouldn't play it so cautious; after all, someone would almost have to be watching for the hyperwave ripples of an X-wing entering the system to have any chance of detecting it. But given the feeling in his gut, there might just be someone doing that.

The roll and yaw he'd put the X-wing in wasn't random, but was designed to give his instruments a full accounting of the surrounding space in the least possible time. While the sensors did their job, Anakin reached out with the sense he trusted most—the Force.

The planet Yavin filled most of his view, its vast orange oceans of gas boiling into fractal, elusive patterns. Its familiar face had marked the days and nights of much of his childhood. The praxeum—his uncle Luke's Jedi academy—was located on Yavin 4, a moon of the gas giant. He could remember watching Yavin in the night sky, a colossal mirage of a planet, wondering what could be there, pushing his evolving Force senses to explore it.

He'd found clouds of methane and ammonia deeper than oceans, hydrogen so stressed by pressure it became metal, life crushed thinner than paper but still thriving, cyclones heavier than lead but faster than the winds of any world habitable by humans. And crystals, sparkling Corusca gems climbing those titan winds, spinning in an ancient dance, capturing what light they could find in the thinner upper atmosphere and gripping it tight in their molecules.

He saw none of this as one might with eyes, of course, but over the nights, through the Force he had felt them, and with references to the library gradually understood them.

In his imagination he had seen more. Pieces of the first Death Star, which had met its end in these very skies, pounded into monomolecular foil by fierce pressure and gravity. Older things, relics of Sith, and species even more lost and distant in time. Once a planet like Yavin swallowed a secret, it wasn't likely to give it up again. Given the other secrets that had turned up in the Yavin system—and the Sun Crusher Kyp Durron himself *had* once managed to pull from the belly of the orange giant—that was for the best.

Just beyond the vast rim of Yavin, a bright yellowish star winked—Yavin 8, one of the three moons in the system blessed with life. Anakin had a friend there, a native of that world who had trained briefly at the academy and returned home. He could feel her, very faintly. Yavin 4 was just around the rim, where he had other friends. In a way, the whole system was like a familiar room to Anakin, the sort he could walk into and immediately know if something was out of place.

And something felt very out of place.

In the Force he could feel the Jedi candidates, for they were all strong with it. He could feel Kam Solusar and his wife Tionne, and the ancient Ikrit, not students but full-fledged Jedi. These were seen as through a cloud, suggesting they were at least trying to maintain the illusion that hid Yavin 4 from the casual eye.

But even through that, one presence shone brilliant, made brighter by familiarity and friendship. Tahiri.

She felt him, too, and though he could not quite hear any actual words she might be trying to send, he did feel a sort of rhythm, as of someone talking quickly, excitedly, without pause for breath.

One corner of Anakin's mouth turned up. Yes, that was Tahiri, all right.

What felt wrong was a little nearer and much weaker. Not Yuuzhan Vong, for they could not be felt in the Force, but someone who shouldn't be there. Someone slightly confused, but with a growing sense of confidence.

"Hang on, Fiver," he told his astromech. "Get ready to run or fight in a hurry. It might just be Talon Karrde and his crew here ahead of schedule, but I'd sooner bet against Lando Calrissian in sabacc than to count on it."

AFFIRMATIVE, the display blinked.

They tumbled into sensor range, and his computer built a silhouette from the magnified image.

"That's not so bad," he murmured. "One Corellian light transport. Maybe it *is* one of Karrde's bunch." Or maybe not. And maybe there were a hundred Yuuzhan Vong ships on the other side of the gas giant or Yavin 4, invisible to his Jedi senses and hidden from his sensors. Whatever the case, waiting around wasn't going to improve matters. He powered up, corrected his tumble, and engaged the ion engines.

He activated his comm system and hailed the stranger. "Transport, acknowledge."

For a few moments, he got nothing, then the audio crackled. "Who is this?"

"My name is Anakin Solo. What are you doing in the Yavin system?"

"We're Corusca gem miners."

"Really. Where's your trawler?"

Another pause, then words underlined with a bit of anger.

"We can see the moon now. We knew it was here all along. Your Jedi sorcery has failed you."

THE TRANSPORT IS ARMING WEAPONS SYSTEMS, Fiver

noticed. Anakin nodded grimly as the other vessel swung toward him.

"I'm only warning you once," Anakin said. "Stand down."

For an answer, he got a blast from a laser cannon, which at that distance he managed to avoid as easily as he might deflect a blaster shot with his lightsaber.

"Gee," Anakin muttered. "I suppose that says it all." He opened his S-foils. "Fiver, give me evasive approach six, but I still want the stick just in case."

ACKNOWLEDGED.

He dropped toward Yavin 4 and the transport at full thrust, spinning and dancing as he went, and when he felt his target firmly enough in the Force, he sliced the night of vacuum with ruby red. The transport returned fire and began its own evasive maneuvers, but that was like a bantha trying to dodge a mace fly.

They had good shields, though. As Anakin completed his first pass, his opponent was still essentially untouched. To make matters more interesting, four winks of blue flame and his instruments agreed that the transport had just fired proton torpedoes at him. Anakin had been preparing to turn for another pass; instead he continued his noseward plunge toward the moon.

"Four proton torpedoes. These guys really don't like us, Fiver."

THE TRANSPORT SEEMS HOSTILE, Fiver acknowledged. Anakin sighed. Fiver was a more advanced astromech than R2-D2, but he missed his uncle's droid's personality at times. Maybe he ought to do something about that.

Two laser blasts hit his shields in quick succession, but they did their job. On his tracker, the proton torpedoes continued to close as Anakin met resistance from the atmosphere. He plunged on, and the ship began to vibrate faintly. His nose and wings were starting to heat up from the upper atmosphere. If he didn't time this exactly right, he would scatter all over the jungle kilometers below.

When the lead torp was almost on him, he cut his engines and yanked the nose up. The atmosphere, still thin, was nevertheless able to give the XJ X-wing a good strong slap, hurling him away from the moon. Servos whined and something somewhere made a startling *ping*. Using the momentum from the atmospheric skip, Anakin turned further spaceward, blood rushing from his head as the g's mounted, then he kicked in the engines again.

Behind him, the proton torpedoes didn't fare as well. They tried to turn after him, of course. Two didn't make it, and continued plunging moonward. The other two skipped along wildly different courses than Anakin and would never find him again before running out of fuel.

"Nice try," Anakin said grimly. Now he was climbing uphill, out of the gravity well, his lasers pumping a steady rhythm. He took another hit from the enemy's more powerful gun, and for an instant the lights dimmed in the cockpit. Then they flared back to life as Fiver rerouted, and Anakin took a hammer to the transport. Their shields faltered, and he slagged their primary generator. Looping around them nose to tail, he drilled laser turrets, torpedo ports, and engines.

Then he tried the comm again. "Ready to talk now?" he asked.

"Why not?" the voice from the other end replied. "You can still surrender if you want."

"That's—" Anakin began, but Fiver interrupted.

HYPERSPACE JUMP DETECTED. 12 VESSELS HAVE ARRIVED, DISTANCE 100,000 KILOMETERS.

"Sith spit!" Anakin muttered, bringing his sensors to bear.

They weren't Yuuzhan Vong ships, he saw that immediately, just a motley collection of E-wings, transports, and corvettes.

They were hailing him. He opened the link.

"Unidentified vessel, this is the Peace Brigade," a voice

crackled. "Stand down and surrender, and you won't be harmed."

They were too far away to hit him. Soon they wouldn't be. Anakin closed his S-foils, rolled, opened the throttle, and raced toward the distant viridian of Yavin 4.

Anakin vaulted from the cockpit of the X-wing into silent near darkness. A twilight line of illumination in the distance was the entrance he had flown through into what had once been a part of an ancient Massassi temple complex, much later the central hangar for the Rebel fleet, and which now saw little use at all, since most ships landing at the academy set down outside.

Anakin's flight boots scuffed the ancient stone surface, and the sound grew around him into the hushed beating of enormous wings. He smelled stone and lubricant and more faintly the musky jungle outside.

Someone was watching Anakin from the darkness.

"Who is that?" a voice asked, each word stretching to fill the abyss.

"It's me, Kam. Anakin."

A faint glow appeared, and then a bank of light panels came on. Some ten meters away Kam Solusar stood, hooking his lightsaber back into his belt.

"I thought it felt like you," Kam said. "But there's been an unknown ship in orbit for several standard days now. We've been trying to keep them confused."

"Peace Brigade," Anakin explained. "And the one ship has friends now, about twelve of them. And they aren't confused anymore."

He'd been walking toward Kam while he spoke, and suddenly his old teacher swept forward, clasping his arm. "It's good to see you, Anakin. And you? You're alone?"

Anakin nodded. "Talon Karrde is on the way with a flotilla. He's supposed to evacuate you and the students. Uncle Luke wasn't expecting the Peace Brigade to show up so soon, I guess."

Kam's eyes narrowed. "But you were, weren't you? You came here without permission."

"I came against orders, actually," Anakin corrected. "That's not important now. Getting the students to safety, that is."

"Of course," Kam agreed. "How long before the Peace Brigade can land?"

"An hour? Not long."

"And Karrde?"

"He could be days."

Kam grimaced. "We can't hold out here that long."

"We might. We're all Jedi."

Kam snorted. "You need a sense of your limitations. I have a sense of mine. We might do very well, but we'll lose kids. I have to think of them first."

They were approaching the turbolift when the door hissed open and ejected a blond-and-orange blur. The blur smacked Anakin at chest height, and he suddenly found surprisingly strong arms wrapped around him in a fierce embrace. Bright green eyes danced centimeters from his own.

He felt his face go warm.

"Hi, Tahiri," he said.

She pushed back from him. "Hi, yourself, great hero-from-the-stars who's too good to keep in touch with his best friend."

"I've—"

"Been busy. Right. I know all about it—well, not *all* about it because we get the news so late here, but I heard about Duro, and Centerpoint, and—"

She stopped suddenly, either because she saw it in his face or felt it in the Force. Centerpoint Station was a sensitive subject.

"Anyway," she went on, "you won't believe how boring it's been without you. All the apprentices have gone off, and that just leaves these *kids*—" She stepped away, and for the first time, he really saw her.

Whatever she detected in his eyes cut her off in midsentence. "What?" she asked instead. "What are you looking at?"

"I—" Now his face felt like it had been grazed by blasterfire. "You look . . . different."

"Older maybe? I'm fourteen now. Last week."

"Happy birthday."

"You should have thought of it then, but thanks anyway. Dummy."

Anakin found himself suddenly unable to meet her eyes. He dropped his gaze. "You're, uh, still barefoot, I see."

"What did you expect? I *hate* shoes. I only wear them when I have to. Shoes were invented by the Sith to keep our delicate toes in anguish and misery, I'm sure of it. Did you think just because I grew a centimeter or two I'd start torturing my feet?"

She looked up at Kam suspiciously. "What's he doing here, anyway? I know he didn't come to see *me*."

Anakin flinched at the hurt he heard in that.

"Anakin's come to warn us of trouble," Kam replied. "In fact, you'll need to do your catching up later."

"Really? Trouble?"

"Yes," Anakin said.

Tahiri put her hands on her hips. "Well, why didn't you say so? What's going on?"

"We need to talk to Tionne and Ikrit," Kam told her, continuing forward into the turbolift.

"*Now*," Anakin added, following him.

"But what's going *on*?" Tahiri shouted at their suddenly retreating backs.

"I'll explain on the way," Anakin promised.

"Fine." She ducked into the lift just as the door was closing.

"The Yuuzhan Vong warmaster basically put a price on our heads," Anakin said. "On *all* our heads, all the Jedi. He announced that if what's left of the New Republic will turn over all of its Jedi to him—and Jacen especially—he won't take any more planets."

"Boy, *that* sounds like a lie," Tahiri said.

"Doesn't matter. People believe him. Like the people in the ships approaching right now."

"They want to turn *us* over to the Yuuzhan Vong? Let them try!"

"Don't worry, they will."

The door opened and they emerged onto the second level. Kam started down the main corridor and then through a series of passages that were utterly familiar to Anakin, though they all seemed somehow narrower than when he had last seen them. The Massassi temple that housed the academy had once seemed impossibly huge. Now it seemed merely large.

They reached the central area, and twenty-odd faces turned toward them. Human, Bothan, Twi'lek, Wookiee— more than a dozen species were represented. All were quite young except one—Tionne, Kam's wife, a graceful silver-haired woman with pearl-white eyes. Her eyebrows lifted in surprise and her lips in pleasure.

"Anakin!" she said.

"Tionne," Kam said gently but urgently, "we need to talk."

"Anakin!" Sannah, a girl of thirteen with brown hair and yellow eyes, waved at him. Even younger Valin Horn was waving, though he wasn't shouting.

"He's busy!" Tahiri told them. But when Anakin went to talk with Kam and Tionne, Tahiri came along.

"Tahiri—" Kam began.

"Oh, no," she said. "You aren't leaving me out of this."

"I wasn't going to," Kam said gently. "I was going to ask you to find Master Ikrit and meet us in the conference room."

"Oh. Okay."

She whirled off down the corridor on bare feet.

* * *

Tahiri was back with Ikrit only moments later. The old Jedi Master padded into the room on all fours, his long floppy ears dragging the ground. His normally bright eyes seemed a little dull to Anakin, and he felt an inexplicable pang.

"Master Ikrit."

"Young Anakin. It is good to see you," Ikrit replied. "Though you bring troubling news."

"Yes." He raced through the details once again, for Ikrit and Tionne.

"They would take our children?" Tionne murmured, more darkly than was her wont.

"The Peace Brigade? Absolutely. Tionne, it's *bad* for Jedi out there right now."

"I understand," she said, then clenched her fist. "No, I *don't* understand. Has the galaxy gone mad?"

"Yes," Kam said softly. "It's an old madness, war."

"You don't have any ships, do you?"

"No. Streen went with Peckhum in the supply ship."

"Where to?"

"Corellia. He should be back soon. Though I suppose they won't, now."

"We'll have to hide them here, then," Anakin said. "Where?"

"Down the river! The cave beneath the Palace of the Woolamander," Tahiri offered. "Master Ikrit's cave."

Anakin raised his eyebrows. "That's a good idea. They'd be really hard to find there, especially if the Peace Brigade doesn't start looking right away."

"What do you mean by that?" Kam said, his voice suddenly cautious. "Why would they delay the search?"

"I'll stay behind," Anakin said. "I'll make it look as if we're still in the temple trying to make a stand. They'll waste time shooting their way through while you and Tionne get the kids to safety."

"You're leaving out one little detail," Tahiri said. "What about *you*? What keeps *you* safe?"

"I'll hide the X-wing. I know a good place. I can slip through them. Then I'll play hide-and-seek until Talon Karrde shows up. Once he's mopped up the Peace Brigade, I'll lead him to you."

"You've been thinking about this," Tionne said.

"All the way down," Anakin admitted. "It's the best way."

"He's right," Kam said.

"Kam—" Tionne began.

"He's right," Kam went on, "except that he's not the one staying behind—I am."

"I'm the better pilot," Anakin said bluntly. "I'm the only one who can pull it off."

"Anakin is correct," Ikrit said in his scratchy voice. "It is part of his destiny. And mine."

"Master Ikrit—"

"You will say I am no warrior. That may be true—it has been long since I wielded a lightsaber, and it was not what I preferred even then. But it is not lightsabers that will prevail here today, not weapons. Not all uses of the Force are aggressive."

Anakin pursed his lips, but he couldn't bring himself to contradict the ancient Master.

Kam gnawed his lip for a moment. "Very well," he said at last. "I don't like it, but we don't have time for a debate. Tahiri, come along. Help me and Tionne get the students on the boats."

"Fine," Tahiri said, "but I'm staying with Anakin."

"No," Anakin said.

"Yes!" Tahiri retorted. "I've been stuck on this mud-ball while you've been out fighting the Yuuzhan Vong. I'm sick of it! I'm ready to do something!"

"You're too young for this," Tionne said.

"Anakin's only two years older than me! He was fifteen at Sernpidal!"

"That's right," Anakin said, "and I got Chewbacca killed. Tahiri, please go with Kam."

Her eyes widened in shocked betrayal. "You don't *want* me with you! After all we—you think I'm a kid, just like they do!"

No, Anakin thought. *I just don't want to see you killed, too.*

"Come on, Tahiri," Tionne said gently. "There's no time to lose."

"Fine. That's just fine," she said, and without another glance at Anakin she darted from the room.

Kam placed his hand on Anakin's shoulder. "It's been hard on her without you here."

Anakin nodded. "Anyway," he said gruffly, "I'd better get to work."

"Be careful, Anakin. You don't have to buy us a lot of time. When you need to go, go. We need you alive."

"I don't plan to die," Anakin assured him.

"Most people don't. It happens anyway. Trust the Force, listen to Ikrit. May the Force be with you."

CHAPTER FOUR

"It will burn you, Anakin," Ikrit's pleasant, familiar rasp solemnly pronounced.

Anakin looked up from his work on the intercom. He and the old Jedi were in what had once been the command center when the Great Temple had been a Rebel base. Most of the wartime equipment was gone, but some remained—the various communication systems, including an intercom that piped information throughout the temple and its surrounds.

"Master?"

"Your anger. You have built yourself a vessel to contain it, but the crucible itself will one day melt from the heat. Then you will burn, and others with you. Many others, possibly."

Anakin slipped the modified data chip in place and straightened. "The Yuuzhan Vong make me angry, Master. They're destroying everything I know, everything I love."

"No. *You* make you angry. People die; you are angry because you could not save them."

"You mean Chewbacca."

"And others. Their deaths are inscribed on you."

"Yes. Chewbacca died because of me. A lot of people have died because of me."

"Death comes to call," Ikrit replied. "You cannot hold water in your hands for long. It leaks away, goes where it

51

is meant to go. To the soil and sky. To ions, and then space, where stars are born."

Frustration hijacked Anakin's lips. "That's poetic, Master Ikrit, but it's not an answer. My grandfather was Darth Vader, and he killed billions. But that was after decades of the dark side. I'm only sixteen, and look what I've done. Darth Vader would be proud."

Ikrit fixed him with luminous blue eyes. "It is to your credit that you feel those deaths, that you mourn. But you did not kill those people. You did not wish them dead and then bring it to pass."

"No," Anakin said. "But at Centerpoint I wished the Yuuzhan Vong dead. I wanted to kill every last one of them. If my brother hadn't stopped me, I would have. I think—often—that I *should* have."

"Your brother didn't stop you."

"You weren't there, Master Ikrit. I would have done it."

"I was there, Anakin. In every important way, I was. Anakin, you must let your anger go. Angry steps have worn a rutted path to the dark side. It is an easy path to follow, difficult to avoid."

Anakin turned to the power generator remote panel and fiddled with it a bit. "This might work," he murmured. "I wish I had time to go out to the generator."

"Anakin." The Master's voice carried a note of command.

Anakin didn't look up from his work. "You know, Master Ikrit," he said, "I used to dream every night that I would turn to the dark side, become my name, what my grandfather became. Now that seems silly. The Force doesn't make a person good or evil. It's a tool, like a lightsaber. Don't worry about me."

"Listen to me, young Solo," Ikrit said. "I never said the Force would lead you to evil. I warned you your feelings might."

"Feelings are tools, too, if you don't let them control you," Anakin said.

Ikrit clucked his soft laugh. "And how are you to know when a feeling controls you? When anger guides your hand or guilt stays it?"

Anakin sighed. "With all due respect, Master Ikrit, we don't have time for this discussion. The Peace Brigade will be here any moment."

"This is the perfect time for it," Ikrit replied. "Perhaps the only time."

"What do you mean?"

Ikrit blinked, very slowly, then scratched out a long breath.

"I am centuries old, Anakin. I came here to Yavin Four to free the spirits of the imprisoned Massassi children, or so I thought. Now I think there was another reason, an even greater one."

"Master? What could that be?"

"The task that drew me here was beyond my power to complete. It was beyond the power of any adult Jedi. You and Tahiri were the only ones who could have done it."

"With your help and advice. Without you, we never could have released them."

Ikrit ruffed his fur. "With or without me you would have done it," he purred. "That is why I say I was drawn here for another reason, slept for centuries for another cause."

"What reason?"

"To see something new born in you and Tahiri. And to give you whatever small help I am able to give to see that birth arrive."

A chill spidered up Anakin's back. He couldn't say why, but Ikrit's words struck something in his core.

Ikrit walked to the window. "They are here," he said.

Anakin bolted over. Peace Brigade ships were settling everywhere.

"I'm not ready!" Anakin said.

"You are ready," Ikrit replied.

"Not as ready as I would like. Ten more minutes would have been nice. I could have brought the automated defenses of the power generator on-line."

"Tell me what you *have* done."

"Well, I've got an energy shield up, though not much of one, and it's only over the compound. A little pounding will bring it down." Anakin switched on the intercom. Faint sounds of speech and movement bustled around them. "It'll *sound* like a bunch of us are in here. And this—" He went to what had once been the local sensor control panel. "—I'm using the old sensory array to generate the illusion of small, local movements in the temple."

"Scurrying," Ikrit said. "As if we're running about."

"Right. Of course, they won't *see* anything, if they get close, but their instruments will tell them we're all over the place."

"They will see also," Ikrit said. "Come."

The Great Temple was a ziggurat with three giant steps. The old command center was on the second tier. The ancient structure had five openings that led out to the flat, paved surface that was the roof of the lowest tier. Anakin and Ikrit made their way to the one that faced the landing clearing and peeked out.

Beyond the vague distortion of the energy shield, Anakin saw five ships settled in the clearing. Two were already disgorging armed Peace Brigaders.

"I hope they go for this," Anakin said. "I hope they believe. If they start a search for Kam, Tionne, and the kids now, they might find them."

"They will believe," Ikrit assured him. "They will believe the children are here because they want to, and because they are weak. Do not worry, Anakin. As I said, a warrior I may not be, but the Force is not weak with me."

"I'm sorry, Master Ikrit," Anakin said. "I should not doubt you."

"Then do not doubt my words. Search your feelings, every day. Keep careful watch. The worst monsters are not those from without." Then the Master closed his eyes, humming faintly to himself. Anakin felt a surge in the Force as Ikrit's will went out to touch the beings below, to nudge their credulity over the edge.

Anakin lifted a remote comm unit and keyed into the outdoor speakers.

"You are trespassing on the grounds of the Jedi academy," he said. "Please leave immediately."

At the sound of his amplified voice, some of the Peace Brigaders dived for cover. A moment later, the exterior speakers of one of the ships boomed on.

"You inside the temple," the voice said. "This is Lieutenant Kot Murno of the Peace Brigade. We have been empowered to take control of this facility."

"On whose authority?"

"The Alliance of Twelve."

"Never heard of it," Anakin replied. "Whoever they are, they don't have any jurisdiction over this system."

"They do now," Murno answered. "We are their authority. Surrender, and you won't be harmed."

"Really? You don't think that the Yuuzhan Vong will harm the children you've come to kidnap when you hand them over to them?"

There was a pause this time before Murno answered. "It is the price of peace," he said. "I regret it, but it is the case. Weighed against what the Yuuzhan Vong could do to every inhabited world in this galaxy, a handful of Jedi isn't much to ask. You brought this disaster upon us. You must pay the price."

"You're blaming the Yuuzhan Vong invasion on the Jedi?" Anakin asked incredulously.

"Jedi have provoked this war at every stage, hoping to use it as a way to embellish their own power. Your plans for the domination of this galaxy have long been known. This time, your tactics have reverse-throttled on you."

"That's the biggest trough of bantha fodder I've ever heard anyone spit up in my life," Anakin said. "You are cowards and traitors. You want us? Come and get us."

He fired his blaster through the narrow window and ducked as return fire heat-spalled the ancient stone. Particle shields like the one he had erected did nothing to stop energy blasts. The thick jungle air filled with the hiss and whine of blasters as the fire expanded to other parts of the temple complex.

"What are they shooting at up there?" Anakin wondered aloud.

"Ghosts of mist and madness," Ikrit told him.

"They don't notice no one is shooting back?"

"Not yet. They believe they see the bolts of energy weapons."

"How long can you keep that up?"

"Longer if the occasional bolt is real."

"Got you," Anakin said, leaning around the door frame. Aiming carefully, using the Force, he blew a blaster rifle out of a hooded man's hands. He continued that way for about twenty minutes, picking his shots carefully. Each second felt like a burden lifted from his shoulders; each movement of the chrono took Tahiri and the rest farther from danger.

"They've found the generator," Ikrit murmured. "Your shield will be down soon."

"It's okay," Anakin said. "We're almost done here. Even after it's down they'll come in cautiously. We'll have plenty of time to get to the hangar and get my X-wing out. Then all we have to do is run their little blockade." He'd noticed three of the five ships had landed facing the closed hangar doors. No surprise there, but what they didn't know was that one of the ion cannons that guarded the hangars was still operational—and had a self-contained power supply good for at least a blast or two.

He leaned out for a parting shot.

A blaster bolt seared by over his shoulder, lanced down into the Peace Brigaders. Anakin jerked his head around.

"That shot came from above us!"

"Yes," Ikrit said. "Didn't you notice? Didn't you know she would come?"

"Notice who?" But in a flash he knew. Tahiri was up there, Tahiri and two other people. All Jedi.

"Hutt slime!" he swore. "Just what I need!" He turned to Master Ikrit. "There won't be room for all of us in the X-wing. Meet me in the deep grotto. I'll think of something on the way."

With that he raced down the corridor, blaster in one hand and lightsaber in the other.

He found them in the refectory—Tahiri, Valin Horn, and Sannah. They had barricaded the outer door with tables and had two blasters between them, no telling where they had gotten them. When Anakin entered, Tahiri waved the gun at him.

"What are you doing?" Anakin exploded.

"Helping you," Tahiri said with a grin.

"How did you—"

"Kam thought we were on Tionne's boat, Tionne thought we were on his. Simple, with a little planning."

"But Valin? Valin's only eleven!"

"Twelve!" Valin said very seriously. "I can help."

"This is insane."

"Fine one you are to talk, Anakin," Tahiri snapped. "You're the one who left Coruscant without permission, aren't you? You get to do everything while we just run away and do nothing? I don't think so, best friend."

"Yeah? Well, my plan was to get away in the X-wing. Now we have too many people for that. What does the brilliant Tahiri propose we do, exactly?"

"Oh." Her green eyes went round. "I hadn't thought that far."

"No, I guess you didn't."

The floor suddenly vibrated like the shell of a Hapan lute.

"What's that?" Sannah asked.

Valin, peeking out the window, answered. "The shield is down. Now they're shooting at the doors. Some men are coming up the stairs, too."

"No more time," Anakin said. "We'll have to think as we go. I told Ikrit to meet us in the grotto."

"Then we'll be stuck underground."

"I didn't have much time to put this together, Tahiri."

"You mean there's more to your plan than hiding in the grotto?"

Anakin blew out a deep breath. "Sure. We'll take a Peace Brigade ship."

Tahiri smiled. "There. That wasn't so hard, was it?"

They reached the turbolift just as a clump of Peace Brigaders appeared at the end of the corridor facing onto the outside stairs.

"Hey! Stop!" one of them shouted.

Two blaster shots pinged against the doors as they closed. Anakin let out a breath as the lift started to descend, then sucked it back in.

"It's going to stop," Anakin said. "At the second level."

"Override it."

"I can't," he said, activating his lightsaber with a *snap-hiss*. "The door will stay open for a few seconds. If they're out there . . ."

The door opened on the muzzles of six blasters. Anakin didn't think. He'd already slapped the "down" button—now he leapt into the midst of his enemies, blocking the first two blaster bolts with his weapon and sending them burning back through the press. He cut a blaster rifle in half and spun. Shouting in alarm, his attackers gave ground, trying to find a range where they could use their weapons. Two came at him with stun batons. He leapt and whirled, disarming one with a cut that took several fingers and another that sheared the baton in half. He felt another blow coming, one he wasn't quite fast enough to avoid.

When he landed, he was facing another lightsaber, its blade a vibrant blue.

Behind it—gripping it and grinning fiercely—was Tahiri. She'd just slashed the force pike in half that had almost impaled him.

He didn't let his astonishment faze him. The turbolift with Sannah and Valin was long gone. *Find Master Ikrit*, he sent after the young candidates, hoping that if they could not make out actual words, they would at least get the sense.

Then he squared his shoulders and faced the Peace Brigaders who were warily regrouping about two meters away. "You don't stand a chance," Anakin told them. "I've been trying not to hurt you. That ends with the next person who fires a weapon at me."

"They can't get all of us," a woman in front said. She had a seamed brown face and dark eyes.

"Of course we can," Anakin said.

"All of us?" She smirked. From behind her came the sound of what could only be reinforcements.

Anakin hit the woman, hard, with a telekinetic shove that took all of her companions down, too. Then he whirled and made four quick slashes that opened a gaping hole into the turbolift shaft.

"Go," he told Tahiri. "You say you're ready for all this? Jump."

Tahiri nodded and without the slightest hesitation leapt down the shaft. Anakin followed her, bolts flashing above him. Together, they hurled through darkness.

CHAPTER FIVE

Anakin reached to Tahiri through the Force, and for an instant met a wall as hard as the stone of the temple. Then she reached back, and they clicked as if they had never been apart, so intensely that it actually frightened him. They fell in a sort of acrobatic dance, Anakin using the Force to slow Tahiri's fall and she slowing his as they spun around a common fulcrum somewhere between them, like two children clasping hands and leaning back, turning around on their feet. If either let go, the other would go whirling off, out of control

An old game, one they had invented long ago.

He noticed something was falling with them—a pair of glop grenades. He sent them humming back up the shaft and out the hole he had cut.

The two young Jedi touched down, feather light, on top of the turbolift.

"Wow!" Tahiri said. "It's been a long time since we did that. That was terrific. And the way you got the grenades, too—that was *art*!"

"I—"

The car of the lift suddenly started again.

Desperately Anakin cut into the power couplings and superconductor casings in the walls. The lift jarred to a stop. Meanwhile, Tahiri sliced into the roof of the car itself and jumped back, in case there was blasterfire.

But there was none.

"I don't feel anyone on the lift," Tahiri said.

"No. I sent it down to the third hangar level below the temple. I think Valin and Sannah got off, and then someone called it back up—probably someone on the ground level. Judging by our drop, we're probably somewhere between—"

An explosion six meters above him cut him off as one of the outer lift doors blew in.

"There's the ground floor, right there," Anakin said. "Come on!"

He jumped down into the car. With his lightsaber, he cut through the car and the wall beyond, revealing an underground hangar that hadn't been used since the battle against the first Death Star.

"You block their shots," Anakin told Tahiri.

As bolts rained down and Tahiri deflected them, Anakin cut the fail-safe magnetic bolts that had locked the turbolift in place. He flicked off his lightsaber.

"Cut your lightsaber, now!"

"But—"

"Quick!"

She did, flattening against the lift walls as blasterfire poured through the hole above them. Another grenade plinked against the lift floor.

"There. Throw that back at them," Anakin said.

The grenade whizzed back up the hole. "Why didn't you do it?" Tahiri asked.

"Because I'm holding the lift car up."

Above them, the glop grenade went off, and Anakin let gravity have the car.

It dropped like a stone.

"Remember to jump up just before we hit bottom," Anakin gritted, as the lift hurled down through the layers of hangars and Massassi caverns below the temple.

"Somebody wasn't paying attention in physics lectures," Tahiri said.

"Nope. Mind the roof." And then they did jump, pushing away from the lift floor with the Force, up through the jagged hole, into the turbolift shaft. Below them, the car hit bottom with a terrific din. Once again they drifted each other down upon it, but this time the car wasn't exactly level. It had wrenched the lowest doors from their hinges, and they were able to step through.

The Rebel Alliance had converted square kilometers of Massassi caverns into hangars, but below that there were chambers and caverns more or less untouched. The turbolift went down only as far as the Alliance had used the caverns. After that it was stairs, winding corridors, and secret panels.

"They'll look up there first," Anakin said. "They'll think we went through into the hangar where I cut the wall. By the time they think to look down here—in fact, hang on." He activated his wrist comm.

"Fiver."

AFFIRMATIVE. Fiver's response scrolled across the small display.

"I need you to fly the X-wing out of the hangar. Avoid all pursuit until I call you again. Got that?"

AFFIRMATIVE.

"Good luck, Fiver," Anakin whispered.

After a long descent, Anakin stopped in front of a blank wall. "Remember this?"

"Is Dagobah up to its neck in mud?" Tahiri pushed a patch in the wall and it swung open. The two stepped through and closed it behind them. Anakin felt around in the rocks and came up with one of the two glow lamps that were usually secreted there.

"Master Ikrit has already been here," he murmured. "With Valin and Sannah."

"Yeah. I can feel them."

"That was, umm, good back there," Anakin admitted. "Where did you get the lightsaber?"

"Anakin Solo. You don't think I can build a lightsaber?"

"I didn't say that. I just didn't think—"

"Right. You didn't think, and you're still not thinking, and you'd better fix that before you say anything else. Now, let's find Master Ikrit."

The pungent, rotten-egg scent of sulfur would have led them to their destination if their memories had not. Ikrit, Valin, and Sannah sat on the edges of an underground hot spring, just outside of a shaft of light that fell from a hundred meters or more above, where some long-ago force, natural or artificial, had cut through the soft stone.

"I've never seen it in daylight," Tahiri murmured.

When they were younger they had come here with Kam and Tionne to drift in the warm water and turn from inward to outward in the Force, to contemplate the stars above and the person within. It was a place all the students knew, but which was never spoken of to anyone else.

"Good that you have come," Ikrit sighed.

"You knew I would," Anakin said.

"Yes. Still, it is good."

"What will we do now?" Valin asked. He was trying to look brave, but Anakin could feel his fear.

"Now? You guys will keep waiting here. It should be safe enough. I'm going to climb up there—" Tahiri elbowed Anakin in the side. "I mean," he corrected, "Tahiri and I will climb up there while we have light to see by. Then we'll hide until dark and stea—er, *commandeer* one of their ships, one big enough for all of us."

"And small enough to bring down here," Tahiri added.

"Right. There's a light transport I think might fit the bill."

"Do you remember the way up?" Tahiri asked.

"You two did this before?" Ikrit asked. "Climbed up to the surface from here?"

"Um, yes," Anakin replied. "When we were bored, once."

"I thought I always had my eye on you," Ikrit said. "I must be getting old."

Somehow, the Jedi Master *looked* old, older than Anakin had ever seen him. He sounded old, too.

"Are you ill, Master Ikrit?"

"Ill? No. Sad."

"Sad at what?"

Ikrit ruffled his fur. "It is inappropriate, my sadness. It is nothing. Go, succeed as you always do. Remember—" Ikrit paused, then began more strongly in a voice that made Anakin feel, suddenly, that he was eleven again. "Remember. You two are better than the sum of your parts. Together, you two could—" He paused again. "No. Enough. I've said enough. Together, that's the important thing. Now go."

They reached the top by nightfall and took shelter in a small cavern just under the lip of the pit. It was a tight fit, but impossible to see unless you were hovering right in front of it. They sat shoulder to shoulder, breathing deeply and working the cramps from their muscles.

"You thought I was going to mess things up," Tahiri said suddenly.

"What brought that up?"

"There hasn't been time to talk about it until now."

"Well, keep your voice down. It's not exactly the brightest thing for us to be talking."

"We'll feel them in the Force long before they hear us."

"Unless they have Yuuzhan Vong with 'em. You can't *feel* them in the Force."

"Really? Is that true?"

"Yeah."

"So?"

"So what?"

Tahiri punched his shoulder lightly. "So you thought I was going to mess things up. Get us all caught."

"I didn't say that."

"No, of course not. Wouldn't want to upset baby Tahiri."

"Tahiri, now you're *acting* like a kid."

"No, I'm not. I'm acting like someone whose best friend has completely forgotten she exists."

"That's ridiculous."

"Is it? When you left the academy with Mara, did you even bother to say good-bye? And since then, have you sent me a single message, or even reached out in the Force? And just a while ago, when we did our old falling dance—you didn't *like* it. I almost had to catch myself!"

"You're the one who resisted," Anakin said. "We were falling like rocks, and you resisted me."

"That was you, you big dumb gundark."

"That's crazy. You—" But the whole scene flashed suddenly though his mind again. Maybe it *had* been him. When he and Tahiri worked together it was sometimes hard to tell who was feeling what.

"See?" she said frostily.

Anakin was silent for a moment, and so, miraculously, was Tahiri.

"I did miss you," Anakin finally said. "No one knows me the way—" He broke off.

"Right," Tahiri said. "No one knows you like I do, and you don't *want* anyone to. You want to keep all of that stuff in you, where no one can touch it. Chewbacca— even last time you were here you wouldn't talk about him. Now you pretend you're past it. And the thing at Centerpoint—"

"You're right," Anakin said. "I don't want to talk about that. Not right now."

Tahiri's shoulders began to shake, just a little, and Anakin realized she was crying.

"Come on, Tahiri," he said.

"What *are* we, Anakin? A year ago you were my best friend in the world."

"We're still best friends," he assured her.

"Then the way you treat your other friends must really stink."

"Yeah," Anakin admitted. Almost without thinking, he reached for her hand. For a few seconds, she didn't respond. Her fingers were cold and motionless in his, and he suddenly believed he had made some kind of mistake. Then she gripped back, and warmth rushed around him like a whirlwind. She nodded her head over onto his shoulder, still weeping, and silence folded around them again. But this time it was an easier silence. Not happy or even quite content, but easier.

After a while her breathing became regular, and Anakin realized she was asleep. By the faint orange light of the gas giant outside, he could make out traces of her features, so familiar and yet somehow different. It was as if, below the girl's face he had always known, something else was pushing up, like mountains rising, driven by the internal heat of a planet. Something you couldn't stop, even if you wanted to.

It made him want to hang on and run away at the same time, and in a mild epiphany he realized he had felt that way for some time.

As children they had been best friends. But neither of them was a child anymore, not exactly.

His arm had gone numb from her weight, but he couldn't bring himself to shift, for fear of waking her.

Anakin woke Tahiri an hour before the orange planet set. The sun was not yet out.

"It's time," he said.

"Good," Tahiri mumbled. "It's getting cramped in here." She shifted into a crouch. "Are the others still okay?"

"I haven't heard or felt anything. Are you ready?"

"Ready as rockets, hero boy."

Carefully they climbed from the pit and padded through the jungle. The spicy scent of bruised blueleaf shrubs suggested a lot of searching had been done in the area, but for the moment it was quiet. Anakin and Tahiri made it to the ship landing clearing without incident.

"I like that one," Anakin whispered, pointing at a light transport a little apart from the rest. "I don't think I'll have trouble flying it, and we can get it down the pit."

"You're the captain, Captain."

Anakin peered more closely at the ship and then began sneaking across the clearing. A guard several hundred meters away glanced in their direction, but it took only a faint suggestion to turn Anakin and Tahiri into shadow and planetlight.

They found a guard in front of the ship, too, sitting on the open ramp. He came quickly to his feet when they saw him.

"You're needed around the other side of the temple," Anakin told him, with a slight wave of his hand.

The fellow hesitated an instant, scratching his chin. "I'm needed elsewhere," he allowed. "I'll go, then."

"See you later," Anakin said as the man started away, pace quickening as he went.

"What the—?" A young man's face stuck around the corner. He looked as if he had just awakened. Seeing Anakin and Tahiri, the fellow's eyes went wide and he reached for his blaster. He stopped with the *snap-hiss* of Anakin's lightsaber igniting, probably because the glowing purple tip was centimeters from one of his gray eyes.

"Easy," Anakin said.

"Hey," the fellow said. "I'm always easy. Ask anyone. Would you, uh, mind getting that a little farther from my face?"

"You have restraining cuffs here somewhere?"

"Maybe."

Anakin shrugged. "I can cut your arms off and get more or less the same effect."

"In the locker over there," the fellow said, pointing.

"Get them, Tahiri. What's your name?"

"Remis. Remis Vehn."

"You pilot this thing?"

"Sure."

"Any surprises I need to know about before I fly her?"

Vehn winced as Tahiri pulled his arms back and snapped them in the cuffs. "Not that I can think of," he said.

"Good. I'll keep you aboard though. If any occur to you, let me know."

Anakin shut his lightsaber down, made his way to the controls, and looked them over. They weren't that different from those on the *Millennium Falcon*, his father's ship.

Vehn cleared his throat. "I just remembered. Before you engage the repulsorlift you have to enter a clearance code."

"Really? Or what happens?"

"The cabin will sort of electrify."

"I'm glad you remembered that," Anakin said dryly. "The code, please?"

Vehn recited it while Anakin entered it. Then the young Jedi turned back to his captive. "Let me explain something to you," he said. "My name is Anakin Solo, and this is my friend Tahiri Veila. We are Jedi Knights, some of the people you came here to betray to the Yuuzhan Vong. If you lie to us, we'll know it. If you try to keep something from us, we'll find it out. The only uncertain factor is how much we'll have to damage you to do so."

Vehn snorted. "They were right. You Jedi and your high-minded ideals—it's all smoke screen."

Anakin shot him a withering glance. "Next time I'm trying to capture children for Yuuzhan Vong sacrifices, I'll be sure to have a talk about 'high-minded ideals' with you. Until then, or until you have something useful to say, you keep your garbage lock cycled shut."

He turned back to the controls. "Hang on, Tahiri. This

might go a little rough until I get the feel of it. And pay attention to Vehn. If you feel the slightest twinge from him, dig it out."

"Yes, sir, Captain Solo."

Anakin engaged the repulsorlifts, and the ship began to rise. Before he closed the ramp, he heard someone shouting outside.

"Call out to Master Ikrit," Anakin told Tahiri. "Use the force to let him know we're coming."

And it's going to be tight, he finished, to himself.

CHAPTER SIX

Talon Karrde clasped his hands beneath his goatee and studied the scene on the *Wild Karrde*'s command deck viewscreen through pale blue eyes.

"Well, Shada," he told the striking woman at his right hand, "it appears that our baby-sitting chore has become somewhat more . . . interesting than anticipated."

"I would say so," Shada D'ukal replied. "The sensor shroud shows at least seven ships in orbit around Yavin Four and another six on the surface."

"None of them are Yuuzhan Vong, I take it."

"No. A mixed bag, but I'd lay odds that they are Peace Brigade."

"Gambling is a foolish occupation," Karrde said. "I want to *know*. And I want to know what they're doing." He ticked his finger against the armrest. "I knew we should have found some way to leave sooner. Skywalker was right." He sighed and leaned forward, studying the long-range sensors.

"There's some sort of firefight on the surface, yes, H'sishi?"

"Looks like it," the Togorian mewled.

"Solusar?" Karrde wondered. "Maybe. How long before we can be there?"

"They outnumber us badly," Shada pointed out. "We should call the rest of our ships before we do anything."

"We should certainly call them, but we can't wait for them. Someone down there is fighting for his life, most likely one of the people I told Skywalker I would protect. What's more, the fact that there are still ships on the surface suggests they haven't finished what they came here to do. That is, they don't have the Jedi children yet. If we wait until they have them aboard, in space, the job of rescuing them will become much more complicated."

"I see that," Shada said. "But it will be more complicated yet if they blow us out of the sky."

Karrde laughed. "Shada, when will you learn to trust my instincts? When have I ever gotten you killed?"

"You have a point there, I suppose."

Karrde pointed at Yavin 4, at the moment a dark disk silhouetted against the larger orange profile of its primary. "So I want to be there, now. Dankin, keep full cloak, but let me know when they notice us."

"Of course, sir."

That point came an hour later, when they were almost sitting on the nearest of the orbiting ships.

"They're hailing us, sir," Dankin told him. "And powering up weapons."

"Put them on."

A moment later, a thick-featured human male with thin, graying hair appeared on the communication holoscreen.

"Transport, identify yourself." He chopped the words out in even syllables.

"My name, sir, is Talon Karrde. Perhaps you've heard of me."

The man's eyes pinched warily. "Yes, I've heard of you, Captain Karrde. It's rude to sneak up on someone like that. And dangerous."

"And it's rude to be given a name and not offer one," Karrde returned.

A look of annoyance crossed the fellow's face. "Don't try me, Captain Karrde. You may call me Captain Imsatad. What do you want?"

Karrde favored the man with a wan smile. "I was going to ask you the same question."

"I don't follow you," Imsatad said.

"You seem to be having some sort of trouble. I'm offering my assistance."

"We need no assistance, I assure you. And to be blunt, Captain Karrde, I don't believe you. I remember you as a smuggler, a pirate, and a traitor to the Empire."

"Then perhaps you remember, as well, what became of those who treated me with disrespect," Karrde said icily. "But if we are being blunt—and perhaps that is best here, since you seem to lack the education for more civilized discourse—I am undoubtedly here for the same reason you are—to collect the bounty on the young Jedi below."

"I don't know what you're talking about."

Karrde leaned toward the screen, eyes glittering dangerously. "You are a liar, Captain, and a poor one. I see no reason for us to play games."

"I trust you've noticed you're outnumbered."

"I trust *you* noted I was able to drop in on you in, shall we say, an unannounced fashion. Do you really think I brought only one ship?"

Imsatad glared at him, then cut his visual. Karrde waited patiently until, a few moments later, the image returned.

"This is none of your business," the man said.

"Profit is always my business."

"There is no profit here, and if there were, you would already be too late."

"Oh, I don't think so. Why are your ships still on the surface? Why do my sensors show what seems to be protracted search activity? You've let your quarry slip through your fingers, Captain." Karrde smiled and leaned back in his chair. "Consider my offer of help. I ask little in return, and I could be a nuisance if you spurn my kindness."

"That sounds like a threat."

Karrde spread his hands. "Take it however you please. Shall we discuss this further or not?"

"You say you ask for little. What, exactly, would that be?"

"A few kind words in the ears of the Yuuzhan Vong. An introduction. You see, Captain, for some years now I've been retired from my chosen profession. But these are very interesting times, exactly the sort of times my kind thrives on, if you know what I mean. I'd like to come out of retirement."

"Go on."

Karrde stroked his mustache thoughtfully. "The Yuuzhan Vong have promised a truce if the Jedi are delivered to them. I would like to bargain for passage through Yuuzhan Vong space, once the borders are established."

"Why should they allow a smuggler to use their space?"

"There may be things they need. I can get them. If not, I would be doing them no harm; all of my activities would be aimed at the scattered remnants of the New Republic. But those remnants are separated, at times, by Yuuzhan Vong–occupied systems. The cost of circumventing them, frankly, would be prohibitive."

Imsatad nodded, and a brief look of disgust wrinkled his features. "I see. You realize I can promise none of that."

"I only asked for a mention of my help in this affair. You can promise that."

"I could," Imsatad acknowledged. "What exactly can you offer me?"

"Better sensors than you have, for one thing. Detailed knowledge of Yavin Four that I believe you lack. A crew that is very, very good at finding things. Certain special defenses against Jedi—and the means of finding them."

Imsatad stiffened, and his voice dropped low. "I was with Thrawn at Wayland. You still? . . ."

"Ah. You know what I mean, then."

"I know you betrayed him."

Karrde rolled his eyes. "How tiresome. Very well,

Captain, if you don't wish my services, there are others who will."

"Wait!" Imsatad chewed his lip for a moment. "I need to consult with my officers on this."

"Take a few moments," Karrde said, lifting a finger. "But do not bore me." He cut the transmission.

CHAPTER SEVEN

"Hutt slime!" Remis Vehn snapped, as the transport scraped along the wall of the pit. "Watch my ship!"

"The controls have too much play in them," Anakin complained.

"No, you're flying like a Twi'lek on spice," Vehn replied.

"Quiet," Tahiri said, "or we'll restrain your mouth, too."

Vehn yelped again as they scraped stone. The fit was tighter than Anakin had thought it would be.

Still, a moment later, they settled into the steaming water of the underground pool. Anakin dropped the landing ramp, and an instant later Ikrit and the two Jedi children were on board.

"Strap in, everyone," Anakin told them. He hit the lifts and back up they started.

An instant later, the whole ship shuddered and their ears were filled with the screech of metal!

"The landing ramp, you vac-brain!" Vehn screamed. "You didn't pull up the ramp!"

Belatedly Anakin flipped the appropriate switch, but all he got was a grinding noise.

"Great," he muttered.

"Anakin," Tahiri said, "I think we may have trouble."

"We'll make it, even with the ramp down. We'll figure out what to do about that later."

"That's not what I meant." She pointed up through the cockpit.

Something dark was eclipsing the morning light.

"Sith spawn. They've moved one of the big freighters over the hole."

"Continue," Master Ikrit murmured.

"But—"

"Continue." The diminutive Master was crouched on the floor, eyes closed, his voice a serene purr. Anakin felt a powerful surge in the Force.

"You should strap in, Master."

"No time."

Anakin nodded. "As you say, Master Ikrit." He throttled up. Banging, sparking, and shaking, they shot up toward the belly of their enemy.

"He's pushing it up," Tahiri said in awe. "Master Ikrit is pushing the freighter up."

And indeed, when they emerged, rather than sitting right over the hole, the freighter was some eighty meters off the ground. Its thrusters were burning, pushing it down, but it wasn't budging. Anakin darted his gaze about. The other ships and people on foot had sidled in on all sides but one, so he cut toward the hole as a brutal barrage struck them.

"My ship!" Vehn howled, as the deck pitched wildly. Not blinking, Anakin took them through the storm, just as two more ships closed in, completing the trap.

"Help Master Ikrit," Anakin told the Jedi candidates. "Push the freighter up farther."

"Master Ikrit is gone, Anakin," Valin said. "He jumped out of the hatch."

"He *what*?"

"There he is!" Tahiri shrieked, pointing ahead of them.

There Ikrit was indeed, walking toward the blocking ships, a corvette and a light freighter. As he approached them, they were parted as if by two gigantic hands.

"I don't believe it," Anakin said. But he gunned forward, nevertheless, aimed at the gap the Jedi Master had created for them. Blaster bolts and laser beams sizzled and hissed in the air, but every shot that might have hit either Ikrit or the ship bent away, missing by centimeters, and still the small Jedi strolled sedately along.

They were almost free now, passing over Ikrit.

"He can't keep that up," Anakin said. "Tahiri, use the Force. Snag him as we go by."

"You bet," she answered. Her confidence rang false; Anakin heard a tremor in her voice.

That was when the first bolt slipped through and struck Master Ikrit. Anakin felt it in the Force, a spike of clarity. No pain, no fear, no remorse, only . . . understanding.

Two more shots hit Ikrit in quick succession, and then fire was pounding their ship again. With a sob of anguish, Anakin jetted the ship through the hole and spun. At the same moment, with an inarticulate growl, Tahiri leapt from the open hatch, lightsaber glowing, and ran toward the downed Master.

"No!" Anakin howled. He brought the forward guns—the only ones under his direct control—to bear, and opened up on the ships that were suddenly closing between him and Tahiri. They returned fire. He caught a glimpse of her, Ikrit's body in her arms, dodging back toward him. Absurdly, his eyes were drawn to her bare feet, white against the brown soil.

The transport turned halfway over under a barrage, and every light in the ship went out. Cursing, Anakin started furiously trying to reroute, and then the power whined back on. The shields were gone.

"Valin, Sannah, one of you!" he shouted. "Get to the laser turret! *Now!*"

He did the only thing he could. In seconds they would be cooked. If he stood any chance of getting Tahiri back on board, he needed a plan.

He spun and fired the jets, leaping above the other

ships, strafing them as he went. He was absorbed now, his senses in the Force stretched to their limits, dodging shots before they were fired, sensing the weakest spots to place his own rounds, pinwheeling and jagging above them.

The ships came up with him. He fought for altitude, all the time aware that Tahiri was farther and farther below him. He could still feel her. She was still alive.

Master Ikrit was not. Anakin felt the old Jedi's life go, felt it pass through him like a sweet wind.

I am proud of you, Anakin, it seemed to say. *Remember—together, you are stronger than the sum of your parts. I love you. Good-bye.*

Gritting his teeth against another concussion, Anakin clenched the tears in his skull. *Cry later, Anakin,* he thought. *Right now you have to see.*

One of his engines was limping. He couldn't win this, not here, not now. With a curse that bordered on being a sob, he flipped, slid between two ships that collided an instant later, and punched toward the upper atmosphere.

Below him, Tahiri's presence dwindled.

Like Chewie. Just like Chewie.

He jerked the ship back around and aimed it at the nearest ship, a corvette, and went to full throttle.

"What the—" Vehn gasped. "You're going to kill us!"

Anakin fired. The other ship held steady, steady.

Anakin pulled up, just slightly, and skipped off the top of the corvette the way a hurled stone might skip across a lake. The collision tossed them up with a terrible shrieking of metal.

The counterforce hurled the corvette down, not far, but far enough to slam it nose-first into the Great Temple. An orchid of flame uncurled from its engines.

A gasp later, the turbolaser in the turret began talking as Sannah took control of the gun. Anakin put the ship into a climb, fighting for distance though every meter he put behind him tore another stitch from his heart.

"I'll be back, Tahiri," he said. "That I swear. I'll be back."

Kam Solusar gasped and sagged against the damp stone wall of the cave. Tionne, nearby, stifled a cry of anguish. Some of the children, the more sensitive ones, began to cry, probably not even sure what they were crying about.

He groped through the darkness until he found Tionne and took her in his arms. He could smell the salt on her cheeks, feel the torn place in her.

Tionne felt things so deep, so strong. She had no fear of the pain that such openness could cause. It was one of the things he loved about her. While he put on armor against the universe, she took it all in and gave it back as something better. Her wound would heal, and from it a song would come. Others thought she was weak, because her powers in the Force weren't so great.

Kam knew better. Ultimately, she was stronger than he.

"Master Ikrit," she whispered.

"I know," Kam replied, stroking her silver hair. "He knew all along."

They stood that way for a few precious seconds, drawing strength and comfort from each other. It was Tionne who moved away first.

"The children need us," she said. "We're all they have, now."

"No," Kam whispered back. "Anakin is still out there."

CHAPTER EIGHT

Talon Karrde was a hostage, but he wasn't supposed to know that. Imsatad probably thought himself clever and subtle for maneuvering Karrde into joining the search party on the moon's surface and equally clever to make certain that there were twenty of his own people to Karrde's four.

Karrde was quite content to allow him that illusion of shrewdness.

"We've already searched here," Maber Yeff, the leader of the Peace Brigade segment of the team, said in his shrill little voice, waving his hand at a long row of vine-smothered ruins.

"I'm sure you did," Karrde replied. "But not with vornskrs."

Yeff's pale, ax-nosed face turned dubiously toward the long-limbed beasts loping ahead of the group. "How do you know they don't just smell womp rats or something?" he asked.

"If they could do that, they would be valuable indeed," Karrde replied. "As there are no womp rats on Yavin Four, it would require hyperwave noses to sniff them out all the way over on Tatooine."

"You know what I mean."

"Vornskrs sense the Force, and especially those creatures that *use* the Force. They are particularly suited for hunting Jedi."

"Yeah? Where can we get some? That would be useful in our line of work."

"Alas, mine are the only tame ones in existence. You don't want to meet a wild one, I promise you."

"Still. We've got plenty more of these Jedi to hunt down, and with all of the advantages their sorcery gives them—and if these things do what you say—"

"Observe," Karrde said. The beasts had pricked up their ears and were panting eagerly. They darted through a crumbling entranceway.

"But we looked in there," Yeff repeated.

"How many Jedi do you estimate are hiding in there? Based on my information, at least two adults and perhaps thirty children. Do you think you could see them if they didn't want to be seen? Or that you would remember them if you did see them?"

"Can they really do that?"

"They can really do that."

"That's what Captain Imsatad said. He also said you have a way around that."

Karrde smile thinly. "Indeed. A certain creature from the same planet as the vornskrs. It projects a bubble that repels the Force."

"That's what your pretty lady has in the covered cage."

From the corner of his eye, Karrde saw Shada's brows lower dangerously, but she continued to play her part. "Exactly. My sweet Sleena is as delicate as they are. She understands their needs."

"Yeah." Yeff spared "Sleena" another leer. "Can I see it?"

"Sunlight harms them, and they are easily agitated. If you wish, after the hunt, I'll show them to you. For the time being, I suggest you have your people ready their weapons. The children shouldn't put up much of a fight, but the adults will be formidable, even without their Jedi powers."

They followed the vornskrs into the ruins, through crumbling galleries incensed with the crushed-spice scent of blueleaf and the grainy, wormy smell of rotting wood. At first the light was dim but sufficient, falling in shards through gaps in the wall and roof, diffused by mist, leaves, and stringy mosslike stuff. But as they followed the vornskrs, it grew darker, and eventually they reached the opening to a stairwell that dropped steeply down into the bedrock foundations of the place.

Karrde drew his blaster and nodded to Shada, on his right. Most everyone else already had theirs out.

"After you," Karrde suggested.

"Your beasts," Yeff told him. "You go ahead."

"As you wish."

The tunnel took them down through ages of stone scribed now and then in alien figures and script. Eventually it debouched into a large cavern. The vornskrs stood snarling and spitting at the darkness.

"Sit," Karrde commanded, the hair on his neck pricking up. Had he just seen a motion, part of a face, or was he just fooling himself? His own life depended on the answer.

He looked again at the vornskrs, at the way their eyes moved. As if watching something walking, very near.

"Where are they? I don't see anything." Yeff swung his lamp around.

"No," Karrde said. "Neither do I." He raised his blaster and stunned the Peace Brigader.

He managed to nail another one before the return fire came, and by then he was already diving for the rocks. Team members Halm and Ferson, alert for his signal, were already doing the same. Shada, on the other hand, was a gyroscoping blur in the midst of their enemies. Too bad Yeff was already stunned; otherwise he would be learning a whole new appreciation for the "pretty lady" right now.

When they had allowed him only three of his crew,

they hadn't known exactly how good Shada was. How could they? Now it was too late.

The air went thick with energy, and the cave strobed.

By his count it was now four to fifteen.

He heard Halm cry out, and regretfully amended his own forces to three. He pulled his other blaster and leapt up, both weapons blazing, searching for better cover.

"Come on, come on," he shouted. "I know you're here! Regards from Luke and Mara's wedding!"

A bolt singed across his arm, and he stumbled on the uneven floor. *I'm getting too old for this,* he thought, rolling on his back. Without cover he would last a few seconds, maybe long enough to shoot two more. Shada might still manage to kill them all, but that would leave the galaxy short one Talon Karrde, which would be a terrible tragedy.

Grimly, he raised his weapons and pointed over his feet. Muzzles flashed.

And suddenly a glowing wand of energy appeared above him, cutting complex hieroglyphs in the air. The blaster bolts that had meant to end the glorious career of Talon Karrde whined off into the cavern.

Karrde blinked up at the man standing over him. "Nice to see you, Solusar. What took you so long?"

Then he opened up on the Peace Brigaders, climbing to his feet as he did so. Solusar was his cover now, deflecting the fire directed at them with that eerie Jedi certainty.

Another lightsaber flashed into existence across the room. That would be Tionne.

Karrde now counted five for his side, an estimated ten on the other.

When the Peace Brigaders were down to three, they fled back up the passageway.

"We can't let them get away," Karrde said.

"They won't," the shadowy figure beside him promised. Then he was gone.

And somewhere behind him in the cavern, Karrde heard the voices of children.

Kam Solusar returned a few moments later. Karrde made out his stern face and receding hairline in the dim light of a glow lamp. Solusar walked up to Karrde and regarded him for a moment.

"You're lucky I didn't cut you down," he said. "Bringing those men down here where the children are. Using your vornskrs against us. What if they had attacked the students?"

Karrde cocked his head. "My pets are very well trained. They attack only on my order. Look, Solusar. I had to find you. I couldn't do it without the interference of those fools, and when I did find you I had to get rid of them. They thought I had an ysalamiri with me, that your Jedi powers would be blocked."

"But you didn't bring one."

"It's an empty cage."

"So you turned on them, not knowing if we were really here or not."

"I know my pets. I was certain you were down here, and I didn't want to cripple you by actually bringing an ysalamiri."

"That was quite a risk."

"I told Luke Skywalker I would take his students off of Yavin Four. If keeping my word requires risk, that's acceptable."

Solusar nodded impatiently. "Understood. But how am I to know you're telling the truth? I know you, yes, and you've been on the right side. But a lot of people are joining the Peace Brigade, and you've changed coats before, Karrde."

"So have you. Have you ever wanted to put the old one back on?"

Solusar's eyes narrowed, then he chopped his head in a single affirmation. "I'll trust you. What now?"

"Now I suggest we get out of here, before they send reinforcements."

Unfortunately, Captain Imsatad had not underestimated Karrde as badly as he might have. When they reached the surface, the forest was teeming with Peace Brigaders.

"Perfect," Kam Solusar muttered, ducking a blaster bolt that vaped a fist-sized hole in the stone near him. "At least before, we were hidden."

Karrde straightened the front of his outfit and glanced casually at his chrono. "Solusar, I'm injured. Don't you have any faith in me?"

"Faith is blind, unquestioned belief. What do *you* think?"

"I think I would cover my ears if I were you." He raised his voice. "Tionne, children. Cover your ears."

"Wha—" Solusar began, but was drowned out by what might have been two hands the size of Death Stars clapping.

Karrde grinned with fierce satisfaction as turbolaser fire set the surrounding jungle ablaze. It was good to have a crew he could trust. He stepped from behind cover and, carefully aiming and picking off the few Peace Brigaders who were still paying attention, trotted toward where the *Wild Karrde* was landing. When the landing ramp came down, Kam Solusar and Tionne shepherded the children on board as Karrde and his crew provided cover fire. In moments, they were all inside.

Karrde was the last aboard, and even as his feet hit the deck, the modified Corellian transport pirouetted and tossed itself at the sky. Through the closing hatch, Karrde saw several enemy ships already on their trail.

He had known it would be a near thing. He almost couldn't believe they had pulled it off.

Of course, he would never say that aloud.

Humming, he went at a brisk but dignified pace to his bridge.

By the time he got there, the sky was already a deep blue bruise getting blacker by the second.

"Well, gentlebeings," Karrde said as he took his seat. "What's the situation?"

H'sishi shot him a harried look from the sensor station. "We did some damage to our watchdogs in orbit, but they're all still flying. Now we have the ships from the surface to deal with as well."

"Well. Deal with them."

"Yes, sir."

The ship shuddered, and the inertial dampeners whined.

"Opur," Karrde shouted at one of his security men. "Make certain the children are secured somewhere. I don't want one hair on their little Jedi heads harmed."

"Yes, sir," Opur said, hurrying off.

"Now." Karrde studied the layout. "They've got us penned in, don't they?"

"Unless we can make the jump to lightspeed."

"With big Yavin right there?" Karrde mused. "No, not today. I think we'll punch through the cage instead." He tapped the console. "Here."

"That's their most heavily armed ship," Shada observed.

"When a pack of vornskrs comes for you, always kick the biggest and meanest one right in the teeth. It will certainly get their attention."

"I believe we already have their attention."

"One can never have too much good wine, beautiful women, or attention," Karrde said. "Go, and keep the throttle open."

"We won't get their shields down before we reach them," Shada said.

"No, we won't. Buy we'll certainly see who blinks first." He reflected for an instant. "Give me the controls."

"I thought you said gambling was a foolish occupation," Shada remarked, as the frigate grew larger on their screens.

"Indeed I did," Karrde replied. "But I'm not gambling. On my mark, release proton torpedoes. Don't fire them—just release them."

"As you wish, sir," the gunner replied, sounding puzzled.

"They're trying for tractor lock," Shada said.

"Yes. Let them have it."

"What?"

"Drop the shields."

This time the dampeners couldn't absorb all of the shock; the deck felt as if it was buckling beneath their feet as the tractor beam caught them, killing their forward motion.

"Torpedoes. Now," Karrde said.

"Torpedoes released." Shada looked up. "The tractor beam has them."

"Good. Arm them and put our shields back up."

"Sir, they've commenced fire on the torpedoes."

"Have they released the tractor beam?"

"No, sir."

"Detonate the torpedoes, then."

He reengaged the drive as the screen went white.

CHAPTER NINE

Treetops snapped as Anakin wrestled with gravity. Vehn's complaints had deteriorated to a steady moan. Valin, strapped in the copilot's seat, looked very ill. Sannah was still firing the turbolaser; from her, Anakin could sense both frustration and anger. Tahiri had been *her* friend, too.

Was *still* her friend. Tahiri was alive. Anakin could feel that as certainly as he could feel his own skin.

The transport cut a smoking swath across the tree line for a kilometer before Anakin saw what passed for a clearing. He dropped in, straining the inertial dampeners well beyond their parameters, fetching up against a wall of vines and secondary growth—dense, but without much mass. If he hit a *big* tree . . .

He tried not to think about it. Instead he dumped a torpedo and reversed direction, traveling into the more open forest beyond on repulsors, drifting back toward the treetops, hiding in the canopy.

The torpedo went, taking a hundred square meters of the forest with it in a carbon-rich plume.

"Come on, you vultures," Anakin muttered.

"Got them," Sannah called softly.

"No," Anakin replied. "Wait."

He could make it out through the smoke, a *Sentinel*-class shuttle.

"They think we've crashed," Valin said.

"Yes," Anakin replied, punching the engines back on.

The modified shuttle tried to swing around as he rose out of the trees, but it was too late. He fired his last proton torpedo, and the Peace Brigade ship became a ball of fire, sinking into the already burning jungle.

"Anakin!" Sannah shrieked.

Instinctively, Anakin threw the ship skyward, but not before multiple impacts ripped through the failing transport.

"There you are," he muttered. "After you, I'm done."

Of the three ships that had chased him halfway around the moon, only this one—an E-wing—remained. Unfortunately, while Anakin's commandeered transport was limping so badly it would soon go down on its own, the speedy little fighter was undamaged.

"You only have to hit it once, Sannah," Anakin said. "Maybe twice."

"I can't get a bead," she shouted back.

The little ship made a pass, and the air suddenly smelled sharply of ozone and vaporized metal as the transport tremored.

"Let me have a shot!" Vehn demanded.

"What?"

"Look, I don't wanna die. This is my ship, those are my guns. I know 'em better than that kid back there. She's never even handled a gun before, that much is clear— yii!" Vehn blanched as Anakin put the ungainly craft in a barrel roll.

"You think I trust you?"

"Use your poodoo-stinking Jedi powers. Can't you tell I'm serious?"

To Anakin's surprise, he really didn't sense deception from the fellow.

"You'd shoot down your own friends?"

"They're not my friends."

Again, no deception.

Anakin made his decision. "Valin, uncuff him. Take

him to the gun. Vehn, I promise you, if this is a trick, no matter what else happens, *you'll* be sorry."

"Sorrier than I am now? I doubt it."

Anakin dropped low again, trying to buy a few more seconds. He had only one engine left on-line, and one more hit would finish that quickly enough.

"I'm on it," Vehn reported from the turret. "Give me a little altitude, that's all I ask."

"You've got it," Anakin said. Once more he put the ship in a climb. The E-wing saw its opportunity then, darting in and chewing what was left of the engine to shreds. It coughed off-line, and for an instant the transport seemed to hang suspended a hundred meters above the treetops. In that in-between moment, Vehn needled red lines across the sky, stitching through the E-wing. It spun wildly out of control. Then the transport was falling, and Anakin hit the repulsors, and the sound of tearing metal deafened him.

Anakin came to with the taste of blood on his tongue. He didn't know if he had been out for seconds or days, and a glance at the controls didn't help. Through the cockpit transparisteel he could see only crushed vegetation.

"Sannah! Valin!"

"They're okay," Remis Vehn said from behind Anakin. "A little battered, but no worse for the wear."

Anakin twisted in his seat and found himself confronting the muzzle of a blaster. He blinked, then looked up at the young man's cool gray eyes.

"You want to put that down, don't you?" Anakin asked, pushing with the Force.

"Well . . . ," Vehn considered.

"You'll put it down," Anakin commanded.

"Sure," Vehn replied. "I'll put it down."

"Great." Anakin unfastened himself from the flight harness. He took the blaster and stuck it in his belt.

"Vaping moffs!" Vehn swore. "You Jedi *are* sorcerers."

"Keep it sealed," Anakin warned him, turning to Sannah.

Sannah was unconscious but breathing evenly. Valin was awake, but the hull near him had crimped in such a way that Sannah's harness was stuck. Anakin sliced through it with his lightsaber. The Melodie girl moaned softly.

"Vehn, carry Sannah out," Anakin told the Peace Brigader. "The ship may have a few surprises for us yet."

"My ship," Vehn said. "I can't believe what you did to my ship."

"Your buddies did it," Anakin said. "The same buddies who just murdered a Jedi Master and took my best friend captive. Don't expect me to cry any tears for you."

"First of all," Vehn said, "they aren't my buddies. I was strictly in this business for the money, and I thought we were taking on adult Jedi, not little kids. Second of all, I don't expect you to get all weepy, but without my ship, how do you plan to get off this snarly jungle?"

Anakin didn't answer Vehn, but examined Valin instead. "Are you okay?" he asked. "Can you walk?"

"I'm fine," Valin answered.

"Good. I want you to go outside and find cover in the trees. Be careful—the jungle isn't exactly safe, though the crash probably scared most everything off."

He then examined Sannah. She was bruised, but he didn't sense anything seriously wrong with her.

"Take Sannah out," he repeated to Vehn. "I'm right behind you."

On his way out, he picked up the stun cuffs.

"This isn't right," Remis Vehn complained. "You just finished talking about how dangerous the jungle is and you not only won't give me a weapon, you've restrained me. What if something comes along wanting lunch?"

"It would have to be a carrion eater to stomach the likes of you," Anakin replied.

"Very funny. I helped you."

"You really think you're going to get thanks from me?" Anakin snorted. "You were saving your own skin, nothing more. Now, quiet."

"Is she going to be all right?" Valin asked, staring down at Sannah.

"I think so." Anakin touched the Melodie girl's forehead and very lightly brushed her with the Force, strengthening her where she was weak, gently tugging her toward consciousness.

With a faint sigh she opened her eyes, blinked at Anakin, then started violently.

"Tahiri!" she gasped.

"Shh," Anakin said. "We crashed. You're banged up, some. How do you feel?"

"Like I've been poisoned by a purella and hung up in its web. Is Valin okay?"

"I'm right here," Valin answered.

"We're all okay," Anakin assured her.

Tears started in the girl's yellow eyes. "No, we're not. Master Ikrit, and Tahiri . . ."

"Master Ikrit sacrificed himself for us," Anakin said, around the gall in his throat. "He wouldn't want us to grieve. He's one with the Force now. Tahiri—"

"She's dead, too, isn't she?" Valin asked.

"No." Anakin shook his head. "I can hear her in the Force." *Calling me,* he added. He could feel her fear, mixed liberally with anger. He didn't get the sense that she was in immediate danger.

Anakin turned toward Vehn, who sat a few meters away, his arms cuffed around a young Massassi tree. "What will they do with her, Vehn? Where were you supposed to take the children you kidnapped?"

"I told you, I didn't know our targets were children," Vehn said sullenly. "And I don't know where we were supposed to take them."

"But you *were* supposed to turn them over to the Yuuzhan Vong."

Vehn studied the leaves above his head. "Yes," he said at last.

"Where? Where is the rendezvous?"

"I don't know."

"You're lying."

"Look—"

"I *can* make you tell me," Anakin warned. "You won't like it." It occurred to him that his brother, Jacen, wouldn't approve of that sort of threat, nor would Uncle Luke. At the moment, Anakin didn't care.

Vehn fidgeted, but said nothing. Anakin suddenly surged to his feet and stalked toward the Peace Brigader.

"Hold it! Just wait a second, Jedi. Don't slag my brain! I don't know much, but I can tell you something I overheard. Something I wasn't supposed to hear at all."

Anakin took another step, then squatted until his ice-blue eyes were millimeters from Vehn's dark gray. "Well?" he prompted.

"I'm not supposed to know this, but—the Yuuzhan Vong were planning to come to this miserable hole already. The Peace Brigade decided to head 'em off, capture you guys before they arrived."

"What, to save them the trouble?"

"Exactly. A present, of sorts. These Peace Brigade guys, they're serious. They really think everyone in the galaxy is doomed unless we give the Vong what they want, and then some."

"Why do you say 'these Peace Brigade guys' as if you aren't one of them?"

"They hired me to pilot. That's all."

Anakin frowned, but let that pass. "What will the Peace Brigade do now that they've botched the job?"

"How do you know they've botched it? They figured out you hid the other kids someplace. They have some pretty good trackers and search equipment with them."

"They won't find anyone," Anakin said. "What will they do? The Yuuzhan Vong might assume the Brigade really came here to hide the kids. At the very least they'll be upset that you were so inept you let thirty or more Jedi slip through your fingers and caught only one."

Vehn looked thoughtful. "They might cut and run. They might try to bluff it out with their one captive. I don't know them well enough to say."

"Anakin," Sannah said softly. "You and Tahiri saved my people. I can't let anything happen to her. I can't."

"Why didn't you think of that earlier?" Anakin snapped. "You three should have gone with Kam and Tionne. You thought this was all some sort of game. It isn't."

"Anakin!" Sannah's eyes widened further, then dropped. "You're right," she whispered. "It is our fault. *My* fault. I could have told Kam, and none of this would have happened. Master Ikrit would still be alive." Tears streamed down her face, and for a second Anakin was happy she was crying, satisfied she finally saw how stupid she had been. He wanted to agree with her.

Grinding his teeth, he quickly stood and walked into the woods.

He didn't go far, but leaned against the bole of a giant tree, breathing heavily, composing himself. Then, when he thought he could do it, he want back into the clearing, where Sannah sat, still crying. Valin was wiping his own silent tears.

"That was wrong of me," he said quietly. "None of you is to blame. You were only trying to help. The Peace Brigade is to blame. The Yuuzhan Vong are to blame. You guys aren't. Feeling guilty isn't going to help us right now. There are plenty more ships on this planet. For all we know they have a perfect lock on us already, so we need to get ready. If they don't, we need to figure out how to get this ship running again."

Remis Vehn vented a bitter laugh.

"We have parts from three ships here," Anakin said evenly. "We ought to be able to cobble something together. Besides that, help is on the way, so maybe all we really have to do is hold out for a little while. Valin, I'm putting you in charge of taking inventory of what food and medicine we have. Vehn, you'll tell him where to find it on your ship—all of it. Sannah, I'm giving you the blaster. I want you to watch the camp, while I go do recon at the other wreck sites. If you hear anything—I mean anything—coming from the sky, you both hide and stay hidden. Understand?"

"Yes," Sannah replied. Valin nodded dutifully.

"Good. And ignore everything Vehn says. Don't touch his restraints, don't go near him. I'll be back soon."

CHAPTER TEN

Karrde didn't black out, but time stretched weirdly as his harness tried to cut him in half and his ship spun madly, power blinking on and off, finally settling on off before minimal emergency systems kicked in. The inertial compensator started up, and gravity reasserted itself, but the screen was a confusing jumble.

"Report!" he snapped. "What's going on?"

H'sishi looked up reluctantly. "Minimal damage to the frigate," she said. "We took a pretty hard bounce, and we're limping a bit."

"Limp *away* from them, at least," Karrde said. "Head for the outer system."

"The hyperdrive core took some of the worst damage," Dankin pointed out. "I don't think we can jump."

"Well, we certainly can't here, not in the hole Yavin's dug for itself."

"The big ships we can still outrun, at least for a while. The frigate will catch us eventually, but we've got a lead it will take them at least an hour to cut down. We've got a couple of E-wings that will be harassing us shortly."

"Good luck to them," Karrde grunted.

"We do have some weak points in the hull, now," Shada pointed out.

"That's why we'll shoot them out of space, Shada my dear," Karrde answered.

"And our shields—"

"Will hold up long enough."

"Long enough for what?" Shada said. "Without hyperdrive—"

H'sishi suddenly grated out a yowling snarl.

"What's the matter, H'sishi?"

"I can give you something better than a working hyperdrive, Captain," the Togorian said.

"And what might that be?"

Her toothy grin nearly split her head in half. "The rest of our fleet, sir."

"You asked what I was waiting on, Shada? Don't ever doubt that the gods favor me. How far out are they?"

"Umm, urr." H'sishi was suddenly more sober. "Two hours at least, sir."

"Well," Karrde said cheerfully. "Then I'm taking suggestions on how to stretch the—it's what, eight minutes now? Into the two hours we need."

The hull suddenly rattled.

"E-wings on us, sir," Dankin reported.

"Well, don't keep them waiting. Show them what this helpless old transport has in store for them. Shada, you have the bridge."

"You're leaving in the middle of a fight?"

"It won't be a long one. When that capital ship catches us, give me a call. I need to talk to Solusar."

Four hours later, a weary Imsatad appeared on Karrde's screen.

"You're a fool, Karrde," he opined.

"What does that make you, Captain?" Karrde replied. "In any event, our positions are now reversed. I have considerably more firepower than your little flotilla."

"And yet, as you once observed of me, you're still here, which means you aren't finished," Imsatad said. "What do you want?"

"By my count, four of the young Jedi are still missing. You wouldn't know anything about that, would you?"

"As a matter of fact, I wouldn't."

Karrde stood and locked his hands behind his back. "I can be a very serious man, at times, Captain Imsatad. This is one of them. I gave my word to deliver the Jedi students and their teachers safely from the hands of scum like you, and I intend to do that. Not in part, but in full."

"You're endangering our work here," Imsatad said. "The Yuuzhan Vong will not stop until they have all the Jedi. If we do the work for them, show our good faith—"

Karrde cut him off with a mordant chuckle. "The Yuuzhan Vong have conquered half of our galaxy in an unprovoked crusade. What about this obligates us to show them good faith?"

"Listen, Karrde. I was at Dantooine, with the military. I saw what they can do. We can't stop them. We *can't*. This is simple self-preservation. Besides, they weren't unprovoked. It was the Jedi who started this war, and it's the Jedi who continue to provoke it."

Karrde sighed and returned to his seat. He tapped his fingers on the armrest. "I don't know if you really believe that sump muck, and I don't care. But it's good you bring up self-preservation, because you are now faced with a crisis in that department."

Imsatad lifted his chin defiantly. "If you suppose I have your missing Jedi, you won't destroy my ships."

Karrde gestured, and Kam Solusar strode into view.

"Let me introduce you. This is Kam Solusar, one of the teachers at the Jedi academy whose curricula you have so rudely interrupted. He is a Jedi, and they can sense one another. Did you know that?"

Imsatad's eyes flicked back and forth between the two. "I've heard such things."

"None of the children are on *your* ship, Captain," Solusar said in a voice that could saw through bones. "Nothing prevents us vaping *you*."

Imsatad blinked, twice. "I do what I do for the good of the galaxy," he said.

"Yes, you've said that already," Karrde said. "Personally, I think you might best serve the galaxy as star food."

Imsatad massaged his forehead. "What do you want?" he asked wearily.

"I want all of your ships grounded so I can conduct a ship-to-ship search."

Imsatad shrugged. "I don't have the children you seek. You may search my ships. Give me eight hours to get them all on the ground."

"You have five." Karrde signed for the connection to be severed.

"He's hiding something," Solusar said. "I can't sense what."

"He doesn't think he's beaten?"

"No, that's the strange thing. He feels utterly defeated. But he *is* being deceptive about Anakin and the others."

"You really think they're still alive?"

"Anakin is, I'm certain of that much. And Tahiri. If they are alive, Sannah and Valin must be. After all, the Peace Brigade didn't come here to kill them, but to capture them."

Karrde nodded thoughtfully. "I'm going to have the *Idiot's Array* come alongside. She's a corvette and her captain is one of my best. I want to get these children we have aboard safe on Coruscant, now."

"An excellent idea, though they won't be safe on Coruscant, not for long."

"No. Luke Skywalker has another plan in the works for that."

"I'm staying until we find the rest," Solusar said.

"I imagined you would. And Tionne?"

"The children need one of us."

"Very good. I'll arrange the transfer, now."

Solusar nodded and held out his hand. "I didn't thank you before. I'm glad I didn't kill you."

Karrde grinned wryly and took the proffered hand.

"The perfect gift for the perfect occasion, that's you, Solusar."

"Sithspawn," Shada snarled from across the bridge.

"What? What is it?"

"Karrde, if you're going to get those children out of this system, I suggest you hurry."

"What? More Peace Brigade?" He stared at the long-range sensors. Blips were appearing—lots of them. "H'sishi, what do we have there?"

The tactician looked up grimly. "Yuuzhan Vong, sir, lots of them. At least two warship analogs and a whole lot of smaller ships."

Karrde gripped the back of his chair until his knuckles turned white, cursing inwardly, trying to keep his face calm.

"How long?"

"No more than an hour, sir."

"Long enough to get the *Idiot's Array* away. Do it now, and have the *Demise* run with her."

"What about us?" Shada asked.

"We can't fight them head-on," Karrde said.

"Anakin and the rest are still down there," Solusar snapped. "If you're thinking of leaving them—"

Karrde cut him off with a wave of his hand. "I'm thinking of no such thing. If we leave this system, they'll button it up so tight only the New Republic Fleet could get in here. But our tactics will have to change. And we need reinforcements. Shada, I want you on the *Idiot's Array*. Bring back whatever it takes."

"You're crazy if you think I'm leaving you here."

"We'll be fine. It's a big system, and we're not without resources. If the Yuuzhan Vong plan on occupying Yavin Four, we can makes things very unpleasant for them. You ought to know by now, Shada, that if there's anything I'm good at, it's surviving. Now go. We have no time to argue about this."

"I'll be back," Shada promised.

"Of course you will. And I'll be here to meet you. Now get going."

CHAPTER ELEVEN

Anakin watched the distant dots buzzing around the crash site. They'd been there for hours, but in the last few minutes they'd been leaving, one by one. He felt a constriction in his belly. If he had one of those fliers, he could get back to the temple and find Tahiri.

And do what? Leave Valin and Sannah with Vehn and a sky full of flitters? Try to drag them all along on another aerial battle and then a rescue?

No. He couldn't pin all of their hopes on that.

He felt a tremor in the tree, and his hand went to his lightsaber. But then he felt Valin, below him, climbing up.

The younger boy reached him and settled in the crotch between two branches. As he watched, the last of the flitters seemed to be moving off.

"You should have stayed in the cave," Anakin told Valin.

"Maybe," Valin replied. "But I didn't." He nodded at the departing craft. "I thought they would search longer," he said.

Anakin shook his head. "Two days is longer than I thought they would give it. They're after the bigger prize—the rest of the students. They've got a time limit, remember? When the Yuuzhan Vong show up, they've got to be successful or gone. The last thing the Peace Brigade would want the Vong to know is that they were the ones who spoiled their mother lode." He motioned down. "Get back in the cave, though. They might make a last-minute sweep."

"Anakin, why do the Yuuzhan Vong want us so bad?"

Anakin blew out a breath. "I'm not sure. Mostly because they hate us. The fact that they don't seem to exist in the Force cuts both ways. We can't sense them or affect them directly, but we can do things they can't understand. And we're the ones who have hurt them most. I guess the last stroke was when Jacen humiliated their warmaster."

"But those guys with Vehn weren't Yuuzhan Vong."

"No, they're worse. They think by turning us in they'll get the Yuuzhan Vong to stop their conquest at the planets they have."

"Will they?"

Anakin snorted. "Senator Elegos A'Kla turned himself over to them. He hoped he could come to understand them, forge a common bond of trust, something to begin the process of finding a peaceful solution."

"They killed him," Valin said quietly. "I heard about that."

"And sent his polished bones back to us."

"But then my dad killed the Yuuzhan Vong who killed Elegos."

Anakin hesitated. He hadn't thought through where his example might lead.

"Yeah," he said briefly.

"But now everyone hates my dad, and not the Yuuzhan Vong."

Anakin shook his head. "No. It's not like that. It's just—it's politics, Valin."

"What does *that* mean?"

"I don't know. I hate politics. Ask my brother, next time you see him, or my mom."

"But—"

"What it means," Anakin interrupted, "is that your father, Corran Horn, is a good man, and everyone with even a little sense knows that. The problem with people is that a lot of them don't have any sense, and a lot of others are liars."

"You mean they would say my dad was bad even if they didn't think so?"

"You got it, kid."

"I'm not a kid."

Anakin looked into the determined young face, and suddenly saw what Kam, Tionne, Uncle Luke, Aunt Mara—all the adults in his life—must be used to seeing by now on *his* face.

"Maybe not," Anakin replied. "But here's what I was trying to get around to saying a minute ago. The Yuuzhan Vong have never shown the slightest tendency to keep their word. I don't think they even believe lying is wrong. And Elegos—well, it was a worthy try, and I honor him. But what the Yuuzhan Vong want from us is our worlds and our people as slaves. They believe our machines are abominations, and they won't rest until they've all been destroyed. The only way to avoid fighting them is to surrender and let them do whatever they want with us. That's the only terms of peace they can understand. The Peace Brigade think they can do something in between. Elegos was brave, noble—and wrong. It cost him his life, and that was his to spend. The Peace Brigade are cowards and they're stupid, and they want to spend *our* lives. Our lives are *not* for them to spend."

Valin nodded, then smiled a little. "You talk more than you used to. Tahiri said she would rub off on you eventually."

It struck Anakin that Valin was right. He'd been practically pontificating, something he wouldn't have dreamed of doing a few years ago except maybe in an argument with his siblings or Tahiri. It was something he wasn't good at, didn't like, avoided like raw cobalt. His father had once joked that it was easier to drag a neutron star with a landspeeder than it was to drag two words out of him.

But more and more, people seemed to want something like this from him. Some of the things he had done had gotten around, and he guessed he had something of a reputation. That part was fine, and though he wouldn't say so out loud, he sort of liked it. It made him feel that he could be like Uncle Luke, back when he was young and fighting the Empire—like a hero, though he knew he wasn't *really* that.

He felt a pang, and suddenly knew where these thoughts were taking him.

"Why did you and Sannah and Tahiri come to help me, Valin? Why didn't you go on with Kam and Tionne?"

Valin looked up at him with guileless eyes. "We want to *be* like you, Anakin. We all do. And you—you would never have run from a fight."

Anakin's lips tightened and his eyes felt gritty and hot. That settled that. He'd lied when he told Sannah and Valin that the Yuuzhan Vong and the Peace Brigade were responsible for this mess. Like Chewie's death, like Centerpoint, this was *his* mess, Anakin Solo's mess.

But this time he would clean it up. Somehow.

"Doesn't look like they took much," Sannah observed, as they picked through the wreck of Vehn's transport. Four days had come and gone since the crash, and a day since they had seen the last of the flitters.

"Why should they?" Valin asked. "There's not much left they would want."

"No," Anakin said. "There's plenty. It would have taken too much time to salvage it, that's all."

"But you think *you* can?" Vehn sneered from where he sat, cuffed hands resting on his knees.

"I can fix it," Anakin replied. "The hyperdrive is fine."

"That's great. We'll just go to lightspeed from here. At

least no one would have to worry about disposing of our remains. And we sure wouldn't have to worry about the Vong anymore."

"If Anakin says he can fix it, he can fix it," Valin snapped.

"Shut up, you smelly little Hutt," Vehn grunted. "I may be your prisoner, but that doesn't mean I have to listen to your smart mouth all day. I—hey! Ow!"

Vehn was suddenly scratching furiously at his legs, then thrashing on the ground.

Anakin straightened. "Stay away from him. It's a trick!"

"Trick?" Vehn screamed. "I'm being eaten alive!"

That's when Anakin noticed Valin was laughing. So was Sannah, but she was hiding hers behind her palm.

"Valin, are you doing that?"

"He deserved it."

"Stop it. Right now. Immediately."

"I just—"

"Now."

"Yes, sir," Valin said. And he didn't sound sarcastic.

Anakin knelt by Vehn. A swarm of multisegmented worms a centimeter in length were detaching themselves from the pilot's arms and face, leaving purplish welts behind. Vehn pushed at them frantically, but when Anakin moved to help him, he jerked away with a hoarse rasp of anger.

When they were all finally off, Vehn turned his head toward Valin. His chest was heaving.

"You did that, didn't you? With some kind of Jedi magic." He rose clumsily to his feet. "I hope the Vong *do* get you. The whole lot of you."

"Yeah?" Valin started. "Well—"

"Valin!" Anakin said a little sharply. "Keep quiet and listen. You know better than that. I *know* you know better than that, because we had the same teachers." He turned on Sannah. "And you were laughing. You think it's funny to use the Force to torture a helpless captive for no better reason than that he called you a name?"

Sannah reddened. "No," she said.

"Valin?"

"No," the boy said. "I guess not."

"There are times to use the Force in self-defense, Valin, and there are times when defense means attack. And if I have to squeeze Vehn's brain to learn what we need to rescue Tahiri, I might even do that. But torture for the sake of torture—never."

Valin nodded and sat down. To Anakin's surprise Valin didn't look so much sullen as reflective. In fact, like a flash, for an instant, he looked almost impossibly like his father, Corran. It was so bright and true that Anakin wondered if it was a real vision of an older Valin or just a striking resemblance.

He cleared his throat. "Let's just get to work, shall we? The engines aren't as bad as they could be. I think with parts salvaged from the other ships we can get it limping, and that's all I need—a way to orbit. At the very least we can get the comm unit fixed."

Anakin actually had his doubts about this, but it would give them something to do while he figured out how he was going to get halfway around the moon to find Tahiri. If they were occupied, they wouldn't worry as much. Meanwhile, Talon Karrde *must* have arrived by now.

And Tahiri—she was still here, and he was pretty sure she was even still on Yavin 4, not in orbit.

Still, it galled him. It made his very bones ache not to set off on foot, though in his head he knew that it would take him months to cross the wilderness separating him from the Great Temple. Maybe he needed the work as much as Valin and Sannah.

With a sigh, he went to see what the power cell couplings looked like.

Something beeped and whistled. His hand was already

on his lightsaber before he realized the sound was coming from his wrist comm. He was being hailed.

He stared at the comm for a moment. It could be a trick by the Peace Brigade, an attempt to triangulate his location. It might be Talon Karrde, trying to find them.

Reluctantly, he acknowledged, and words began to scroll across the display.

PURSUIT EVADED. X-WING BADLY DAMAGED. AWAITING FURTHER INSTRUCTIONS.

"Fiver!"

AFFIRMATIVE.

"Fiver, lock on this signal and come straight here. Where are you?"

252.6 KILOMETERS FROM YOUR PRESENT POSITION.

"Great. How long will it take you to get here?"

20 STANDARD HOURS.

"What? Why?"

REPULSORLIFT MOTIVATION ONLY. SHIP BADLY DAMAGED.

"But you're okay?"

OPERATIONAL.

"Good. Good going, Fiver. Get here as soon as you can. We need you."

AFFIRMATIVE, ANAKIN.

"Anakin?" Despite everything, Anakin grinned. The astromech hadn't been memory-wiped lately. He was starting to develop a few quirks. Flying the X5 X-wing alone—a task Fiver wasn't really built for—had probably contributed. In fact, Anakin couldn't believe the little droid had really done it. He'd thought he was sacrificing his ship and Fiver as a diversion. Finding that it hadn't worked out that way was an unexpected break. He now not only had more parts to work with, but an astromech droid to help with repairs.

Things weren't exactly looking up, Anakin thought, but maybe he could take his eyes off his feet, at least.

CHAPTER TWELVE

Darkness wrapped around Anakin like a cloak and whispered to him like a mother. It promised him a face of durasteel and a heart of ferrocrete. It offered him supernovas of power and the unflinching will to use it.

He had been to this place before, often. It was his oldest dream, perhaps dreamed for the first time when the clone of the Emperor Palpatine touched him through his mother's womb. And when he learned about his namesake, his grandfather Vader, the dreams grew stronger, more detailed. He saw futures in which he was grown, his blue eyes gone as gray as hull plating. He saw himself in Darth Vader's mask, the Knight of Darkness reborn.

He had made a sort of peace with his dreams in the cave on Dagobah, the same cave where his uncle Luke had faced his own dark side and failed. But peace did not mean silence, and here, on a moon as deeply stained by the dark side as the Sith themselves, the dreams were particularly troubling.

But now, something broke, a dam holding back ebon waters that hit him so cold and strange that the tattoo in his chest stopped, as if a fist had closed on his heart.

Soft laughter began, familiar yet strange; the pitch and timbre were wrong, but the cadence was as known to him as his father's speech. A woman's laughter, throaty and sardonic. It made the hair on his neck prickle up.

He turned and saw her.

Her hair was gold, the gold of a vein in a sunset on

Coruscant or of the sudden spark from an inferno. One of her eyes was jade and the other obsidian. Her lips were fringed by a hundred incisions, and a white scar ran from the top of her forehead to her chin. Armor of a black-and-gray-banded chitinous substance fit close to her body, a very adult, very human body, though the armor was plated and jointed like an insect's. Knobs and spurs stuck out from her shoulders and elbows.

She smiled at him through those split lips and held up something baton-shaped, which flexed in her grip like a sluggish pupa. Sudden light blazed from one end of it and resolved into a blazing blue blade. Dark-side energy crackled around her, calling to him, and he felt a sudden terrible attraction to her, every part of him yearning for her in a way he had never even begun to feel before.

She grinned more widely and laughed again, and with sudden understanding Anakin realized that she wasn't looking at him at all, but at someone else in the vision, someone Anakin couldn't see.

"The last of your kind," the woman said, her voice made whispery by what had been done to her mouth. "The last of *my* kind." And she raised the blade, and Anakin recognized her.

"Tahiri!" he shrieked. She paused, as if she might have heard something very far away. Then she came forward, sweeping the weapon down, and Anakin choked on the look in her eye, the mixture of glee and despair, joy and sickness.

He awoke still choking. A strong hand was clamped over his mouth. He squirmed, but the grip on him was sure and strong. He tried to get his feet under him and failed.

Calm. No fear, he thought. *Get it together, Anakin. You're supposed to be on watch. They won't even hear this, in the cave, if you die.*

He used the Force to twist the hand away from his mouth and shove his attacker sprawling, and in the next instant got his feet under him and his lightsaber in hand. In its sudden light he made out a bearded face, a blaster. He leapt foward.

"Wait! Jedi! I'm—I'm a friend."

"Yeah? Why did you attack me?"

"Didn't know—didn't—" He wheezed off, his voice sounding strange, weak, as if he rarely used it. "Name's Qorl. I have been a friend to Jedi. I didn't know who you were."

"Qorl? My brother and sister knew a Qorl. He made them fix his ship at blasterpoint."

"Jacen. Jaina," the old man said. "Qorl also saved them from the Shadow Academy."

"You were a TIE fighter pilot, stranded here when the Death Star was destroyed. You went off—"

"And came back. I left as an enemy to your brother and sister. I came back their friend. You're really their brother?" He squinted. "Can't see so well anymore."

"What are you doing here?"

"Saw some ships fly over, fighting. Thought I saw one go down, so I followed to see." He shrugged. "Seven days later, here I am."

"So you are." Anakin struggled to remember what he knew about this grizzled old man. Jacen and Jaina had found his wrecked TIE fighter and set about fixing it, not realizing its pilot was still around, hiding in the jungle, unaware that the war was over. Qorl had forced them to finish the repairs and left them to die, but had later helped them escape the Shadow Academy. Anakin remembered that Qorl had ended up back on Yavin 4, but none of the details. He did know that Jacen and Jaina counted him a friend, and Uncle Luke had been content to leave the old man alone.

Qorl gestured at the lightsaber. "Could you put that away, please?"

"Oh. Sure."

"Who were you fighting?"

"Peace Brigade."

"Who?"

"Er—how long since you've had news from the outside, Qorl?"

"I don't know. Old Peckhum dropped off some supplies for me, maybe two or three years ago. I told him not to come back."

"Oh. Well, this will take some explaining, then. A lot of explaining."

"Will it explain the new ships I've seen? The strange ones?"

Anakin felt his chest constrict. "What ships?"

"They look like—*growths* of some kind. Ugly."

"Oh, no," Anakin whispered. "Okay, I'll have to tell this as fast as I can, and then—" He remembered his vision, that future Tahiri, a dark Jedi with Yuuzhan Vong scarring and implants. "And then there's something I have to do, no matter what."

"I need to talk to you, Vehn." Anakin settled down across from the man.

"So talk. Hey, who's the old guy?"

"A hermit of sorts. I'm putting him in charge of you."

"What do you mean?" Vehn asked suspiciously.

Anakin drew a deep breath and plunged into it. "Okay. Here's the thing, Vehn. I need your help."

"I've been telling you that for a while."

"And you were right."

"Yeah, well—too bad. You've treated me like Hutt slime. Why shouldn't I return the favor?"

"The Yuuzhan Vong are here."

That got his attention. Vehn's face closed over his fear, but Anakin could still feel it.

"Qorl's seen their ships."

"They'll find us," Vehn said flatly.

"Why should they? They aren't looking for us. Unless the Peace Brigade tells them about the crash—but I don't think they will. It would only show their incompetence, right? So the Yuuzhan Vong see us only if they notice us on a random patrol, and the odds of that—"

"Depends on how many ships they have patrolling," Vehn interrupted. "You don't know the one, so you don't know the other."

"True. The thing is this—I'm going after my friend, back at the temple. I'm going now. I want you and Qorl to get Sannah and Valin off of this moon."

"What? Have you got some kind of fever?"

"You can finish the repairs on your ship, can't you?"

Vehn continued to stare at him as if he was crazy. "No. The sublight drive—"

"Is nearly repaired. I'll show you."

"Impossible."

"Nope. You still need some parts, but Qorl knows where you can get them. And you have Fiver. I've programmed him with everything you'll need."

"And why should I do this again? I keep missing that part."

"Because it's your only chance, too. You think the Yuuzhan Vong are going to hail you as an ally when they find you? I doubt it very much. You say you were only in the Peace Brigade for the money, you say you don't really share their cause—let's say I'm going to take you on your word about that. Get these kids to safety, and I can guarantee you a profit."

"How do you know I won't just fly straight to the Vong and turn Valin and Sannah over to them?"

"A couple of reasons. The first is that Qorl will blast a very large hole in you if you try it. I don't completely trust the man. He was an Empire stalwart twenty years after the death of the Emperor. By the same token, he would never turn humans over to the Yuuzhan Vong—or let you do it. He might take off for the Imperial Remnant the instant he gets the chance, but the way I see it, that's parsecs better than staying here.

"The second is that I think you'll do whatever gives you the best chance of getting out of this with a whole skin—and you're smart enough not to gamble on the milk of Yuuzhan Vong kindness. The third—" He leaned close. "Third, if you bring any harm to Valin or Sannah, you'd better pray I'm dead. Because if I'm not, no matter what, I will find you. That I swear."

"Ease up, Jedi. I'll do it. Anything has to be better than hanging out in the jungle waiting to die of a lizard bite. But I don't want you to threaten me again. I'm really sick of that."

"I've said what I meant to say. I won't say it again." Anakin raised his voice. "Qorl. Could you come here, please?"

The old pilot shuffled over and treated Vehn to a thorough once over. He knelt on creaky joints and shook his finger in Vehn's face. "I know you," he muttered.

"You're crazy," Vehn said. "I've never seen you before in my life."

"Oh, no. Even if you saw somebody like old Qorl, you wouldn't recognize him. You don't have the database. On the other hand, old Qorl has seen a hundred like you. You won't give Qorl any trouble. You'll do what he says."

"Right," Vehn said. "Just . . . stay away from me, yeah? Or take a bath, at least. You smell like a Wookiee's armpit."

Qorl laughed brusquely, put his hands on his thighs, and rose painfully to his full height. He looked squarely at Anakin. "You sure about this, then?" he asked.

"I've got to do it," Anakin said. "The Force is pulling me to do it."

"The Force. Huh. Will the Force get you halfway around the moon in less then a year? Because that's how long it will take you to walk it, if you don't get gobbled by piranha-beetles or die of creek fever. You might as well wait until we have the ship fixed."

"I don't have to walk," Anakin said. "The repulsorlift system in the E-wing was salvageable. I cobbled together something that will pass for a speeder."

"Already?"

"Days ago. But until you came along, I couldn't really talk myself into going. I couldn't take Valin and Sannah, and I couldn't leave them behind." *But now I have two signs,* he finished to himself, *Qorl, and my dream.* It felt right to go. It felt terribly wrong not to. It felt— Chewbacca's face flashed in his mind, as he had last seen it, and Tahiri, alone, surrounded.

Tahiri, grown, wearing Yuuzhan Vong armor and wielding dark-side Force.

It was a risk he had to take.

"I'm going to explain this to Valin and Sannah now," Anakin said. "I'll leave in the morning."

CHAPTER THIRTEEN

Commander Tsaak Vootuh aimed his opalescent eyes at the trembling human, restraining the part of himself that wanted to put the pathetic creature out of its misery.

Which was most of him.

"You are Imsatad?" he asked.

"Yes, sir."

"Straighten yourself," Vootuh snarled. "The mewling of a Yuuzhan Vong infant in a crèche has more fierceness than your whine." As he spoke, he cherished the thin hiss of breath through the deep chevrons that cut through his cheeks. He clasped his hands behind his back so that the cloak gripping into the flesh of his shoulders fell open to reveal the full glory of the tattoos and burn puckers that adorned his torso. He silently praised Yun-Yuuzhan for not condemning him to be one of these smooth, honorless infidels.

"Yes, sir," Imsatad replied, his voice slightly firmer.

"You explained to my subordinates that you are an ally of ours? One of the—" He frowned, trying to remember the name of the group in Basic. "*Peez* Brigade?"

The tizowyrm in his ear translated the first word as "willing and appropriate submission from the submissive to the conqueror."

"Yes, sir."

"I wonder how you will confirm that," Tsaak Vootuh said. "Our information was that this moon was home to many young *Jeedai*. And yet I find none at all. This is peculiar, and I suspect you are to blame."

"No!" Imsatad said. "We came here in good faith, to keep the terms of the peace your warmaster Tsavong Lah proposed."

"And failed miserably to do so. Where are the *Jeedai*?"

Imsatad hesitated. "We have one. The others are with Karrde."

"The commander of the flotilla that fled our approach?"

"That's him. He tricked us into—"

"I have no interest in the details of your failure. Two of this Karrde's ships made the jump to hyperspace. I assume those ships contained the prize you let slip through your fingers."

"With all respect, Commander, if it weren't for me and my crew, you wouldn't have even one Jedi. Karrde would have taken them all before you arrived."

"Perhaps, perhaps not. But tell me—why does he remain in this system?"

Imsatad frowned. "Does he?"

"Yes. He has withdrawn to the edge of the system, but remains there. I do not complain, for it will give me and my warriors combat when I feared we must sit idle. But I wish to know his reason. I do not imagine that he would stay for the sake of a single immature *Jeedai*." He leaned close, dropping his voice to a whisper. "What have you failed to tell me?"

The human cleared its throat. "There—I think there are perhaps a few more Jedi here on the moon. I think one of them might be Anakin Solo."

"Solo?"

"Brother to Jacen Solo, whom Tsavong Lah so desires."

"Interesting, if true."

"I would like to offer my ships and crew to help find him and any others who might still remain on Yavin Four."

Tsaak Vootuh fixed a venomous stare on the creature. "You have helped us quite enough. As for your ships, they are abominations and will be destroyed."

"But what—how will we return home?"

Tsaak Vootuh allowed himself a grim smile. "How indeed, Imsatad?" he said. "How indeed?"

"Now, wait a minute—" Imsatad began, but Tsaak Vootuh cut him off with a look.

"I wish to see the captured *Jeedai*," he told the human. "You will take me, now."

"I'll do no such thing until you—"

Tsaak Vootuh nodded in a certain way, and Imsatad was suddenly staring in astonishment at the head of an amphistaff poking out of his belly. He looked questioningly at Tsaak Vootuh, coughed blood from his mouth, and died. Vo Lian, Tsaak Vootuh's lieutenant, withdrew the amphistaff he had struck through the man's back.

Tsaak Vootuh gestured at the human who had been standing behind Imsatad. "You. Take me to see the *Jeedai*."

"O-of course," the creature stammered. "Whatever you wish."

Tsaak Vootuh nodded and stood. Before leaving the room, he turned to Vo Lian. "Supervise the landing and make secure the space around this moon. I want the damutek on the ground within the next cycle. I will give the shapers no cause for complaint."

Vo Lian snapped his fists against his opposite shoulders. "*Belek tiu*," he said. "It will be done, Commander."

PART TWO

THE SHAMED AND
THE SHAPERS

CHAPTER FOURTEEN

Borsk Fey'lya, Chief of State of the New Republic, offered an apologetic expression that looked as false to Luke as it was well-practiced. His words followed suit.

"I'm sorry," he demurred, violet eyes unblinking. "I can be of no help in this matter, Master Skywalker."

Luke fought down the urge to shout and sought the calm he so often implored of his students. "I beg you to reconsider, Chief Fey'lya. Lives are at stake." Grief over Ikrit's death was still raw.

The Bothan nodded. "I am painfully aware of that, Master Skywalker. However, whereas you are concerned with the lives of four—count them, four—Jedi, I must consider a great many more. I must consider the lives we will lose in an attempt to retake the Yavin system, a system with no tactical or strategic advantage. I must consider, further, that this action would quite effectively end the truce with the Yuuzhan Vong and cost even more lives in renewed warfare."

"They've already broken the truce," Luke replied, still trying to keep his voice even. "They promised not to take any more of our worlds if Jedi are turned over to them, something that the whole galaxy seems eager to do. And yet they've now taken Yavin Four."

"Of course, neither I nor the senate sanction the purported purge of Jedi."

"Purported?" Luke allowed the word to absorb all of the incredulity he felt at Fey'lya's implication.

"And as for Yavin Four," the chief continued evenly, "it is not one of 'our worlds,' not if by the use of the plural pronoun you mean the New Republic. Yavin Four is *your* pet project, Master Skywalker. You Jedi have made it clear that you are not bound by the laws and decisions of the senate. You fight unsanctioned battles and provoke needless dissent. And now, suddenly, after spurning our wishes, you desire our aid? Really, can't you see the hypocrisy in that?"

"Chief, putting aside for the moment that you are confounding the action of a handful of Jedi with our order as a whole, these are *children* we're talking about. They've done nothing, and they don't deserve to suffer for the mistakes of others."

"But you would ask me to jeopardize millions, perhaps billions for those same mistakes? Your mistakes? Listen to yourself."

"That's the most—" Jaina Solo exploded. Luke was surprised she had kept silent for so long.

"Quiet, Jaina," he said.

"But he's twisting—"

"Child, you have all of your mother's fire and none of her common sense," Fey'lya said. "Listen to your Master."

"There's no need to insult my niece," Luke said. "Her brother is one of those missing."

"Would this be Anakin Solo, who forged a fake departure authority in order to leave Coruscant surreptitiously?"

"Anakin is a little . . . overeager."

"He did not proceed under your authority?"

"No, Chief Fey'lya, he did not, but he thought the students at the praxeum were in imminent danger. As it turns out, he was correct."

"Another example, however, of what I'm talking about. Young Solo ran off against orders, breaking several laws in doing so, with no say-so from anyone. This, so far as I can tell, is the essence of what the Jedi have become."

"I'm coming to you now, Chief Fey'lya."

"Yes. Now that the matter is too large for you to handle on your own. And I note that you did not come here first. At the very least, you went to General Antilles—and, I suspect, to others. And they all sent you here."

"I was inquiring into what was possible," Luke said. "Not making requests."

"How diplomatic. And where is your sister in all of this? She and her husband also seem to have disappeared."

"That's not relevant to this," Luke said.

"Oh, isn't it? Are they engaged in yet more unsanctioned covert activity? Are they a part of the little government you're trying to run on the side, as if the elected officials of the New Republic are incompetent to do their jobs?"

"We're following our Jedi mandate, Chief Fey'lya. We protect. We serve. I'm sorry if these goals are incompatible with yours."

"The arrogance," Fey'lya said. "The sheer arrogance. And you wonder why you are disliked."

Luke felt matters rushing to a heated conclusion and knew part of it was his own fault. Perhaps the rage he felt pulsing from Jaina was partially responsible, but he was dangerously near losing his own head in the matter. He placed his palms together. "Chief Fey'lya, if you won't consider military action, at least consider a diplomatic solution."

The Bothan reclined in his chair. "The matter has already been brought to our attention. Negotiations have been and are occurring."

"Brought by whom?"

"The Yuuzhan Vong, of course. The Yavin situation has already generated a good deal of tension."

"What? You knew?"

"The Yuuzhan Vong assure us that their occupation of the system is temporary. They went there in search of raw materials, not captives. They knew nothing about your Jedi praxeum."

Luke bore down on the chief of state with his gaze. "I ask again," he said softly. "You *knew* the Yuuzhan Vong were going to Yavin, and didn't see fit to warn me?"

"Don't be absurd," Fey'lya snorted. "Do you think I could keep that from your Jedi spies? No. The Yuuzhan Vong entered the Yavin system peacefully. There was already some sort of scuffle between smugglers going on when they got there, and some of those smugglers remain and continue to harass the Yuuzhan Vong water-mining activities on Stroiketcy. It took considerable diplomatic effort to convince them that these outlaws have nothing to do with the New Republic." He cocked his head. "You know nothing of these pirates, do you, Master Skywalker? This wouldn't be yet *another* example of unsanctioned Jedi activity, would it?"

Luke narrowed his eyes. "You sold my students out. I won't forget that. Ever."

"I see. Instead of answering my question, you threaten me." Fey'lya waved the back of his hand. "You've taken up enough of my time, Skywalker. Let me just leave you with a warning. I'm formally cautioning you that the Yavin system is off-limits to you and your followers. If the forces there are in any way connected with you, you will recall them. Under no circumstances are you to go there yourself or send Jedi in your stead. If you make any move in that direction, you will be placed under arrest. You are already, I rather needlessly point out, under close observation. Is that clear?"

"Oh, it's clear all right," Luke replied. "Suddenly, a lot of things are very clear indeed." He felt Fey'lya's mind snap down and vacuum seal. The interview was over. He turned to go—and stopped when he noticed that Jaina wasn't moving, was standing stock-still, tears of anger streaming down her face.

"Chief Fey'lya," she said in a quiet voice. "You are a poor excuse for a sentient being. I hope one day you really smell the stink in your heart and choke on the fumes."

Fey'lya returned her gaze. "You're very young," he said. "When you've accomplished a fraction of what I have for the people of this galaxy, come back and we'll talk again."

"It makes a certain amount of sense from his perspective," Jacen said later, when Luke and Jaina had returned to the Jedi Master's quarters. Luke had just finished relating the substance of his talk with the chief of state to Shada D'ukal, Tionne, Mara, and Jacen.

"I do *not* believe you said that," Jaina snapped. "This is Anakin we're talking about. It's the praxeum!"

"You don't have to remind me who my brother is," Jacen said. "But that's the point, don't you see? We can hardly be impartial in this case."

"Vape impartiality!" Jaina replied. "Fey'lya's not impartial."

"No, he's not. But his concerns are different."

"Yeah. He's more concerned about the Vong than he is about his own citizens."

"That's not true," Luke said gently. "To be honest, I never thought he would send ships to the Yavin system. I had to ask, though, and we did learn some things."

"Right. Like Fey'lya sent the Vong there in the first place."

"I doubt that very much," Luke said. "I think things happened pretty much as he said. When the Yuuzhan Vong showed up they found Karrde fighting the Peace Brigade, and when they took occupation, Karrde turned on them. They then contacted the New Republic. And Fey'lya's right—I should have seen this coming, long ago. The Yavin system has been at risk for months now.

Only the concentrated effort of the Jedi there even allowed us to think it was safe."

"That's perfect, Luke," Mara said. "Blame yourself."

Luke lifted his eyebrows, surprised at the brittle anger in her tone. "I'm not trying to allocate blame, Mara."

"Then spare us your apologies for Fey'lya and the senate. What are we going to do?"

"What Anakin did," Jaina said. "Talon Karrde is out there right now, fighting a holding action for help that will never come. He'll stay there until they pick all of his ships off, one by one. Won't he, Shada?"

"Yes."

Luke fixed her with his gaze. "I understand your concern, Jaina, but what good will one more X-wing do Karrde *or* Anakin?"

"More good than sitting here. And we can contact Mom and Dad, have them bring the *Millennium Falcon*."

"First of all, Han and Leia are still out of contact. More important, you heard what Fey'lya said."

"Oh, *please* let them try arresting us," Mara grunted.

"You think I care even faintly what that scruffy Bothan said?" Jaina chimed in. "Uncle Luke, we can't do *nothing*."

Luke placed his hand on Mara's arm. "Listen to me, all of you. I'm not worried about arrest as such, and I think you all know that. But things aren't good for the Jedi now. If we have *any* friends left in high places, we can't afford to alienate them. We're already considered rogues. We *can't* allow ourselves to be cast as enemies of the state."

"If they're stupid enough to think *that*, let 'em," Jaina snarled. "They're hopeless."

"Right," Jacen said sardonically. "That's really what we need right now, Jaina—a civil war within the New Republic, as if the war with the Yuuzhan Vong isn't already enough. Besides, Uncle Luke is right. I don't think the weight we could add to the battle would help, not considering the situation as Shada outlined it."

"What, then?" Shada asked. "Karrde can't do it alone."

"What if we added a Star Destroyer to the equation?" Luke said.

Shada looked thoughtful for a moment, then nodded slightly. "If the Yuuzhan Vong don't get more reinforcements—maybe."

"Terrik," Mara said.

"Terrik," Luke agreed.

"I thought you said you couldn't find him?" Jacen asked.

"No, but I have some ideas about where to look. All I need is someone to look for him."

Jaina stared. Jacen nodded. "Yes," he said.

"No, now wait a minute," Jaina said. "You want us to chase halfway around the galaxy for a Star Destroyer we might never find—"

"Jaina," Jacen interrupted. "Do you think Anakin is dead?"

She hesitated fractionally. "No. I *know* he's not."

"Right. I don't think he's dead either. I don't even think they've caught him. Anakin knows Yavin Four as well as we do, maybe better. The Yuuzhan Vong don't know it at all. If they didn't catch him when they landed, it would take a miracle for them to find him."

"Unless he ran right up to their ships, lightsaber swinging, which is just what Anakin is likely to do," Jaina said.

"He's headstrong," Jacen said, "but he isn't stupid. He knows help is on the way. He probably knows Karrde is there already. The problem is, he can't get to Karrde or Karrde to him because the Yuuzhan Vong are in the way. Uncle Luke is right—a couple more X-wings or even the *Falcon* won't change that equation much. The *Errant Venture* would."

Jaina's nostrils flared. "Uncle Luke, you aren't just trying to get us out of the way, are you?"

Luke shook his head. "How do you plot *that* course? No. Jacen's laid out the situation perfectly. Let me add to that the fact that since Valin is Booster Terrik's grandson, Booster will be more than happy to help."

"And Terrik isn't tied directly to the Jedi."

"What are you talking about?" Mara interrupted. "Corran Horn is Valin's father, and last I heard, he was with Booster."

"Corran distanced himself from us after Ithor," Luke replied. "Fey'lya might suspect something, but he won't be able to prove it. Which reminds me—Shada got here without revealing she has most of the Jedi candidates with her. If they turn up here on Coruscant, with us, Fey'lya will know we're behind Karrde being there. That may or may not be a situation I can control. But they aren't safe here anyway. When you go to find Terrik, I want you to take the candidates with you."

"What, in an X-wing?"

"We have Shada's ships—" Jacen began.

"Oh, no," Shada said. "They aren't my ships, they're Karrde's, and he needs them. I'm returning to the Yavin system, and I'm doing it very soon, no matter what you work out here."

"We'll take the *Jade Shadow*," Mara said. "I can convert some space. It may still be a little cramped, with all of the kids, but she'll do the job."

"You and I can't leave Coruscant," Luke said bluntly.

Mara's eyes flashed. "Skywalker, if this is about my 'delicate state,' you can shove—"

"It's not, Mara. We can't attract suspicion. Fey'lya's watching us. It'll be hard enough to get Jacen and Jaina out without raising eyebrows, but that can be done."

Mara seemed to roll that around in her mouth. *I don't like playing these games,* she practically hurled at him.

I don't either, he replied.

The room was silent for a score of heartbeats, during which time Luke realized that everyone else in the room was staring at them. Their mouths were admirably closed, but their read in the Force was purely gape-jawed.

No, not all of them are surprised, Luke suddenly knew.

It was typically Jaina who broke the silence. "Mara? You're? . . ."

"Bright kid," Mara said. Her eyes narrowed a little. "Jacen?"

Jacen seemed to be trying to see the individual atoms in the floor. His face was redshifting.

"You *peeked*," Mara accused.

"I, uh, didn't *mean* to," he mumbled. "But when I started using the Force again at Duro . . ." He looked around helplessly for support.

"We were going to tell you soon, anyway," Luke said.

"That's wonderful!" Jaina exploded. "Mara, congratulations." Her brows scrunched a bit. "I guess? I mean, I didn't think—"

"What?" Mara said, nailing the younger woman with a pointed gaze. "Didn't think what?"

"Oh, I—nothing," Jaina replied, her face suddenly twinning her brother's in hue.

"It's just suprising," Jacen said, for her. "You were sick for so long."

Mara nodded. "Yeah. Well, the universe surprises you sometimes. And sometimes—on rare occasions—in a good way."

"In the *best* way," Jaina burbled. "Congratulations. To both of you."

"Thank you," Luke said.

" 'Cousin Jaina.' I like the sound of it."

"So do I," Mara replied, lips twitching in a smile. "But that doesn't solve the immediate problem. So, 'Cousin Jaina'—why don't you take the *Jade Shadow* and go find Booster, already?"

Jaina's eyes widened. "You're offering me your ship?"

"Loaning it for a good cause. Just don't get her dinged up, understood?"

"Understood," Jaina replied. "But if we don't find Booster within a standard week—"

"We will find him," Jacen interjected.

"Either way," Jaina warned, "you won't keep me away from Yavin Four. Not if I have to fly there on a repulsorsled."

CHAPTER FIFTEEN

Anakin sped over what might have been the billows and curls, thunderstorms and circlestorms of a vast sea of green clouds. The illusion was nearly perfect as the sun reddened, puddled, and shrank against the horizon like a fusion explosion going in slow reverse, condensing back into the bomb that had released it. The real clouds were orange-and-umber lace, and the gas giant was just slipping under the horizon as well. A rare true night was settling, the first in the three standard days since he'd left the crash site.

But the green clouds were an illusion, a potentially deadly one. They were really treetops, and if he passed through one at this speed, he wouldn't experience the slight dampness and negligible turbulence that flying through a cloud produced; he would shatter his makeshift speeder and possibly his own bones against them.

And so he closed his eyes and used the Force, feeling the life below him, watching for it thrusting too high.

It was exhilarating to be flying again, so much so that for moments at a time Anakin nearly forgot what he was doing and where he was going. He kept reaching for the throttle, to really open her up, to feel the wind in his face turn into a fluid, cheek-biting sheet of speed.

But the throttle was already open; the "speeder" quite simply wasn't. He'd tinkered with it as much as he could, but no amount of jury-rigging could transform a cannibalized A-wing repulsorlift welded to an awkward strut-work chassis into a fleet steed of the winds. The pilot seat from his X-wing perched atop the improbable cagelike thing, and before him were exactly four controls—an on-off switch, a throttle and lift control circuited to the repulsor, and a tiller that wagged a large aluminum rudder behind him. Not the most wieldy craft he'd ever flown, and his maximum speed was a poky ninety klicks an hour. Still, it would get him there faster than walking or waiting for the repairs on the transport.

He stretched out farther in the Force, touching Tahiri again. She was in a dark place and he felt pain, or the fading of pain. He couldn't tell where.

Anakin.

That startled him. His name rang like an H'kig chime, nothing fuzzy about it.

"I'm coming, Tahiri," he whispered.

Anakin . . . But the sense of words dissolved into emotion. Fear, grief, hope. Wordlessly, he reached for her, to give her the equivalent of a squeeze on the hand, and found himself instead in a tight, desperate embrace.

I'll find you, he projected to her. *Just hang on.*

No! He couldn't tell if she was warning him away or responding to the blade of pain that suddenly cut between them, tore her away from him, leaving him once more alone with the treetops.

He searched for her again, but found nothing, not even a faint presence.

"You're okay, Tahiri," he mumbled. "I know you are."

He did sense someone else, however. It was like seeing a faint star, the faintest star in the sky.

"Jaina," Anakin said. "Hello, Jaina."

But he couldn't tell if she felt him back.

Days passed, blurred and monotonous. The forest broke into narrow savannas and sparkling stretches of marsh and then ocean that shimmered like planished copper beneath Yavin and liquid gold by sunlight. He watched the crawling, V-shaped wakes of behemoths he had no names for and could make out only as shadows in the deep. He flew day and night, sleeping only in tiny naps, drawing on the Force to replenish himself. He ate the last of his rations after ten days, but even two days later did not feel hungry. He felt light and humming, like a flash of lightning given human form.

Water he did need, and stopped to distill it when his body required more. But mostly he flew, and lost himself in the life around him. He searched for Tahiri, trying to understand what was happening to her, trying to give her hope.

Yavin eclipsed the sun and then rolled under the sky, and once more Anakin found himself in full darkness. He was slipping into the arms of fatigue, considering a short nap, when he heard an odd noise. At first he thought he was imagining it, for he felt nothing in the Force, but as it grew louder, he opened his eyes, turning carefully to see what it might be.

Pacing him, perhaps fifty meters away, was something large and dark. Something that did not exist in the Force at all.

"Oh, Sithspawn," he muttered under his breath. Otherwise he froze, watching the thing. It was flying perfectly parallel to him, which couldn't be an accident. It wasn't as big as a coralskipper, but not much smaller, either. A speeder analog, maybe? Something better designed for atmospheric flight than the ships he had thus far seen? He couldn't make out a silhouette, only a tactile impression of size. And there, again, he could be wrong.

Did they think he hadn't seen them yet, or were they still trying to figure out what he was?

He got his answer a few moments later, when the craft subtly changed course and their flight paths began to converge.

"This is no good," Anakin muttered.

He turned the lift control down two-thirds and dropped through what felt like a small gap in the treetops. A branch caught under one corner of the speeder and flipped it over, and with no gyro to correct, Anakin found himself hurling toward the ground. Desperately, he wrenched at the craft with the Force, flipping it back over with a very raw, unsubtle use of strength, exactly the kind of thing his brother was always berating him for. "The Force isn't a torch for you to weld plating with," Jacen might say.

Of course, without that macrofuser, Anakin would be a bag of broken bones on the forest floor right now. The Force was about everything, wasn't it?

Stabilizing in the midlevel canopy of the forest, Anakin was in more complete darkness than before, deprived even of starlight. He dropped his speed a little; his rudder was too crude to allow him the kind of hot flying that might take him between the great boles at full throttle. He let the Force guide his hands on the rudder and used his gaze to track the dark for any sign of his pursuer.

But it was his ears, again, that alerted him. Something crashed through the treetops behind him, and all of the hairs on his neck stood up. What was he facing? A living ship? A beast?

He dropped and cut a sharp turn, slipping between two trees, scraping one of them. For an instant, he thought it had worked, but then he heard the whirring turn to follow him.

How does it see? he wondered. Infrared? Or, given that the Yuuzhan Vong used only living technology, maybe it smelled him. Whatever the case, it certainly had a lock on him. It was faster, too, though less maneuverable in the trees due to its greater size.

He thought he was evading it pretty well until something hissed past his ear—not a branch, not anything he could feel in the Force. Desperately he increased his evasive tactics, spinning and rolling, coming as near the trees as he dared, slipping through the narrowest spaces he was able to.

Dark things licked past him, hissing in the leaves, and then something caught the speeder in a grip that stopped it dead in the air.

Anakin didn't stop, however. With all of the forward momentum that had just been stolen from his craft, he was hurled into the night, a rocket of blood and bone. He tucked and spun, slowing himself with the Force, and dropped onto a branch bigger around than he was.

He turned and found himself facing a hole in the night.

A thin tendril whipped out from the thing and wrapped around his waist, cinching painfully tight. With a hoarse cry, he snapped on his lightsaber and cut, just as the strand started to tighten further, as if reeling him in. Incredibly, the strand—it seemed no thicker than his thumb—resisted the first cut, though it yielded to the second.

By then he had been jerked off the branch, and once again he was falling. Closing his eyes, he nudged his course to another branch and used it as a springboard to propel himself toward the next unseen landing place. He never made it. Another of the strands caught him in mid-air. He managed to twist himself and chop it, but by that time another had fastened on him. He managed to cut it, too, but noticed the severed pieces weren't dropping off, but retained their grip on him. If this kept up . . .

He saw pretty clearly what he had to do. The next time his feet hit a branch, he hurled himself up and out, feeling the breath of several strands passing beneath and by him. He aimed himself at the hole in the Force.

The problem with that, of course, was that he couldn't sense a landing place. He came down on top of the craft, but the surface was uneven, and he slipped, bounced once on the rear of the thing, and slid off. He caught a projection as he fell, and for a brief moment felt an odd disorientation, as his inner ear suddenly told him that *down* was in two different directions, as if he stood on the dividing line between two different gravities.

In a flash, he knew what that must mean. Whatever this thing was, it was, like other Yuuzhan Vong craft, propelled by a dovin basal, the creatures that somehow generated gravitic anomalies. He was hanging next to the craft's lifts.

The craft jerked and spun over. Anakin lost his grip, but he had a fix on the gravity source now. The Yuuzhan Vong and their creatures might not exist in the Force, but gravity did.

As he fell, he hurled his lightsaber up, guiding it with the Force. It struck at the heart of the gravitic anomaly, and sparks showered the canopy below. As Anakin fell through the first layer of leaves he saw his lightsaber rupture into a bright purple flare.

Concentrating on the weapon, Anakin glanced off a branch, falling like a rag doll. Trying to focus through the pain, he found the forest floor, pushed against it, pushed . . .

Until it pushed him back. All of his breath coughed out in a rush, and he folded around his gut, sucking for wind that would not come.

The morning sun found Anakin turning blue and black over much of his body, but still functional. In the dim light, he cautiously climbed from his hiding place in the hollow of a tree and looked around.

The Yuuzhan Vong craft was down, perhaps eighty meters away. It reminded Anakin of some sort of flat, winged sea creature, though it looked as if it were grown from the same stuff as the coralskippers. It was fetched up against a tree. The cockpit was a transparent bubble extruding from the top. The pilot inside looked quite dead.

Anakin found he'd been right about the dovin basal. It looked roughly the same as the larger ones he'd seen, except it had a huge, oozing gash in it. His lightsaber lay nearby. When he picked it up and tried to activate it, his fears were confirmed—nothing happened.

"Perfect," he murmured aloud. "No weapons at all. Perfect."

He found the remains of his speeder, still attached to the cable snaking from the Yuuzhan Vong craft. It didn't take much of an inspection to tell him that this time he wouldn't be salvaging anything.

From here on out, he was walking.

CHAPTER SIXTEEN

Nen Yim watched the damutek ships settle amongst the alien trees, with a giddiness she tried hard to conceal. No reward could come from a display of emotion, especially childish ones. A shaper was circumspect; a shaper was analytical. A shaper did not stare in wonder and joy and wave the tendrils of her headdress in abandon.

So Nen Yim did none of that. But by the gods, she *felt* like doing it. This was a planet! Perhaps technically a moon, but a world, an unknown world! The unfamiliar smells of the place, the unanticipated movement of the air, the unimagined oddness of a gravity that wasn't exactly right had her senses buzzing. But the real excitement came from within her. Like the thick-trunked damutek, she was a seed, finally come to the right soil to sprout in.

Soil. She reached down, bent, and scratched up a fistful of the rich black dirt. It smelled like nothing she had ever known—a bit like the sluices beneath the mernip breeding pools, or the exhalations of the maw luur of the great worldships. The latter took in waste through its vast capillary network and digested it into nutrients, metals, and air. As a child, she'd often stood where the maw luur exhaled; until now, it was the only wind she had ever known.

"Your first time on a true world, Adept?"

Nen Yim turned, thinking to find one of her fellow adepts speaking to her, but suddenly arranged the tenta-

cles of her headdress into genuflection when she saw it
was no such lowly creature, but her new master, Mezhan
Kwaad.

The master let her finish, then beckoned her to face
her. "You may turn your eyes on me, Adept."

"Yes, Master Mezhan."

Mezhan Kwaad was a female nearing the final edge of
youth. If she were not a shaper, she might yet bear a
child, but of course that was the one form of shaping forbidden to masters of their caste. She was lean but still
wore the form of a mature female, despite her high status.
Her broad, high-cheekboned face bore the ritual forehead scars of her domain, and her right hand was an
eight-fingered master's hand. Her other alterations, in
keeping with the aesthetic of the shapers, were more discreet. The marks of her sacrifices were not external, as
they tended to be for the other castes. She wore the body-
hugging oozhith of a master, its tiny cilia rippling in
subtle waves of color as it sought and captured the alien
microorganisms in the atmosphere to feed itself.

"And answer my question," the master went on.

"Yes, Master. I have never before known a world outside of our worldships."

"And what are your impressions?"

"Our worldships are built for centuries, perhaps millennia. Yun-Yuuzhan created planets and moons for
millions and billions of cycles. The resources in the
moon's interior are released slowly, by tectonic processes,
or by life adapting to lack." She looked back down at the
dirt beneath her feet. "But it does feel so strange, the un-
imaginable wealth I'm standing on. And the life! Different from our own, and varied, and none of it made to
serve us!"

The master shaper narrowed her eyes. "It *is* made to
serve us," she said quietly. "It is the will of the gods that
life serves us. You were taught this."

"Of course, Master," Nen Yim said. "I only meant we have not shaped it yet. But we shall."

"Yes, we shall," Mezhan Kwaad agreed. "And I emphasize *we*. Do you know why you are an adept, Nen Yim? Do you know why you are here, and not correcting the mutations of methane-fixing recham forteps in a decaying maw luur?"

"No, Master."

"Because I saw your work on the endocrine cloister in the worldship *Baanu Kor*."

Nen Yim knotted her headdress in a humble posture. "I only did what needed to be done," she said.

"You did it optimally. Many would have stopped short at the molding of tii, but you went beyond that. You applied the Vul Ag protocol, though such has never been used in an endocrine cloister."

"I thought it would make the outer osmotic membranes more efficiently transpire—"

"Yes. Tradition and propriety are of absolute importance to our task, and yet immersion in those qualities can lead to hidebound thinking. I need adepts who are resourceful, who can use the sacred, unchanging knowledge in new ways. Do you understand?"

"I believe so, Master," Nen Yim answered cautiously. A small lump of fear formed in her throat. Did the master *know*?

But she couldn't. If she knew that Nen Yim had dabbled in heresy, she would never have promoted her. Unless she herself—

No. Not a master. That was impossible.

"Don't believe," the master said. "Know, and you shall go far. Do you see? As you say, after generations we have a whole new galaxy of life at our fingertips. It is time to demonstrate exactly what Yun-Yuuzhan intended us for."

Nen Yim nodded, watching the damuteks again. They were already splitting from their protective skins and beginning to expand, to grow into highly specialized shaper compounds.

"Come, Adept," the master said. "It is time to receive your hand."

"So soon?" Nen Yim asked.

"Our work begins tomorrow. We have one of the *Jeedai*, you know. Only one, but we shall have more. Supreme Overlord Shimrra himself is watching what we do here *most* carefully. We will not disappoint him."

Nen Yim stepped from the ceremonial bath into a darkened oozhith. At her touch it wrapped itself firmly about her, and she felt the tingle as it inserted cilia into her pores. It was not a full-skin oozhith, but a shortened garment that left her arms and most of her legs bare. She smoothed back her short dark hair and held out her right hand, looking at it as if for the first time rather than the last. Then she allowed the attendant to escort her into the darkened grotto of Yun-Ne'Shel, where the master waited.

The grotto smelled of brine and oil. It was close and damp and reacted faintly to the touch. The grotto was a distant relative of the yammosk; what you felt in the chamber came back to you, enhanced.

And so now both her eagerness and her trepidation had her pulse hammering as she knelt at the mouth of the grotto, a hole the size of a fist surrounded by a massive bulge of muscle. Without pausing or flinching, she placed her hand through the opening.

For a moment, nothing happened. Then the teeth slid out of their sheaths, eight of them, and pricked into her wrist.

Sweat started on her brow as she surrendered to the pain, as the teeth, with glacial slowness, sank through tissue, grated into bone. The lips closed occasionally to suck away the blood. The grotto gave her back her pain, amplified, and her breath went choppy. She lost her sense of time; every nerve ending in her body was raw, as if the cilia of her garment were writhing needles.

Until, finally, the teeth met in the center of her wrist; she felt them click together. She tried to take a long, calming breath to prepare for what was to come next.

It happened quickly. The mouth suddenly rotated ninety degrees. Her arm twisted with it no more than a degree or so, and then the hand came off with a wet *snick*. Nen Yim held up the stump of her wrist and stared at it in dull astonishment. She barely noticed the attendant taking her by the shoulders, guiding her toward the dark basin in the center of the grotto.

"I can do it," she whispered. She knelt by the basin, her head spinning. Dark things moved in the waters, five-legged things that came to the scent of her blood eagerly. She pushed her gushing stump into the water.

She had thought her body could feel no greater pain than it already had. She was wrong. She didn't feel it in her hand at all, but in a great spasm that arched her body like a bow and kept it cramped there. She couldn't see the creature grappling with her wrist. For a horrible moment, she didn't want to. A great flash of light exploded in her head, and for a time she knew nothing.

She awoke, and tears of shame started. Through them she saw the master standing over her.

"No one has ever endured it without a brief lapse the first time," she said. "There is no shame, on this occasion. If you ever receive your master's hand, it will be different. But you will be ready."

Hand. Nen Yim raised it before her.

It was still seating itself, a thick greenish secretion marking the line between it and her wrist. It had four narrow fingers and a thumb protruding from the thin but flexible carapace that now served as the top of her hand. Thousands of small sensor knobs covered the fingers and palm. The two fingers farthest from her thumb ended in small pincers. The finger nearest the thumb had a thin, sharp, retractable claw.

She tried to wiggle the fingers; nothing happened.

"It will take some days for the nerve connections to complete themselves, and some time after that for your brain to become used to the finer modifications," the master said. "Rejoice, Nen Yim—you are now truly an adept. You will join me in shaping the *Jeedai*, and will bring glory to our caste, our domain, and the Yuuzhan Vong."

CHAPTER SEVENTEEN

Anakin sank farther beneath the roots of a marsh-grubber tree and submerged himself up to his mouth, peering through the twisted growths at the elusive sky. For long moments he thought perhaps he had been mistaken, that the noise from above had been his imagination, but then he saw a shadow much too large to be any native bird pass across the fetid U-shaped lake that concealed him.

His hand went to his useless lightsaber and then fell away.

For three days he had been avoiding the Yuuzhan Vong speeder analogs. It helped that he knew the sounds of the jungle moon; the irritated cries of woolamanders in the distance or a flight of a group of lesser kitehawks had become his best allies, warning him of approaching fliers kilometers before they passed overhead. Still, as he approached the site of the academy, the searchers came with greater regularity. He didn't think they were random flights, but rather that they were part of some sort of expanding search net spiraling out from the flier he had brought down with his lightsaber.

Well, at least now he knew better than to cut into a dovin basal. From what he could tell, his weapon had passed through or very near the part of the thing that warped gravity; the crystal in his weapon had been subtly warped, then fused by the energy it generated. That was both good news and bad; focusing crystals had been found on Yavin 4 before, in the old Massassi temples, and they could be used in lightsabers. Unfortunately, Massassi temples had been in short supply lately.

Sighing, he renewed his grip on the makeshift staff he had managed to cut with his utility knife. He doubted very much that it would be of any use whatsoever against Yuuzhan Vong armor, but it was better than nothing. He'd run across some explosive grenade fungi earlier—a local plant that, when dry, could generate a respectable bang. At the moment, however, they weren't available. He'd stashed them on dry ground before hiding here.

So he sat, waiting for the shadow to return, and tried not to think about what would happen when he finally reached Tahiri and her captors. How many Yuuzhan Vong were there? Why were they still here?

All good questions, all totally moot if Anakin Solo died or was captured on the way.

He would have to face the answers soon enough, of course. By his calculations, he was only about twenty kilometers away from the academy.

He was so busy watching the sky that he didn't notice ripples of a wake approaching him until it was nearly too late.

Even then he first thought it was a large crawlfish, one of the harmless crustaceans that had been furnishing him with food since he came to ground. He caught a glimpse of mottled chiton as it approached.

But crawlfish got to be only a meter or so long, and he suddenly realized that this creature was more on the order of three meters.

He quickly lowered the sharpened end of his staff, which was promptly yanked from his hands by something very strong. The head surfaced then, a nightmare of mandibles and hooked feelers reaching for him. For an instant, fear and shock got the better of him, then he grabbed its mass with the Force and *pushed*. As it blew back and up, he got a good view of it: flat, wide, and segmented with thousands of legs.

It splashed down, milled about, and started for him again. Quickly, he clambered out of the water.

Someone called behind him, in a language he didn't understand. He spun and saw one of the Yuuzhan Vong craft, side extruded open. A Yuuzhan Vong warrior was just stepping out.

The warrior hesitated for a second, then stepped back into the craft. As it rose into the air, Anakin uttered a brief curse and ran. He paused only long enough to grab his pack.

The flier stayed with him, but kept its distance. Adrenaline hummed in Anakin's blood, but his mind was curiously calm. He dodged through the undergrowth, looking for a cave, temple ruins, any place to remove him from his observer. His fatigue sloughed from him like dead cells in a bacta tank, and the Force flowed through him like a river, wild, almost frightening in its sheer, joyous strength.

It was not a state he had quite ever achieved before, an utter awareness of everything around him. Yavin 4 was so *alive*. And in that matrix of living, pulsing Force, the fliers were bubbles of nothing. The Jedi had learned to detect the Yuuzhan Vong by not detecting them, but before it had always been a matter of focus. He would look at a suspected Yuuzhan Vong, and if he felt nothing, that was likely what he had.

But this was different. It was like suddenly noticing the spaces between words. It was a fragile thing, probably something he could never have achieved if he had tried for it, something that might go away if he thought too hard about it.

But for the moment he wasn't doing much thinking. He knew before he should have that the first Yuuzhan Vong he came across on foot was there. The warrior sprang from behind a tree, long, snakelike amphistaff held in a guard position. He was missing two fingers at the knuckle, and his ear had been cut into fringe. He wore the usual vonduun crab armor and an expression of gratification.

Anakin snapped a heavy tree bough, already rotten and fatigued, and yanked it with more than the force of gravity down upon the warrior. The Yuuzhan Vong was quick and nearly dodged, but nearly wasn't enough as half a metric ton of tree crushed him into the ground. Anakin didn't know if the warrior was dead or alive, injured, or merely compromised. He didn't care, but changed beats, aiming himself away from the bubbles of nothing crawling at the edges of his expanded senses, tightening themselves around him like a vast noose.

The next Yuuzhan Vong caught him by surprise, telescoping his amphistaff across the path so it caught Anakin just below the knees. Pain was a bright line across his shins, but he wrapped himself in the life of the forest and lifted himself up, returning to ground three meters away. The Yuuzhan Vong was charging by then, weapon retracted but ready to flip out once more. Anakin spun to face him, dancing back from the attack, until his enemy whipped the weapon out with a peculiar snap of the wrist. Not entirely limp or stiff, the amphistaff arced over Anakin's shoulder, poisonous fangs aimed at some spot on his lower back.

Anakin didn't try to parry; the staff would only wrap around his weapon and find its target anyway. Instead he leapt toward and to the left of the warrior, closing the distance so quickly that the staff slapped painfully against his shoulder. The head, however, snapped short, and by then Anakin was ducking, driving the point of his weapon up into the warrior's armpit. He pushed his own body and the staff away from the forest floor with the Force, resulting in a blow that sent the warrior hurling almost vertically, three meters in the air.

Again, without waiting to see what the effect was,

Anakin hurried on, opening his pack and tossing out the dried fungi he had gathered earlier. He didn't let them fall, but held them gently aloft with the Force, spread out around and just ahead of him. Two exploded because his Force grip was too tight, but then he was in the zone again, one with everything but the Yuuzhan Vong.

A pair of warriors hit him next, but he hardly slowed down. Each got two explosive grenade fungi. One of the Yuuzhan Vong managed to block one of the spheroids with his amphistaff, but the resulting explosion broke the warrior's concentration, and the next hit him in the head. His companion went down as well, venting a hoarse cry of anger.

The net was tightening, but there was a way out. Anakin could feel a hole in their search pattern. He lunged on ahead, lifting a virtual cloud of stones and sticks to join his remaining fungi. He was like a strange, strong wind, rushing through the trees.

Then something thudded dully into his left shoulder, and he stumbled, his legs refusing service. He hit the forest floor, wondering what had happened. The forest resounded with the sounds of his explosive grenade fungi rupturing on the ground.

He tried to sit up, then he saw the blood, spattered on the dead leaves and along the sleeve of his flight suit.

A Yuuzhan Vong stepped from out of the bushes, holding something about the size of a carbine, a tube that swelled into a sort of stock or magazine.

Grunting, Anakin struggled to his feet. The whole left side of his body felt curiously numb. He reached back and found that a hole had been gouged in his shoulder. He felt something hard in the hole and pulled it out.

It was a mass of cracked chiton.

His legs threatened to buckle again. The Yuuzhan Vong was advancing, weapon trained on him. All around him, Anakin could hear more enemies rushing toward him.

Oddly enough, he still didn't feel frightened or angry. He didn't feel much of anything, except the Force.

And a familiar presence, something not too far away. Not one presence, really, but one that was legion.

"Two can play that game," Anakin whispered.

He dropped his weapon and held his hands up. "Nice going," he told the Yuuzhan Vong. "You shot me in the back with a bug. Very brave."

He could see three or four of them now, with his peripheral vision.

He hadn't expected the warrior to answer, but he did, in Basic.

"I am Field Commander Sinan Mat. I salute your bravery, *Jeedai*. I must deny you the embrace of death in battle. For this I apologize."

A little closer, Anakin thought. *If they don't mean to kill me . . .*

"Will you fight me, Sinan Mat? Just you and me?"

"That is my desire. It cannot be. I am to bring you living to the shapers."

"I'm sorry to hear that. And . . . well, I'd feel worse about this if you hadn't shot me in the back, but . . . forgive me."

Mat frowned and touched his ear. "The tizowyrm doesn't know that word, *forgive*. What—" Then his eyes widened. The forest was screaming a song of death.

The piranha-beetles fell upon the Yuuzhan Vong in a cloud. Sinan Mat dropped his weapon and clawed at his face as it disintegrated beneath the fierce mandibles. The piranha-beetles didn't spare the other Yuuzhan Vong, either, and a chorus of pain and rage rose counterpoint to the strident song of the insects.

Anakin picked up his staff and hobbled away, knowing his legs wouldn't carry him much farther. He needed to find a place to hide.

Ten minutes later, he leaned heavily against a tree. In the distance the ravenous piranha-beetles had finished their task, and now, finally, Anakin felt his control of the Force slipping. His shoulder at last understood what had been done to it, and the pain was like burning liquid, dripping down his ribs, drooling across his chest and the side of his head. Each footstep brought a new wave of dizziness and nausea.

He tried to take another step and found he couldn't. With a sigh, he sank down onto the moss. Just a little rest, and then—

A shadow fell across him. He looked up to find two Yuuzhan Vong warriors looking down at him, obviously not a part of the group he had just killed.

He called on all of his energy, trying to find the piranha-beetles again, but they were a distant presence and gorged now, not as easily attracted to a meal by Anakin's will.

A third warrior appeared from the forest behind the first two. He looked different, somehow—mutilated like every other Yuuzhan Vong Anakin had seen, but he was more strikingly grotesque. Unlike the other two, this one was empty-handed.

The newcomer snarled something in his language, and the other two turned.

Anakin wondered, then, if he had slipped into a dream. The first two warriors grunted and spat words at the third. Anakin had heard the tone before—when the Yuuzhan Vong spoke of machines, or other things that they considered abominations. It was a tone of pure contempt.

For a moment the newcomer seemed to cringe beneath this abuse, but then he grinned, all needle teeth and malice. Then he slashed one of the warriors in the neck with the edge of his gloved hand. The other warrior gave a hoarse cry of outrage, lowered his amphistaff, and thrust at the attacker. The unarmed warrior caught the shaft, leapt high in the air, kicking with both feet and striking the staff-wielder in the face.

The first warrior down was coming back up, clutching

his throat. The unarmed one grabbed him by the hair and drove stiffened fingers deep into his eyes, lifting him from the ground by the sockets. The warrior went rigid, and when the newcomer let him drop he fell to the forest floor, twitching.

The warrior who had been kicked in the face didn't get up. Anakin suspected his neck was broken. The unarmed Yuuzhan Vong was the only one still standing. He squatted next to Anakin and peered at him with eyes like algae-infested pools of water.

He looked—sick. The Yuuzhan Vong showed their rank by scarification and the sacrifice of body parts, but this one looked like an example of that gone horribly wrong. His hair hung in dank patches, and his face and neck were covered with scabs and open wounds. His scars looked swollen and unhealthy. Spiky growths that looked like dead or dying implants moldered on his shoulders and elbows. He stank of putrefaction.

After observing Anakin for a long moment, the Yuuzhan Vong rose, approached one of the bodies, and dug into its ear. He pulled out what looked like a worm of some sort and fed it into his own ear—or, rather, the festering hole that might once have been an ear. He shuddered, and his body spasmed as if in great pain. A thin drool of blood leaked from the orifice.

He turned back to Anakin and held out his hand.

"I am Vua Rapuung, *Jeedai*. You will come with me. I will help you."

CHAPTER EIGHTEEN

The young *Jeedai* fell, her body gripped with convulsions. A strangled cry filled the vivarium.

"Interesting," Mezhan Kwaad said, watching the reaction. "Do you see, Adept Yim, that—"

"I fail to see what interests you, Master Mezhan Kwaad," a voice said from behind.

Nen Yim turned and immediately supplicated. Another master had just entered the vivarium, one so incredibly ancient the signs of his domain were entirely obscured. His headdress was a fragile, cloudlike mass, and both hands were those of a master. Both of his eyes had been replaced by yellow maa'its. He was accompanied by an adept aide.

"Master Yal Phaath," Mezhan Kwaad said. "How good to see you, Ancient."

"Answer me, Mezhan Kwaad. What so interests you about this creature's agony? She is an infidel and cannot embrace the pain. There is no surprise in that and nothing interesting in it."

"It is interesting because the provoker spineray causing her pain has been designed to do so selectively," Mezhan Kwaad replied, "one nerve array at a time. What we have just seen is a reflex unknown in Yuuzhan Vong. We may now confidently map a part of the human nervous system that has no counterpart in our own."

"And this is of what use?" Yal Phaath asked.

"We cannot shape what we do not know," Mezhan Kwaad answered. "This species is new to us."

"It strains the protocol," the older master said. "What can be discovered that is not codified already?"

"But, Master," Nen Yim said, supplicating as she did so. "Surely in a new species—" She broke off when the master flicked the gaze of his maa'its toward her.

"Are all of your adepts so insolent?" he asked dryly.

"I should hope not," Mezhan Kwaad said stiffly.

Yal Phaath turned back to Nen Yim. His headdress writhed slightly in the air, turning a pale blue. "Adept, if knowledge is not to be found in the archives and sacred memories, what then does a shaper do?"

Fear glittered in Nen Yim's nerves. What could he see, with those strange eyes? The maa'its probed the hidden regions of the spectrum, of course, and the domain of the microscopic, but did they peer farther yet, into the sins crouched beneath her skull? She contracted the tendrils of her headdress into a ball, a deep supplication. "We petition the Supreme Overlord, Master, that he might ask of the gods."

"Correct. There *are* no new species, Adept. All life comes from the blood and flesh and bone of Yun-Yuuzhan. He knows them all. Knowledge cannot be created; that is the stuff of heresy. If the gods do not grant us knowledge, it is for good reason, and to seek further is an attempt to steal from them."

"Yes, Master Yal Phaath."

"I suspect this is not your fault, Adept. It is your own master who uses the provoker spineray so. You are susceptible to her influences."

Mezhan Kwaad smiled gently. "The protocol of Tsong specifies the use of the provoker in just such a manner."

"I am aware of that. But you strain the intent of that protocol. Not to breaking, perhaps. And yet who knows what I might have observed had I arrived a little later?"

"Are you accusing me of something, Master?" Mezhan Kwaad asked mildly. "If not, one might believe you are merely jealous because Lord Shimrra chose Domain Kwaad for the honor of this shaping."

"I accuse you of nothing, nor am I jealous. But dangerous heresies have surfaced in recent years, most often among Domain Kwaad."

"I have never been accused of heresy, nor have any of my subordinates," Mezhan Kwaad said. "If you try to bathe me in the filthy secretions of slander in a pitiable attempt to regain the favor of your domain with Lord Shimrra, you will discover I can be a most unresting foe."

The old shaper drew himself very erect. "I do not slander. But I watch, Mezhan Kwaad. Rest assured, I watch. And now—"

He broke off suddenly and staggered. His aide caught him. Nen Yim was still wondering what had happened when she suddenly felt something pressing her entire body, as if she were deep under water. Her lungs labored to draw the syrupy air and her pulse hammered.

Through flashes of blue and black, she saw that Mezhan Kwaad and Yal Phaath's aide were also struggling to breathe.

The pain increased sharply. Soon her eyeballs would collapse, then her heart. Striving for calm, she spun her failing gaze around the room.

The young *Jeedai* stood at the side of the vivarium, hands pressed against the transparent membrane. Her green eyes blazed and her teeth were drawn back from her lips in a rictus of fury. Nen Yim saw murder there, and suddenly understood.

She staggered toward her master. Mezhan Kwaad had already collapsed. The ol-villip that controlled the provoker spineray had fallen from her hands. Nen Yim took it up and stroked the variable tissues, all of them at once.

The *Jeedai* screamed and pounded on the membrane, and for an instant the pressure actually increased, crushing so hard that Nen Yim couldn't breathe at all. Then, more suddenly than it had come, the uncanny pressure relented, and her lungs jerked in a much-needed breath.

The *Jeedai* writhed on the floor of her chamber. Nen Yim watched her, reaction starting to set in.

An eight-fingered hand fell on Nen Yim's shoulder.

"Adept," her master said, in a strained voice. "The ol-villip, please. Before the specimen dies."

Nen Yim nodded dumbly and handed Mezhan Kwaad the organism. Mezhan Kwaad adjusted it until the *Jeedai* stopped her contortions and succumbed to unconsciousness.

"That was well-wrought thinking, Adept," Mezhan Kwaad told her.

"What happened? Tell me," Yal Phaath demanded impatiently.

"The *Jeedai* did it," Mezhan Kwaad replied. "Surely you've heard of their powers."

"Do not insult me. I am, of course, current on the information concerning the *Jeedai*. They can move objects, communicate with one another as villips do, even influence the minds of weaker creatures. But there has never been any evidence that they can affect Yuuzhan Vong. Quite the contrary."

"I beg the master for permission to speak," Nen Yim said.

Yal Phaath gave her a reluctant glance. "Speak."

"The *Jeedai* did *not* affect us, not directly. She affected the molecules of the atmosphere, compressing them."

"She tried to crush us with our own air?"

"And would have succeeded but for my adept," Mezhan Kwaad observed.

"Amazing. And this power—it is not generated by implants of any kind?"

"She has no implants, either biological or"—her voice lowered—"mechanical. From our earlier interrogation, she believes that she is manipulating a kind of energy produced by life."

"Ridiculous," Yal Phaath said. "If such a power existed, why would the gods deny it to the Yuuzhan Vong?"

Mezhan Kwaad smiled a carnivorous smile. "The gods have not denied it to us, they merely withheld it for a time. And now they have delivered it." She stepped to the vivarium membrane and parted it with a flick of her fourth finger. She knelt by the unconscious *Jeedai* and stroked her face.

"She is young, her body and mind still pliant to shaping. The warriors promise us more like her, soon." She stood, looking down at the creature for a few moments, then stepped away and resealed the membrane.

The old master shrugged. "For the glory of the shapers and the Yuuzhan Vong, I wish you success." He sounded doubtful.

"You may observe anytime you wish," Mezhan Kwaad said. To Nen Yim it seemed as if her master was taunting Yal Phaath.

But the old master ran a negative ripple through his tendrils. "Among other things, I've come to take my leave. The new project awaits me, a shaping that will end this *Jeedai* threat forever."

Mezhan Kwaad stiffened a bit. "Oh?" she said politely.

"Indeed. Under interrogation, the infidels who serve us admitted that they were tricked by those who presently harass our ships in space. From this information came a most interesting item, about a certain sort of beast, one that can sense and hunt these *Jeedai*."

"The infidels knew where to find these beasts?"

"No," Yal Phaath said. "Not those on this moon, at any rate. But we have sources in their senate, and one of them was able to discover and provide the information. As it turns out, the beasts are native to a world already in possession of our Lord Shimrra, a planet the infidels call Myrkr. I am to oversee the shaping of these beasts."

"Interesting, about these beasts, if true," Mezhan Kwaad allowed. "For the glory of the Yuuzhan Vong, I wish you well. I also wish you success in leaving the system. Apparently the infidels have been quite successful in preventing outgoing traffic."

"I have no fear," the ancient master replied. "If Yun-Yuuzhan wants my life, it is his to take. But I suspect he has many tasks for me yet."

"Captain, one of the Yuuzhan Vong warships has broken orbit," H'sishi said. "It has a substantial escort."

Karrde stroked his mustache. "Get Solusar up here. Meanwhile, close distance, and have the *Etherway* and the *Idiot's Array* lay down a barrage. Let's keep her in the gas giant's mass shadow for as long as we can."

"Yes, sir," Dankin, the pilot, returned.

"And get Solusar up here," Karrde repeated. "We'll need him for this."

"I'm already here, Captain Karrde."

Indeed, Solusar was standing just behind him. "Ah. Perfect. The Yuuzhan Vong are trying to punch a ship through our defenses, presumably to leave the system. My question is, should I let them go?"

"You haven't let any others go," Solusar pointed out.

"True. But none of those tried in such force. If we fight here, I'll lose ships, more than we can spare. If I thought relief was on the way, I might risk it. As it is, I need to know—are there Jedi on that ship?"

For an instant, Karrde saw a twinge of what might pass for fear in the Jedi's eyes.

"I can't be certain," Solusar said stiffly.

"Why not?"

"I can't sense the Yuuzhan Vong in the Force. Their ships might as well be lifeless asteroids as far as my senses are concerned."

"Then I should think the children would stand out in quite a spectacular manner."

"They should, and they don't. If it weren't important, I would say there are no non–Yuuzhan Vong on any of those ships. But it *is* important. If I'm wrong, we might end up letting them go—then we'd be fighting here for nothing."

"How might you be wrong? I don't understand."

"The Yuuzhan Vong not only don't exist in the Force—they make me doubt my Jedi senses altogether. They make the whole area . . . *murky,* somehow. I've no better way to explain it."

Karrde looked back at the screen. The Yuuzhan Vong had scrambled fighters.

"I can't wait much longer, Solusar. I have to decide. Forget the ships; try to sense them on the moon. If they're still there, they can't be on that warship."

"I'll try," the Jedi said. He closed his eyes.

Karrde watched the enemy fighters race closer. So far, he had managed hit-and-run operations at minimal risk to his people. He'd made good use of mines and asteroids and other classic guerrilla weapons of intrasystem war.

But if he had to stop that ship, he would have to commit to a real stand-up-slug-it-out battle, a battle he could win—at the cost of the war.

Maybe that was all they wanted. His instincts certainly told him that this was a decoy of some kind, not what he was fighting for. Solusar seemed to concur. But if they couldn't be sure . . .

"First fighter wave in thirty seconds," H'sishi said tonelessly.

"Get ready, people."

A good crew. They would die if he asked them to.

"*Tahiri,*" Solusar breathed. His face was beaded with sweat.

"What's that?"

"Tahiri. And Valin. Sannah. Anakin. They're all down there." His voice dropped lower, into a register of anguish. "Tahiri's been tortured."

"But they're down there."

"Yes. I'm sure of it."

"Thank you, Jedi Solusar. Dankin, break off the attack. We're letting this one go. Lay down minimal cover fire and tell the other ships to burn jets. We'll fight another day, people—when it really counts." Karrde took a deep breath, trying to release the pent-up tension in his neck and shoulders.

"And hope those Solo kids find that rogue Terrik before we have to fight that fight. After this, I'm definitely looking into getting my own Star Destroyer."

CHAPTER NINETEEN

Anakin arched his back and tried not to cry out as whatever the Yuuzhan Vong put on his wound sent cosmic flares of pain through his body.

"You hate pain," Vua Rapuung said with evident disgust.

Anakin couldn't and didn't disagree. He just gritted his teeth and waited for it to pass. He knew the Yuuzhan Vong venerated pain in themselves and others. It was one of many unlikable tenets of their unhealthy religion.

"What hit me?" Anakin asked instead.

"A nang hul," the warrior grunted. "Thud bug."

"Poison?"

"No."

The two sat in a damp cave behind a waterfall. It was slick with fungus and moss. The Yuuzhan Vong had evidently been hiding in the cave for a day or two, for various of his possessions were already in it, including the patch he had just applied to Anakin's shoulder. He'd peeled it from a pale green, roughly rectangular pad several centimeters thick. The pad consisted of many thin layers, like leaves of flimsiplast glued together. Rapuung had pressed one of these detached skins over Anakin's wound. Like everything else the Yuuzhan Vong used, it was alive. Anakin could feel it squirming, digging into his wound. It occurred to him that the warrior might be poisoning him or something even worse. But if Vua Rapuung wanted him dead, he could have accomplished that anytime. After all, he had made short work of two Yuuzhan Vong warriors, and Anakin didn't have the strength to fight off a wokling.

"You saved my life," Anakin said reluctantly.

"Life is nothing," Vua Rapuung said.

"Yeah? Then why take the trouble?"

Vua Rapuung's black eyes glimmered murkily. "You, *Jeedai*. You fight your way toward the shaper compound. Why?"

"Your people have a friend of mine. I'm going to get her back."

"Ah. The female *Jeedai*. You wish to save her life. How pitiful. What a pitiful goal."

"Yeah? Well, I didn't ask for your help, you offered it. So explain or kill me. I haven't got time to waste."

"Revenge," Vua Rapuung said, his voice low, his eyes slitted. "Revenge, and to prove that the gods—" His eyes suddenly went hard and glittering. "I need not tell you, human. I need explain nothing to you, unsanctioned offspring of machines." He spat the last word out as if it were poison he'd suddenly discovered in his mouth.

"You need know only this," he continued. "I will stand at your side or your back. Your foes are my foes. We will kill together, embrace pain together, embrace death together if such is Yun-Yuuzhan's wish."

"You'll help me rescue Tahiri," Anakin said dubiously.

"It's a stupid goal, but finding her will serve my purposes well."

Anakin searched that black diamond gaze, trying to understand. There was nothing there, nothing. The Yuuzhan Vong was more like a holo than a person, an image, an appearance. How could such a thing have feelings to be understood? Without the Force, how could he hope to comprehend such an alien creature?

"I don't understand," Anakin said. "What did your people do to you? Why do you hate them so?"

Vua Rapuung slapped him, hard, and bounded to his feet, chest heaving.

"Do not mock me!" he shrieked. "You have eyes! You see! Do not mock me! The gods did not do this to me, they did *not*!"

As the Yuuzhan Vong started toward him again, Anakin hefted a rock with the Force and sent it straight for the warrior's sternum. It caught Rapuung completely by surprise, smacking him against the side of the cave. He sank down, looking a bit dazed.

Anakin hefted the rock again and poised it over Rapuung's head.

The Yuuzhan Vong looked up at the stone and suddenly started hacking as if he had the Dagobian swamp cough.

It took half a minute of this before Anakin recognized it as laughter.

When he calmed down, Vua Rapuung fixed the young Jedi with a curious gaze. "I saw what you did to the hunters, but still, to have it turned on me—" His face hardened again. "Tell me the truth, one warrior to another, if you can. In the warrior caste there are rumors. It is said your *Jeedai* powers come from machine implants. Is this true? Are your people that sick?"

Anakin returned the challenging stare. "Our powers do not come from machines. Furthermore, some of your people must know that, because they've had ample opportunity to dissect some of us. Your rumor is a lie."

"Yes? Then the *Jeedai* Master does not have a machine hand?"

"Master Skywalker? He does, but—" He broke off. "How do you know this?"

"We hear many stories from converts and spies. So it is true, then. The leader of the *Jeedai* is part machine." Rapuung's face probably couldn't have shown more disgust without being surgically altered.

"One has nothing to do with the other. Master Luke

lost a hand in a great battle. He had it replaced. But his power, like mine, flows from the Force."

"Do you have implants like your master?"

"No."

"Will you receive them as you attain rank?"

Anakin laughed briefly. "No."

Vua Rapuung nodded. "Then it is as I said. We will fight together."

"Not if you keep flying off course like you did a minute ago," Anakin replied. "I may be injured, but as you've seen, I'm not without resources."

"I see," Rapuung growled, "but do not challenge me. I dislike it."

"You keep the same thing in mind, pal. Now. You say we're going to fight together but you won't tell me why. Can you at least tell me how?"

"The shapers have planted five damuteks on this moon. That is where your *Jeedai* companion is held."

Anakin let pass the precise definition of *damutek* for the moment. "Why? What will they do to her?"

Murder flashed in Rapuung's eyes again, but this time he mastered it without an outburst. "Who can know the mind of a shaper?" he said, softly. "But you can be sure they will *shape*."

"I don't understand. What is a shaper?"

"Your ignorance is—" Rapuung stopped, blinked his eyes slowly closed, open, closed, and started again. "The shapers are a caste, the caste nearest the great god, Yun-Yuuzhan, who shaped the universe from his body. It is they who know the ways of life, who bend it to our needs."

"Bioengineers? Scientists?"

Rapuung stared at him for a second. "The tizowyrm that translates for me makes no sense from those words. I suspect they are obscene."

"Never mind. There was a Jedi named Miko Reglia. Your people tried to break his will with a yammosk. They tried to do the same to another Jedi named Wurth Skidder. Is that what you think they'll do to Tahiri?"

"I do not care what they do to your *Jeedai*. But what you describe is—" He grimaced. "I once knew a shaper who spoke of such things, of warriors who thought they could do the task of shapers, as you describe. But breaking is not shaping. It is a child's parody of it. Understand, the shapers make our worldships. They *make* the yammosk. They will not try to *break* your *Jeedai*—they will *remake* her."

A chill seeped into Anakin's veins, and he remembered his vision of an older Tahiri.

He knew what they would make of her. And they would succeed, if Anakin failed.

What Rapuung offered might be a cruel trick, a part of some devious plan; Anakin would have to take that risk. Without the Force to guide him, he could never be certain the Yuuzhan Vong wasn't telling the truth. Now was no time to dither. Any course that would take him closer to Tahiri was worth plotting, even if he had to let someone he didn't trust do some of the figures.

"Okay," he said. "Let's go back to an earlier vector. You said something about damuteks?"

"The sacred precincts within which the shapers live and work."

"How many of them? How many shapers?"

"I don't know for certain. Around twelve, if initiates are included."

"That's all? That's all the Vong on this world?"

Rapuung spat something Anakin didn't understand. He didn't seem to be so much angry as in genuine shock.

"Do not—*never* refer to us in that way," he sputtered. "How can you be so ignorant? Or do you *wish* to insult?"

"Not that time," Anakin said.

"To use the word *Vong* alone is an insult. It implies that the person so addressed does not have the favor and kinship of gods or family."

"Sorry."

Rapuung didn't answer, but stared out into the forest.

"We should go," he said, "I have hidden our scent from the trackers, but they will find us soon enough if we stay still."

"Agreed," Anakin said. "But first—how many Yuu-zhan Vong on this moon, total, would you think?"

Vua Rapuung considered briefly. "A thousand, perhaps. More warriors in space."

"And we'll fight our way through all of them?"

"Was that not *your* plan?" Rapuung asked. "Does the number we face mean anything to you?"

Anakin shook his head. "Only in terms of tactics. Tahiri is there. I'll find her and get her out, no matter how many Yuuzhan Vong I have to walk through."

"Very well. You can walk, now?"

"I can walk. Soon I can run. It might hurt, but I can do it."

"Life is suffering," Vua Rapuung said. "We go."

CHAPTER TWENTY

Vua Rapuung gnashed his teeth. "No, ignorant one," he growled. "Not that way."

Anakin didn't look at him, but kept his gaze wandering through the whispering Massassi trees, searching for shadows that did not agree with the wind in their motion.

The two stood at the divide of the ridge top; one stone spine snaked down and away to Anakin's right, the other continued up and to his left. Anakin had started up the steepening trail.

"Why?" he asked. "The search craft are over there." He waved toward the lowlands off the left ridge.

"They are not 'craft,' " Rapuung snapped.

"You know what I meant."

"How do you know where they are, when you cannot sense Yuuzhan Vong or the life shaped for us?"

"Because I can sense everything native in this forest," Anakin replied. "Every whisper bird and runyip, every stintaril and woolamander. And the ones over there are agitated. I get flashes."

"This is so? How many fliers? Five, yes?"

Anakin focused his concentration. "I think so."

"They will split into a lav peq pattern, then. First the lowland, then arcs tightening to the highest point. If they find us up here, they will converge and release netting beetles."

"What are netting beetles?"

"If we do not isolate ourselves on an elevation, you will not find out. This is not air warfare, *Jeedai*, and unless you plan to fortify this high spot and fight all of the warriors on this moon, altitude is of no use to you."

"I want a look at the lay of the land."

"Why?"

"Because you've gotten us lost, that's why. You no more know where the Vo—the Yuuzhan Vong base is than a mynock knows how to play sabacc."

"I can find the shaper damutek. But if we slash a straight line toward them, they will snare us."

"I know this moon," Anakin said. "You don't." He stopped, staring suspiciously at the warrior. "How did you find me, anyway?"

"I followed the search parties, infidel. You *were* slashing a straight path, weren't you? Yes. Without me, you would have been captured ten times by now."

"Without you, I would have been in your shaper base by now."

"Yes. I just said that," Rapuung said. He closed his eyes, as if listening to something. "What do your *Jeedai* senses tell you now?"

Anakin frowned in concentration. "I think they've split up," he said reluctantly.

"I can hear them," Vua Rapuung said. "Not as well as I once could. Once my ears were . . ." He reached and lightly touched the festering, oozing scar tissue on the side of his head. He snarled and dropped his hand.

"We go down," he said.

"I go up," Anakin replied. He started up the trail. He didn't look back, but after he had gone perhaps thirty strides, he heard what he guessed to be a Yuuzhan Vong profanity and the sound of footsteps pacing up behind him.

"Gee," Anakin breathed. Tears stung his eyes.

He stood at the crest of the height, where he could see

the familiar meander of the Unnh River. He'd seen this spot from the air maybe fifty times, and knew it as well as he knew any place.

Except that things had changed. The Great Temple—which had stood for untold thousands of years, watching the passage of the people who built it, of Jedi dark and brilliant, the destruction of the Death Star—was gone without a trace.

In its place near the river were five spacious compounds formed like many-rayed stars. The walls were thick and perhaps two stories high, and probably had chambers in them. The inner courtyards were open to the sky. Two seemed to be filled with water, another with a pale yellow fluid that probably wasn't water. Another had structures in its central space—domes and polyhedrons of various shapes, all the same color as the larger structure. The fifth was full of coralskippers and larger spacegoing ships. Lots of them.

It looked like canals had been dug from the river to connect the compounds.

"We must descend before they scent us," Vua Rapuung insisted again.

"I thought that stuff you rubbed on us fools the sniffers, or whatever they are."

"It causes confusion. It gives us time to hide. There is no place to hide here, and they will *see* us. There is no fooling that."

There is for Jedi, usually, Anakin thought. But he could no more cloud a Yuuzhan Vong mind than he could dance on the surface of a black hole.

"There's cover," he said. The hill was blanketed mostly in scrub and lacked the high canopy that grew over most of the moon's land surface, but the bushes were usually more than head-high.

"Not from heat-pit sensors," Rapuung demurred. "Not from netting beetles. No water."

Anakin nodded thoughtfully, but he was really still examining the shaper base, barely paying attention to the Yuuzhan Vong beside him.

"Outside of the big compounds—all of those little structures that look like somebody just threw them down and let them grow—what's all that? It looks like a shantytown."

"I don't know that word, *shantee*. That is where the workers and slaves and Shamed Ones live."

"Support colony. They do the drudge work."

"If the tizowyrm translates correctly, yes."

"Workers and slaves I know. What are Shamed Ones?"

"Shamed Ones are cursed by the gods," Rapuung said. "They work as slaves. They are not worth speaking of."

"Cursed how?"

"When I say they are not worth speaking of, how do my words confuse you?"

"Fine," Anakin sighed. "Have it your way."

"My way is to leave this ridge, work spiralwise toward where the gas giant sets. Quickly."

"That's the wrong direction! We're only a few kilometers away!"

"All the forest below is trapped," Rapuung said. "The river, too. There is only one way in for us, and I know it."

"Tell me what it is, then," Anakin said. "Convince—" But he stopped. "Listen."

Rapuung nodded. "I hear them. They are weaving the lav peq. I was foolish to trust you. You think with something other than your brain." He pressed his frayed and ulcerous lips together in an expression of contempt.

"We aren't caught yet. Is there a weak spot in this search pattern?"

"No."

"We'll make one, then. These fliers they're using—"

"Tsik vai."

"Right. Are they the same as we've seen before?"

"Yes."

"They're just atmospheric fliers, right?"

Rapuung looked wary. "How do you know that?"

"They look like they have some sort of air intake vents—gills—on the side."

"Correct."

"Come on, then." Anakin started down the hill. Rapuung started after him, for once without objection.

Anakin was feeling considerably better today. Jedi healing and relaxation techniques had drained much of his weariness, and Vua Rapuung's artificial skin—or whatever it was—seemed to have done its part with his shoulder. He loped down the hill in a series of long, flat, Force-aided leaps. Rapuung kept up, barely, winding nearly soundlessly through the dense underbrush. It actually raised the hackles on Anakin's neck to look at him. It was hard to believe something so deadly looking could be sentient at all.

Most of the trees were gone, no doubt burned off in one of the many battles that had occurred on the jungle moon since the Rebel Alliance located its resistance here before the battle against the first Death Star. What remained was waist-high scrub. Farther down, the trees began again, a green necklace around the hill, and Anakin suddenly understood what Rapuung was concerned about. Fire burned *up*. Anything caught up here when the blaze started had probably died. If these netting beetles were anything like fire . . .

He realized, reluctantly, that Rapuung was right. Anakin thought too much like a pilot, where the high ground was everything. He wasn't a pilot right now; he was prey.

But dangerous prey—a feral rycrit, not a tame one, he reminded himself, when the first tsik vai flier came over.

Anakin didn't hesitate; he knew what he wanted to do. He reached in a ten-meter radius and lifted everything that wasn't fastened down—leaf litter, twigs, stones—and hurled them in a cyclone at the intake slits on the side of the flier.

"Fool!" Rapuung shouted. "*That* was your plan?"

The tsik vai swooped in low, and the tentaclelike cables fired out at them. Anakin dodged, keeping up his barrage. Undeterred, the flier followed close, dropping lower. A tentacle caught Rapuung. The warrior leapt, gripped the upper part of the tentacle in his hands, and started climbing, a grim expression on his scarred face. Getting the idea, Anakin tried to do the same, but without the Force to give him certainty—without being able to feel the tentacles as well as see them—he missed.

The flier suddenly made a peculiar whine, and its flexible wings began to shiver as if in spasm. The tentacle holding Rapuung released him, and he instantly leapt for the ground. The flier hung there, shaking itself.

"Run," Rapuung shouted. "It will clear its lungs quickly. These tsik vai were not shaped by idiot children, as you seem to think."

Anakin fell into step with him. "Where are the other fliers?"

"They know where we are now. They will seed the netting beetles into the lowland, as I told you."

"I wish you had told me what these things do."

"They draw fibers from tree to tree, from bush to bush. They come in waves that overtake one another, the first wave weaving and the waves behind feeding to replenish their fiber. They move very quickly."

"Oh. That's not good." A sudden thought occurred to him. "You were climbing toward the flier when it had you. Did you think you could capture it?"

"No. I thought I might die gloriously rather than ignominiously. My bare hands are not capable of forcing open the cockpits."

"But if we can get above the net, somehow . . ."

"Some of the beetles will draw strands up into the air and cross them above our heads. If we could fly at this very moment, we might escape."

Anakin came to a halt. "Why are we running, then?

Whichever way we go, we're only coming nearer to the net."

"True. And if we go uphill, we will only delay our confrontation with it. Do you have your *Jeedai* blade-that-burns? It might cut the fibers."

"No." Anakin was peering downhill. The trees started perhaps a hundred meters away, but he had enough elevation to see their swaying tops stretching off to the horizon, bending this way and that in a fickle wind.

Except in a strip, where they weren't moving at all. Following the strip, he saw it curving around the hill.

"That's it, isn't it," he murmured. "The net is holding them together."

"Yes. The fibers are very strong, the net very fine."

Even as Anakin watched, more trees froze in place, and the strip deepened.

"Will the netting beetles eat us?"

"They will attach to our flesh and draw fiber, using some of our cells in the process. It will not be fatal."

"Right. Because it's not going to happen." Anakin stopped, knelt, and took off his pack. After an instant of rummaging, he'd found what he was after: five phosphorous flares.

"Are those weapons? Machines?"

"Not usually," Anakin said. "Don't look directly at this." He struck one alight, then, using the Force, hurled it in a long arc downhill.

He struck another and hurled it similarly, along a different vector.

"I don't understand," Rapuung said. "How will the light stop the netting beetles?"

"The light won't. The fire will. The beetles can't attach to trees and bushes that aren't there."

He struck another flare. As he cocked his arm back to throw it, Vua Rapuung backhanded him in the face.

Anakin's nostrils filled with the iron scent of blood, and he fetched hard against the ground before he could react to cushion himself. Rapuung was all over him, snarling like a beast, fingers curled around his neck. He smelled sour and sick.

Spots dancing before his eyes, Anakin did the only thing he could. He found a stone with the Force and hit the crazed warrior right between the eyes with it. Rapuung's head snapped back and his hands came away. Anakin hit him in the chin so hard that sparks of pain exploded in his knuckles. The Yuuzhan Vong fell off of him, but by the time Anakin had scrambled to his feet, Rapuung was up, assuming a martial stance.

"Sithspawn!" Anakin snapped. "What are you doing?"

"Combustion!" the Yuuzhan Vong roared. "The first abomination is the use of fire from a machine!"

"What?"

"This is forbidden, you stinking infidel! Don't you understand what you've done?"

"You're insane!" Anakin shouted back, rubbing knuckles that felt shattered, drawing breath through an aching windpipe. "You were just asking me if I could use my lightsaber! You think that's not a machine?"

A look of what might have been horror dawned on Rapuung's face. "I . . . yes, I prepared myself for that, But *fire*, the first of all sins—"

"Wait," Anakin snapped. "You're not making any sense. The Yuuzhan Vong have used fire breathers against us in the past."

"Living creatures producing flame is another thing entirely!" Rapuung shrieked. "How can you possibly imagine it is the same as what you've just done? As well say that the hand of a Yuuzhan Vong warrior and the metal grip of one of your made-thing abominations are the same because either can hold an amphistaff."

Anakin took a deep breath. "Look," he said. "I don't pretend to understand your religion. I don't even want to. But you've chosen to fight with an infidel against your own people, haven't you? You were perfectly willing for me to use my abominable lightsaber. Now you deal with this or go your own way. Unless you've got another way out."

"No," Rapuung admitted. "It's just the shock . . ." He dropped his head. "You really don't understand. The gods don't hate me. I know they don't. I can prove it. But if I soil myself like this, they will have reason to hate me! Ah, what have I become?"

The wind shifted, and the charred pepper scent of burning blueleaf set Anakin to coughing. The last flare had gone only about three meters, and now the bushes upwind of them were blazing merrily. It was the dry season, and jungle burned very well in the dry season.

"You'd better get a grip fast, Vua Rapuung, or the first abomination is going to eat you alive."

The Yuuzhan Vong stood there for a long moment, head cast down, but when he raised his head, his eyes were beacons of rage. Anakin tensed, preparing to fight again.

"*She* has driven me to this," the warrior said. "These sins will settle on *her*. I leave it to the gods to judge."

"Does that mean we can go?" Anakin asked, watching the fire sweep toward them. Down the hill, smoke poured thickly from where the other flares had lodged.

"Yes. Let us go. We still embrace pain together, *Jeedai*."

The fire drove them around the side of the hill and up it; the change in the wind seemed to be a lasting one. Smoke boiled and crept close to the ground.

The jungle burned *fast*.

"My opinion of you as a strategist improves," Rapuung said. "The fire drives us directly into the other side of the net. We have our choice of being burned to death by the first abomination, or being captured and then burned."

"The wind shifted. My plan was to follow along the

fire's exhaust, walk on the ashes. The net will collapse where the fire burns through, and then we're clear."

"Then perhaps the gods have spoken after all," Rapuung said. He coughed violently on the smoke, which was becoming so thick that Anakin was seeing spots in front of his eyes. He remembered most people who died in a fire were dead before the flames ever reached them.

"Keep low," he said. "The smoke rises."

"Low. Crawling like a tso'asu."

"If you want to live, yes."

"I do not fear death," Rapuung choked out. "But my revenge will not be thwarted. I . . ." He convulsed in another series of racking coughs, fell, climbed back to all fours, and collapsed again.

"Get up!" Anakin exhorted him.

Rapuung quivered but did not move.

Through the smoke, the yellow teeth of the fire appeared, chewing toward them.

CHAPTER
TWENTY-ONE

Everything went pale gold as Anakin dropped to his knees next to Vua Rapuung. His breath felt like broken shards in his lungs, and his head rang like an alarm.

He lay flat, trying to find sweeter, cooler air, but if it was there, it was traveling in disguise. If he was going to find something he could breathe, it would be somewhere above him. Sure, it would be smoky up there, too, but it was worth a shot.

Anakin reached up and *pulled*, creating a tube that sucked higher air straight down on him and the Yuuzhan Vong. His breathing eased immediately.

The fire liked it, too. The underbrush exploded like a bomb. Anakin felt the heat briefly, heat he knew would blacken and crack his flesh in seconds. He had not tried to alter energy before, but Corran Horn could do it. Their lives depended on his success. Anakin opened himself again to the Force, focused his efforts, and leached the fire's heat from a radius around them both.

How long he kept this up, Anakin did not know. He slipped into a sort of fugue state, each breath pulling life from the sky, each exhalation bleeding heat into the crust of Yavin 4. But eventually he blinked and realized it was over, that the fire had burned past him and he knelt in ashes.

Vua Rapuung still lay motionless. Anakin shook him. Where did one check for vital signs on a Yuuzhan Vong?

Did they have hearts like humans, linear pumps, something stranger?

He slapped Rapuung, hard, and the warrior's eyes flickered open.

"Are you okay?" Anakin asked.

"Pray me you are not one of the gods," Rapuung muttered. "If you are, death will be tedious."

"Yeah, you're welcome," Anakin replied. "Can you walk? We need to go before the fliers think to look here."

"Smoke and heat will confuse them," Rapuung said. He sat up and looked around. "The fire—it passed over us."

"It did."

"And we live."

"We do," Anakin assured him.

"This was your doing? Another *Jeedai* sorcery?"

"Something like that," Anakin admitted.

"Then you saved my life. How disgusting. How unfortunate."

"No, don't gush on so," Anakin said. "It was nothing, really." He offered his hand to help Rapuung up. After a long moment of staring at it as if it were nerf dung, the warrior took it.

"Come on," Anakin said. "Now all we have to do is follow the fire."

Under cover of the smoke, they slipped through the ruins of the netting beetle web. The strands themselves had not burned, but lay silvery and glistening in the ashes, draped like shrouds on the smoking trunks of trees. When Anakin's foot tangled in some, he found that it had cut into his boot a little. None of the web had broken, and he didn't try to tear it with his fingers, but instead gently untangled it. After that he was more careful where he stepped.

The fire had burned on past the end of the web. Anakin could see fliers nosing around in front of it. One made a pass back, far to their left.

They pushed right, eventually cutting out of the path of the fire into unburned, unnetted woods, and though they did not slacken their pace for another two hours, Anakin felt suddenly safer, surrounded by the living pulse of the forest.

But in that pulse was a raw edge of pain.

Only then did it strike him what he had done. To save himself, he had burned countless square kilometers of forest. He had felt beasts dying, peripherally, but in the moment his own pain had been paramount. Now the forest's anguish hit him like a hard slap in the face. He was a swarm of stintarils, clustered in the top of a tree, the fire climbing after them. Their fur was beginning to singe. He was a big, harmless runyip, too slow to outrun the flame, trying to nose its calves ahead to safety, but not herself knowing where that was. He was charred flesh and scorched lungs. He was dead and dying.

"You were right," he told Rapuung later, when they stopped to splash water on themselves, to clear the ash from their eyes, nostrils, and lips.

"About what, infidel?"

"What I did with the fire. It was wrong."

The Yuuzhan Vong's eyes narrowed. "Explain."

"I killed innocent life to save us."

Rapuung laughed harshly. "That is nothing. Killing and dying are nothing; they are the way of the world, part of the embrace of pain. What you did was wrong because it was an abomination, not because you killed. Do not fool yourself. I see now how determined you are to rescue your *Jeedai* companion. If you could reach her only by filling in a chasm with corpses to walk over, you would do it."

"No," Anakin said. "I wouldn't."

"A goal desired so lightly is not a goal at all."

Anakin sighed. "We'll get her. But I don't like to kill."

"Then the warriors will kill you."

"Warriors are different," Anakin said. "I will defend

myself with extreme prejudice. But the forest did nothing to me to deserve what I did to it."

"You make no sense," Rapuung said. "We will kill who and what we must."

"And I say no."

"Indeed. So you would have me pollute myself with the first abomination in order to achieve your purposes, and yet you will force me to cling to a childish fear of killing? All life ends, *Jeedai*."

Anakin felt that one. Did the Yuuzhan Vong really think nonbiological technology was as wrong as the Jedi philosophy taught indiscriminate killing was? Intellectually he supposed he'd understood that, but it had never reached his gut. Only now, when they both agreed something terrible had been done—but for absolutely different reasons—did it make any kind of sense to him at all.

If only he could feel Rapuung in the Force. If only he could tell if the Yuuzhan Vong were of the light or of the dark side.

Or was that even a relevant question, without the Force? Were Jedi so dependent on their Force-given senses that without them they were moral cripples?

Rapuung had kept a stinging gaze on Anakin as the Jedi searched for a response. Now he suddenly looked away toward some middle distance.

"You make no sense," Vua Rapuung said. "But . . . I acknowledge you have saved my life. My revenge will owe to you, when it is complete."

"You've saved me a couple of times," Anakin replied. "We're not even yet."

"Not what? What is that word?"

"Never mind. Vua Rapuung, what is this revenge you seek? What has been done to you that would make you turn against your own people?"

Rapuung's eyes hardened. "Do you really not know? Can you really not see? Look at me!"

"I see your scars fester. You have implants that seem

dead or dying. But I don't have the faintest idea what that means."

"It does not concern you," Rapuung said. "Do not presume, infidel."

"Fine. Then tell me this plan of yours, the one that will get me to Tahiri."

"Follow and see," Rapuung answered.

They crouched in a tangle of roots at the water's edge on a tributary of the great river.

"We're farther away from the shaper base than we were yesterday," Anakin complained.

"Yes, but in the right place, now," Rapuung said.

"Right place for what?"

"Wait. See."

Anakin's mouth twitched around a retort but didn't form it. Was this what people were complaining about when they accused *him* of being tight with words? Rapuung was as stingy with facts as a Bothan courier. Six days running and fighting together, and Anakin still knew nothing about the warrior except that he was mad about something. Maybe even crazy. He'd mentioned some "she" and seemed to have an obsession with his worthiness before his gods.

But maybe all Yuuzhan Vong were like that. It was not like Anakin had chatted with a lot of them. Maybe Rapuung was as normal as normal could be. Maybe he kept his motives and plans secret because that's just the way Yuuzhan Vong were.

Or maybe he was afraid—afraid that if Anakin knew what he was up to or knew how to get into the shaper base, Anakin would kill him or abandon him.

He sneaked a glance at the fierce, flat-nosed visage and gave that a silent negative. He couldn't imagine Vua Rapuung being afraid of anything. Maybe *prudent* was a better word.

So Anakin waited, quietly, and found himself gradually mesmerized by the gentle flow of the stream. He stretched out tentatively to the life around him, feeling again the shadow of the pain and death he had caused.

I'm sorry, he told the forest.

How close was he to the dark side? Was Rapuung right?

He'd argued with Jacen that the Force was a tool that was neither good nor evil, but that could be used, like any tool, to do good or evil with. Could evil be as simple as not thinking? He supposed so. Corran Horn had once told him that selfishness was evil and selflessness good. In that light, selfishly causing death to save himself was evil, regardless of the fact that he simply hadn't considered the consequences of his actions at the time. And yet he wasn't just fighting for himself, was he? Tahiri's life was at stake. Maybe more than her life, because if the Tahiri of his vision ever came to be, it could mean the end of a great many people.

If he was honest, he had to admit he hadn't been thinking about those larger consequences, either. He'd had a problem to solve, and he'd solved it, the same as he might solve a mathematical equation or a problem with the hyperdrive motivator in his X-wing. He just hadn't thought about the problems his solution might cause, which seemed pretty typical of him lately.

Mara Jade had pointed out this tendency of his ages ago, when they were camping together on Dantooine. Apparently he hadn't learned anything. Maybe it was time he started to.

Which brought him back to Vua Rapuung. The man was self-admittedly out for revenge, and if there was one thing that had been drilled solidly into Anakin, it was that revenge was of the dark side. If he continued working with Rapuung, would he be implicated in that revenge? What tragedy was he helping to bring about by cooperating with this half-crazed Yuuzhan Vong?

Something stirred the life of the forest. A thousand

voices changed slightly as they smelled and heard something unfamiliar, something not included in their limited vocabulary of predator and prey, hunger and danger.

Something new to Yavin 4 was approaching, on the river.

"Are you expecting someone?" Anakin asked.

"Yes."

Anakin didn't ask who. He was tired of asking questions that he knew wouldn't be answered. Instead he sharpened his senses and watched.

Soon something appeared on the river, coming upstream.

At first he thought it was a boat, but reminded himself that if it was a Yuuzhan Vong boat, it was something organic, as well. Studying it, he picked out the details that proved him right.

The major visible portion was a broad, flat dome poking up from the water, banded with scutes or plates. Whatever moved it was below the surface of the water, but it did move. Now and then something that might be the top of a head broke the water in front of it. If it was a head, it was a big one, nearly as wide as the visible portion of the shell, and scaled and dull olive in color.

Sitting on top of it was a male Anakin could not feel in the Force, but the closer he came, the less he looked like a Yuuzhan Vong. At first Anakin didn't understand why he got that impression; he had the same sharply sloping forehead, and his nostrils were set nearly flat into his face just like every other person of that species Anakin had seen.

But he had no *scars*. Not one. Not a single tattoo that Anakin could detect, and he could see most of the fellow because he wore only a sort of loincloth.

Now and then he touched something on the surface of the carapace, and the boat creature altered course slightly.

"Stay hidden," Rapuung said, and stood.

"Qe'u!" he called.

Through the concealing roots, Anakin saw the other man's head snap around in surprise. He uttered a string of words Anakin didn't understand, and Vua Rapuung replied in kind. The floater began turning in their direction, and Anakin dug himself lower.

The two Yuuzhan Vong continued their conversation as the floater drew nearer to shore.

Anakin took several deep, steadying breaths. He'd been thinking about Vua Rapuung's prudence; it was time to start thinking of his own. When would the Yuuzhan Vong stop needing him? Now? When they reached the shaper base? When he'd exacted whatever revenge he was after? It could be anytime. He remembered what he had told Valin about the Yuuzhan Vong and their promises. Was there any reason to believe Rapuung would keep his?

Anakin suddenly noticed that the two had stopped talking. Just as he was thinking about taking a look, he heard a loud splash.

"You may come out from cover now, infidel," Rapuung said in Basic.

Anakin rose warily from his hiding place. Rapuung stood on the floater. Alone.

"Where did he go?" Anakin asked.

Rapuung gestured toward the water on the other side of the floater. "In the river."

"You threw him in? Will he drown?"

"No. He is already dead."

"You killed him?"

"A broken neck killed him. Mount the vangaak and let us depart."

Anakin stood there for a moment, trying to master his anger.

"Why did you kill him?"

"Because to leave him alive was an unacceptable risk."

Anakin almost retched. Instead, he climbed up onto

the floater, trying not to look at the corpse floating beyond.

That was one innocent, unarmed sapient being dead because Anakin had saved Rapuung's life. How many more would there be?

Rapuung began manipulating several knobby projections on the carapace. Anakin assumed they were nerve clusters or something of the sort.

"Who was he?" he asked, as the floater turned sluggishly downstream.

"A Shamed One. A person of no consequence."

"No one is of no consequence," Anakin said, trying to keep his voice steady.

Rapuung laughed. "The gods cursed him at birth. Every breath he drew was borrowed."

"But you knew him."

"Yes."

They continued down the river at a leisurely pace. "How did you know him?" Anakin persisted. "What was he doing up here?"

"Trawling the stream. It was his usual route. It used to be mine."

"You're an angler?" Anakin said incredulously.

"Among other things. Why so many questions?"

"I'm just trying to understand what happened."

The warrior grunted and held his silence for five minutes. Then, almost reluctantly, he turned to Anakin.

"To find you, I had to disappear. I faked my death out here, on the water. I made it appear as if some water beast had eaten me. They gave Qe'u my route. I will return and tell a story of how I survived, lost on this strange world, until I came across the vangaak, pilotless. I will not know what happened to Qe'u. Perhaps a *Jeedai* killed him, perhaps he met the same water beast I did."

"Oh. And they'll let us through the security on the river. But why should they believe that story?"

"They will not care. He was a Shamed One. His death

will be of no concern. Even if they suspect I killed him for some reason, no one will question my story."

"And how will you explain me?"

Rapuung grinned nastily. "I won't. They won't see you."

CHAPTER
TWENTY-TWO

Nen Yim found her master staring into the waters of the succession pool—the heart, lungs, and liver of the damutek. It rippled slightly as the native food fish of the moon investigated her shadow. It smelled faintly of sulfur, iodine, and something oily and burnt, almost like singed hair.

Master Mezhan Kwaad's headdress was woven into an expression of deep contemplation, so Nen Yim stood behind her, waiting for her attention.

A drop of something plunked into the succession pool, just below the master's feet. Another followed, and another.

When Mezhan Kwaad finally turned, Nen Yim saw it was blood, drizzling from her nostrils.

"Greetings, Adept," the master said. "Have you come in search of me, or of the succession pool?"

"Of you, Master. But if you would speak at another time . . ."

"There will be no better time until my cycle of sacrifice is complete and my Vaa-tumor is removed. You had your first implanted yesterday, did you not?"

"I did, Master. I cannot feel it yet."

"Bear it well. It is one of the oldest mysteries." She cocked her head, focusing her regard on Nen Yim's face. "You wish to know what it does, the Vaa-tumor?"

"I am content in the knowledge that the gods desire this sacrifice of our caste," Nen Yim replied dutifully.

"Once passing to adepthood, you enter the mystery,"

Mezhan Kwaad said, as if speaking in a dream. "As warriors take on the outward aspects of Yun-Yammka, so we take on the inner qualities of Yun-Ne'Shel, she-who-shapes. The Vaa-tumor is her most ancient gift to us. Yun-Ne'Shel plucked a fragment of her own brain to make it. As it grows, it models our cells, changes our very thoughts, takes us nearer the mind and essence of Yun-Ne'Shel." She sighed. "The journey is painful. It is glorious. And, regrettably, we must return from it, excise her gift from our bodies. But though we return to a semblance of who we were, each time that we are vessels for that pain and glory we are forever changed. Something of it remains with us. Until . . ." Her words seemed to fail her.

"You shall see," Mezhan Kwaad finally said. "And now—what have you come to tell me?"

Nen Yim glanced around, making certain no one was within hearing.

"It is quite safe here, Adept," Mezhan Kwaad assured her. "Speak freely."

"I believe I have finished mapping the *Jeedai*'s nervous system and brain structure."

"That is good news. Very commendable. And how would you proceed now?"

"It depends on what results we want. If we wish her obedience, then we should use restraint implants."

"Why, then, have we mapped her nervous system?"

Nen Yim felt her headdress fidgeting and tried to calm it. "I don't know, Master. It was your command."

Mezhan Kwaad tilted her head and smiled faintly. "I am not trying to trick you, Adept. I chose you for very particular reasons. I have told you some of them; about others I have remained silent, but I suspect you are bright enough to know what they are. Suppose, just for a moment, that there are no protocols to be followed. In the absence of direction, what would you do? Hypothetically."

"Hypothetically," Nen Yim said. She felt as if she were

poised over the digestive villi of a maw luur. She could almost smell the sour scent of the acid. If she answered this question truthfully, she might be revealed as a heretic. If what she had come to suspect about her master was wrong, this conversation would be her last as a shaper, and one of the last in her life.

But she could not surrender to fear.

"I would modify the provoker spineray to fit our expectations of her nervous system, to give us very fine control."

"Why?"

Nen Yim did not hesitate this time. It was already too late, whichever way it went.

"Despite the assurances of the protocol we followed, what we have now is only an educated guess concerning how her nervous system functions. All we have done is to map unknowns onto knowns. But the 'knowns' are Yuuzhan Vong norms, not human ones, and we know already that she lacks analogs to some of our structures and has others that have no comparable configuration in ourselves."

"Are you saying, then, the ancient protocol is meaningless?"

"No, Master Mezhan Kwaad. I am saying it is a starting point. It asserts certain things about how the *Jeedai*'s brain works. I suggest that we now *test* those assertions."

"In other words, you would question the protocols given us by the gods."

"Yes, Master."

"And you understand this is heresy of the first order?"

"I do."

Mezhan Kwaad's eyes were oily pools, utterly unreadable. Nen Yim met her gaze steadily, without flinching, for a very long time.

"I have searched for an apprentice like you," the master shaper finally said. "I have asked the gods to send you to me. If you are not what you appear to be, you will not be forgiven. You will not profit from any betrayal of me, I promise you that."

That gave Nen Yim a start. The thought that the master might be afraid of *her* had never crossed her mind.

"I am your apprentice," Nen Yim said. "I would not betray you. I have put my life and my position in your thirteen fingers."

"They are well placed, Adept," Mezhan Kwaad said softly. "Proceed as you have just suggested. Do not speak to anyone but me about this. If our results are to the liking of our leaders, I assure you they will not look closely at our methods. But we must be discreet. We must move with caution." She glanced once more at the pool and touched her head.

"When the pain of the Vaa-tumor reaches its peak, there are colors to be seen that have never been seen before, thoughts to be had, strange and mighty . . . Well, you will see. At times I am almost ashamed to have it removed, to retreat from the final embrace of it. I should like to know where it would take me." She gave Nen Yim a rare genuine smile. "One day the gods shall ordain it. Until then, I have much work to do for them." She draped her eight slender fingers on Nen Yim's shoulder.

"Let us go see our young *Jeedai*, shall we?"

The *Jeedai* watched them come in. Only her green eyes moved, following them closely, like one beast seeking the soft throat of another.

"I would advise you not to attack us with your *Jeedai* tricks," Mezhan Kwaad told her. "The provoker has been told to stimulate you to great agony if we are afflicted in any way. Though in time you will come to understand agony, at the moment you seem to dislike it, and it clearly disrupts your concentration. There are worse things we could do to you."

The *Jeedai*'s eyes widened. "I can understand you,"

she said. Then she stopped, looking even more confused. "I'm not speaking Basic. This is—"

"You speak our language now, yes," the master shaper said. "If you are to be one of us, you must speak the sacred tongue."

"Be one of *you*?" The *Jeedai* sneered. "Thanks, but I'd much rather be the slime under a Hutt."

"That's because you perceive yourself an infidel," Mezhan Kwaad said reasonably. "You do not understand us, and there are things that confound us about you and the other *Jeedai*. But we will understand you, and you will understand us. You will become a tissue connecting the Yuuzhan Vong and the *Jeedai*, nurturing both. You will make it possible for understanding to flow both ways."

"That's what you want from me?"

"You are the path to peace," Mezhan Kwaad assured her.

"Kidnapping me won't get you peace!" the *Jeedai* shouted.

"We did not kidnap you," Mezhan Kwaad said. "We rescued you from the other infidels, remember?"

"You're twisting things," the *Jeedai* returned. "The whole reason they captured me was to give me to you."

The master's headdress rearranged itself into an expression of mild anger.

"Memory is a most malleable commodity," Mezhan Kwaad said. "It is mostly chemical. For instance, you now know our language. You did not learn it."

"You put it there," the *Jeedai* said.

"Yes. Your memory of the words, the grammar, the syntax. All introduced to you."

"So you can implant memories. Big deal. We Jedi can do that, as well."

"Indeed. I have no doubt those *Jeedai* abilities could do much to confuse one as young as yourself. How many of your memories are real? How many manufactured? How could you tell the difference?"

"What's your point?"

"My point is this. Right now you think you are—what is it, Taher'ai?"

"My name is Tahiri."

"Yes. Tahiri, a young *Jeedai* candidate, raised by a tribe strange to her—"

"Sand People."

"Of course. But soon enough, you will remember. After we've stripped away the false memories and undone the disgusting modifications made to your body, you will remember who you are."

"What are you talking about?" the *Jeedai* exploded.

"You are Riina of Domain Kwaad. You are one of us. You always have been."

"No! I know who my parents were!"

"You know the lies you were told, the memories you were given. Fear not. We will bring you back."

Mezhan Kwaad signaled, and Nen Yim bowed and followed her from the room. Behind them, the young *Jeedai* wailed in the first sign of true despair that Nen Yim had heard from her.

"Do not wait for tomorrow," Mezhan Kwaad said. "Make your modifications and begin your trials. We must show results, soon."

CHAPTER
TWENTY-THREE

Anakin rode in the belly of the beast.

Literally. And it *stank*. The Yuuzhan Vong equivalent of an organic gill, the gnullith Anakin wore did nothing to buffer the confused and odious smells of river crawl-fish, silman eel, rotting wetweed, the viscous mucus that coated the inside of the vangaak like jelly—or of the breather itself, which insisted on reminding him, by slowly and constantly writhing, that he had a live animal shoving its tentacles down his throat and nostrils.

The only bright spot was that he hadn't eaten anything for a day and a half.

It had been better, earlier, when the trawling-boat creature was still making its catch, swimming with its mouth expanded into a flattened funnel ten meters across. The water passed through and out the filtering membranes in its posterior, acting as the underwater equivalent of a fresh breeze. Now that the belly was bloated, the lips had sucked in on themselves, and water flow was cut to the minimum necessary to sustain the live catch squirming all around him.

He was reminded of the story of how his mother and father had met, on the Death Star, a story he'd heard far too many times. Seconds after seeing each other for the first time, they'd ended up fleeing stormtroopers into a garbage hold.

"What an incredible smell you've discovered," his father had sarcastically told his future wife. He hadn't been very happy with her at the time.

I've found a better smell than you did, Mom, he thought.

The thought of Rapuung above, in the warm breezes of Yavin 4 and no doubt delighted over the discomfort of his infidel ally, did nothing to improve Anakin's mood. If he'd had a working lightsaber, he would have long ago slashed his way through the vangaak even if it meant facing a hundred Yuuzhan Vong warriors. Some things made death seem pretty.

He immediately regretted that thought. There were beings in the galaxy who endured misery that made what he was going through look like a day in a garden on Ithor.

Well, back when Ithor had gardens.

Still, he was more than ready to get out. He passed the time by getting to know his bellymates, gently convincing the more adventurous ones he wasn't something to nibble on. He tried to relax and forget his body and the unpleasant sensory data it was processing. He found Tahiri—in pain, but alive. He thought he briefly found Jaina, then lost her again. Time stretched and ceased to have meaning.

Some strange motion jarred him. Had he been asleep? It was difficult to tell.

The motion came again, a sudden contraction that squeezed water-dwellers against him.

Then a stronger contraction hurtled him forward, blasting into the light in a stream of fluid and fish, then plunging into new water. Something strong caught his arm and hauled him up, and he found himself staring blearily into the face of Vua Rapuung.

The warrior set him down on his feet and detached the gnullith. Anakin coughed up water and then took deep, grateful breaths. He looked up at Rapuung.

"I've just been vomited by a fish," he said.

Vua Rapuung cocked his head. "Obviously. Why are you telling me?"

"Never mind. Where are we?" The vangaak had disgorged its prey at the narrow end of a wedge-shaped pool. The larger end of the wedge, about twenty meters away, opened into an even larger aquatic space. Anakin and Rapuung stood on a landing, of sorts, bounded by slightly uneven coral walls six meters high. Every six meters or so, the walls were marked by ovoids the size of doorways, obvious because of their darker shade. The vangaak had apparently entered this complex through one canal opening at the end of the wedge. Anakin could see daylight and swaying Massassi trees beyond.

He could see the sky above, too.

"I see," Anakin said. "We're in one of the—what did you call them?"

"Damuteks."

"Right. They're shaped like rayed stars. We're at the end of one of the rays. This is one of the compounds filled with water."

"Each damutek has a succession pool. Some have coverings over them so the space can be used for other things."

Anakin pointed at the canal. "We came up that. It goes to the river, right?"

"Correct again."

"Why is the water in the canal flowing toward the river, then?"

"Why ask after such irrelevancies? The succession pool is filled from below. Its rooting tubes seek water and minerals. The outflow goes to the river. And that is enough talk."

"You're right," Anakin agreed. "Let's find Tahiri and get out of here."

Rapuung glared at him. "It isn't so simple. First we must disguise you. An unbound human, walking free? Then we must locate your other *Jeedai*."

"I can find her."

"I surmised as much, from what I have heard of *Jeedai*. You can sniff each other out at a distance, yes?"

"Something like that."

"Then you will be my hunting uspeq. But not yet. Even when we know where she is—"

"We have to chart the course. I get it. You'll figure the layout of the place. And your revenge? What about that?"

"When we find the other *Jeedai*, we will find my revenge."

The coldness in Rapuung's voice touched a worry in the back of Anakin's mind. "Your revenge is not against Tahiri, is it?" he asked. "Tell me now if it is."

Rapuung showed his teeth in grim humor. "If I wanted revenge on your *Jeedai*, I need only to let the shapers have her. Nothing could be worse than to be in Mezhan Kwaad's fingers."

"Mezhan Kwaad?"

"Don't repeat that name," Rapuung snarled.

"But you just said it."

"If you repeat it again, I will kill you."

Anakin drew himself taller. "You're welcome to try," he said softly.

Rapuung's muscles bunched and tensed and his mauled lips twitched. Again he seemed more like a dangerous, poisonous animal than a person. But then he rasped a sigh. "Here, *I* know what is best. You must learn to listen to me. How else would you have entered the perimeter of the base? But from here, the dangers we face have increased. You must make peace with my commands. Furthermore, the longer we argue, the more likely it is that we will be thwarted here and now. We're lucky no one has yet chanced by. You have passed through the nostrils of this beast, but you will not live to find the beating heart without me."

That was probably true, Anakin reflected. Pride was not the way of the Jedi. Rapuung kept pricking at his pride, and he kept twitching like a Twi'lek's lekku. He could almost hear Jacen and Uncle Luke scolding him now.

"I apologize," Anakin said. "You're right. What do we do now?"

Rapuung nodded curtly. "Now we make you a slave."

Anakin had thought he'd been through some hard things before; but nothing had prepared him for the ordeal of letting Vua Rapuung implant the coral growth on him. It looked exactly like the sickening, ulcerous growths he'd seen on more Yuuzhan Vong slaves than he could count. He'd watched and sensed sentient beings lose their reason, grow thin and vanish in the Force, become mindless drones for the Yuuzhan Vong, because of just such infections.

"It is not real," Vua Rapuung told him, "but you must respond as if it is real. You must follow certain commands."

How do I know this isn't a trick? Anakin's brain screamed at him. *How do I know this wasn't the plan all along, to march me into the shaper base and have me willingly give up my very being?*

Again he felt as if his eyes had been struck out, his tongue cut off, the nerves of his fingers numbed. He had absolutely no way of knowing what Vua Rapuung was thinking.

But it seemed somehow unlike the mutilated warrior to play out such an elaborate charade.

"So I have to act like a mindless drone?"

"No. We do not use that form of restraint on most work slaves anymore. It proved too debilitating to them. What use is a slave that dies or becomes stupid? The implant merely insures you can be restrained if need be. If it tingles, pretend pain and paralysis. If it actually gives you pain, pretend to die."

"Got it."

So Anakin let the Yuuzhan Vong warrior prick the

thing into his flesh, tried not to wince as it rooted. He concentrated on recognizing the first sign—any sign— that his will was being taken from him.

When Rapuung was done, he felt violated, as if his own flesh had become a hateful thing, but he still felt in control. For the moment.

"Where can I hide my lightsaber?" Anakin asked. Rapuung had made him shed his clothes and gear back in the jungle. The broken weapon was the only possession he retained.

"It does not work."

"I know. Where can I hide it?"

Rapuung hesitated for a moment. "Here," he said. "In the far corner of the succession pool. It will be unnoticed in the organic material on the bottom."

Anakin reluctantly followed Rapuung's advice. It was a hard thing to watch the lightsaber he had built with his own hands sink into the water. But right now, it could only get him caught.

Moments later, Anakin was suddenly surrounded by Yuuzhan Vong, hundreds of them. They'd exited the larger compound at the same point the boat creature entered it, walking along the quay that ran parallel to the canal. The latter he could see curved off to join the river.

Between the river and the damutek complexes was the shantytown he had observed from the ridge. Unlike the orderly compounds, the dwellings here seemed placed almost at random, a series of organic domes and hollow circles pierced by openings. Most seemed barely large enough to sleep in, and he didn't see many people coming in or out of them. Most of the Yuuzhan Vong he saw were like the angler Rapuung had killed. They were unscarred or had very few scars. Some had malformed or festering scars like Vua Rapuung, and they wore the same sort of loincloth that Rapuung and now Anakin had donned.

Of course it wasn't a cloth at all, but something alive.

If he pulled it away from his flesh, it slowly sealed itself there again.

He also had a tizowyrm secreted in his ear, and the speech of those around him reached him in little starts and flurries. But almost no one was talking. They went about their business quietly, rarely making eye contact.

He wasn't the only non–Yuuzhan Vong either, he saw. There were a fair number of them, all with the coral re-straining implants. Their expressions he readily recog-nized; they ranged from utter hopelessness to mere misery. Now and then he caught a glimmer from one that sug-gested he or she still hoped for escape. Like the Yuuzhan Vong, none gave him more than a glance.

"You!" a voice called from behind. Rapuung turned toward it, and Anakin shambled around more slowly, trying to keep the expression of the humans he had seen.

The Yuuzhan Vong who had addressed them was a warrior, the first Anakin had seen here. He struggled to keep still; up until now being this close to a warrior meant a fight to the death, and he had had more than his share of those.

The warrior twitched when he saw Rapuung's face, and for a brief moment he looked almost as if he were about to genuflect. Then his eyes turned to obsidian.

"It *is* you. They told me at the port you had returned."

"I have," Rapuung answered.

"Many thought you had fled your shame. Many were glad not to have to look upon it."

"The gods know no shame is on me," Rapuung answered.

"Your flesh says otherwise," the warrior answered.

"So it may be," Rapuung replied. "Do you have a command?"

"No. What task has your executor given you?"

"I go to speak to him now."

"The trawling schedules are filled for another four days. Perhaps you may spend that time in sacrifice and penitence begging Yun-Shuno to intercede for you. A word could be planted in your executor's ear."

"That is most generous, Hul Rapuung. But I do not require favor."

"It is no favor to be given time to beg, even of the gods," Hul Rapuung answered. "Go." He turned brusquely and started to leave, then turned back. "The slave. Why does it accompany you?"

"I found it wandering aimless. I take it to my executor for assignment."

"Aimless, you say? You know that in the wilderness several *Jeedai* skulk."

"This one was here before I was lost. He has always been of a forgetful nature."

Hul Rapuung lifted his chin. "Is it so?" His voice lowered. "There is a story—a rumor, really, that one of these *Jeedai* is not a *Jeedai* at all, but a Yuuzhan Vong, driven mad somehow by their powers."

"I know nothing of such rumors."

"No. They began only a short time ago." He spat. "Go to your executor."

"I go," Vua Rapuung said.

"Vua Rapuung. You are a Shamed One," Anakin said, as soon as the warrior was out of earshot. He kept his head down and tried not to move his lips too much.

Rapuung looked briefly around, grabbed Anakin's arm, and propelled him into the nearest structure. Inside, it was cozy, but smelled sour like an unwashed Bothan.

"Did I tell you to hold your tongue?" Rapuung snapped.

"You should have told me," Anakin replied. "If you want me to keep quiet, then make it so I'm not surprised every ten seconds."

Rapuung clenched and unclenched his fists several times. He gnashed his teeth.

"I must act the part of a Shamed One. I am not."

"First of all, what *is* a Shamed One? And don't give me that 'they aren't worth speaking of' fodder."

"They *aren't*—" Rapuung began, then stopped. He closed his eyes. "Shamed Ones are cursed by the gods. Their bodies reject proper scarring. They do not heal well. The implants of utility and rank that set us apart as castes and individuals are rejected by their feeble bodies. They are useless."

"Your scars. Your sores. Your implants have rotted out."

"I was a great warrior," Rapuung said. "A commander. None doubted my ability. And then one day, my body betrayed me." He started pacing suddenly, slamming his palms on the coral, cutting them. "But it was not the gods. I know who did it. I know why. And she shall pay."

"The female whose name you told me not to repeat again."

"Yes."

"And she's the one you want to kill."

"Kill?" Rapuung's eyes widened, then he spat. "Infidel. You think death, which comes to all, is punishment in itself. My revenge will be to force her to admit what she has done, so everyone will know that Vua Rapuung was never shamed! So the Yuuzhan Vong will know *her* crime. My revenge will be to know that when she does die, however she dies, it will be in ignominy. But kill her? I would not give her the honor."

"Oh," Anakin said. That was all he could think of. Despite Rapuung's secrecy, Anakin had at least thought he knew *what* the Yuuzhan Vong meant by revenge. In two quick reversals, everything he knew about Rapuung fell apart.

"Is that enough of my blood in your ears for the moment?" Rapuung asked in a low, strange voice.

"One more question. The warrior we just met. Part of your name is the same as his."

"As it should be. He is a sibling of my crèche."

"Your brother?"

Rapuung inclined his head slightly in the affirmative. "We go to the executor now. I will suggest you once worked clearing fields for growing lambents. Those slaves live the longest. We will meet when I can manage it without suspicion. Play your part. Do not falter. Use your powers to locate the nearest point where the other *Jeedai* is. I will see you in seven days or so. Until then we will not speak another word. Watch the other slaves. Speak as they speak or not at all. Now, come."

He glanced outside, then walked out, towing Anakin by the arm. No one seemed to notice. Together, they walked toward the largest building, unnoticeable among the other slaves and Shamed Ones.

Or so Anakin hoped.

CHAPTER TWENTY-FOUR

A spike of pain drove through Anakin's forehead, so unexpected and strange that his legs buckled and he fell to his knees on the black jungle soil, grasping for the wound in his forehead. It felt as if it had been gashed from his hairline to the bridge of his nose. The blood stung his eyes and brimmed his nostrils.

But when he brought his hands down, they were clean. Chapped, blistered, and friction-burned from days of pulling tough weeds from the soil, but not bloody.

Cautiously he felt his head again. The pain still throbbed, but now he felt only unbroken flesh.

"You! Slave!" the tizowyrm chittered in his ear, apparently translating the brutal shout from one of the guards. The coral growth on his neck gave him a faint shock, and he knew he was being given the force of command. He went rigid and fell to the ground, jerking spasmodically. It was easy, given the agony already creeping into his head.

When he thought he'd played that role long enough, he climbed back to his knees and went back to work, knotting his chapped, raw hands around plants and uprooting them.

The Yuuzhan Vong did not care for machines even as complicated as a lever. They had biotic methods of clearing fields other than slaves, but they seemed determined to go through the slaves they had, first.

Grab weed, wriggle, pull. For the ten billionth time.

The pain reverberated behind his eyes, fading a bit, and he began to pick out details through the static.

Not his forehead, not his blood, not his senses. It was Tahiri who had been cut. Scarred like a Yuuzhan Vong.

It was almost too much. He had been feeling her pain sporadically since her capture. Sometimes it was like an itch, sometimes like burning methanol poured down his nerves. But this time it was somehow real, intimate. He could smell her breath and taste her tears. It was like holding her, in that last moment of peace they had had together.

Except she was bleeding, and here he was pulling weeds. If his lightsaber was working . . .

But that was the problem, wasn't it? Or one of them. And it was days before he would see Rapuung again.

"Slave." An amphistaff lashed lightly across his back, and it took everything in him not to leap up into the guard's face, take his amphistaff, and kill every Yuuzhan Vong in sight.

What are they doing to you, Tahiri?

But he didn't. Instead he stood compliant, arms at his side.

"Go with this Shamed One," the guard told him.

He then turned to the person indicated, a young female with no obvious scars. She had a deeply worn look to her, but her eyes had a certain brightness many of the other Shamed Ones' did not. "Go to the third lambent field, nearest the perimeter. Show him how to harvest."

"I will need more than one faltering slave to make my quota," she said.

"You feel it is your place to argue with me?" the warrior snapped.

"No," she replied. "I think it is a prefect's place to assign workers."

"The prefect is busy today. Would you rather make your quota alone?"

She maintained an expression of defiance for another

beat, then grudgingly hung her head. "No. Why are you doing this to me?"

"I treat you as I treat everyone."

She narrowed her eyes, but did not reply. Instead she beckoned Anakin. "Come along, slave. We have a long walk."

He followed her, trying to reestablish contact with Tahiri. She was still alive, he could get that much, but more distant than the stars.

Almost as if she was fighting contact.

"What's your name, slave?" the woman asked. It so shocked Anakin that his step actually faltered. "Well?"

"Begging your pardon, but when did any Yuuzhan Vong care to dirty her ears with the name of a slave?"

"Where did a slave get the idea that insolence would go unpunished?" she responded.

"My name is Bail Lars," he replied.

"What's wrong with you, Bail Lars? I saw you nearly collapse. So did that filth-bather, Vasi. That's why he sent you with me, so I'll fail to meet my quota."

"He has something against you, personally?"

"Puul. It's what he *couldn't* get against me that bothers him."

"Really? I would think—" He suddenly thought better of what he was saying and didn't finish the sentence.

The female did, however. "Would think what? That I wouldn't refuse a warrior?"

"No, that's not it," Anakin said. "I suppose I thought they—the rest of the Yuuzhan Vong, I mean—were . . . well, that they didn't think Shamed Ones were, you know, desirable."

"We aren't, not by normal people. Not even by each other. But Vasi is *not* normal. He likes sick things. He can command a Shamed One to do things that no true caste would ever do, or want to do, or want done."

"But he commanded you and you didn't?"

"He knows if he commands me, I will make him kill

me. So he didn't command me. He wants me to come to him." She stopped and dropped her eyeridges angrily. "And this is not your business. Never forget—what I am to them, you are to me. One day Yun-Shuno will grant me redemption, and my body will take the scars and implants. I will become true caste, while you will forever be nothing."

"Do you really believe that?" Anakin asked. "I don't think you do."

She slapped him then, hard. When he did not react to the pain, she nodded thoughtfully. "Stronger than I thought. Maybe we can meet my quota," she said. "If you help me do it, I will find some reward for you."

"I would do it for no other reason than to disappoint Vasi," Anakin replied. "Though I may feel differently if you keep slapping me."

"You say filthy things, and don't expect to be punished?"

"I didn't know it was filthy."

"I have heard you slaves are infidels, but even infidels must know the gods and their truths."

"I would think that not knowing that is exactly what makes me an infidel," Anakin said.

"I suppose. It makes no sense, and I've never spoken to an infidel before, not like this." She hesitated. "It is . . . interesting. Perhaps as we work, we can pass the time. You can tell me of your planet. But restrain yourself— Shamed I may be, but I have not abandoned myself to shame."

"It's a deal," Anakin said. "Will you tell me your name?"

"My name is Uunu." She pointed ahead, to a low coral wall. "We're nearly to the lambent field now. They are just past there."

"What is a lambent?"

"Another moment, and you shall see. Or, rather, you shall hear them."

"Hear?"

But suddenly he did, a faint, buzzing rattle, like the voices of small animals.

And yet this didn't come from the Force, not exactly. It didn't have the familiar touch, the depth. It was more like having a staticky comlink in his head.

They rounded the wall. Beyond was a field tilled into concentric circular ridges. On them, spaced perhaps a meter apart, grew plants that resembled a nest of short, thick, green knives. From the central clump two, three, or four short stalks grew, and at the end of each of these was a sort of hairy, bloodred bloom. The blooms were roughly the size of his fist, and it was from these that the telepathic murmur seemed to come.

"What are they?"

"Start working now. I'll explain what they are later, if it looks as if we are approaching our quota."

"What do I do?"

"You will follow me. I will stroke the down from the blossoms—like so." Almost tenderly she rubbed away the red, hairlike petals until all that remained was a yellowish bulb. "This attunes it. Once that is done, you must harvest it. That is more difficult. Hold still, please." She withdrew something curved and black from a pouch in her garment.

"Place it on your thumb."

He looked at it. It resembled a spur, about eight centimeters long. It looked very sharp. It was hollow, and when he slipped his thumb into the hollow he winced as what felt like many small teeth bit into him.

"It's alive," he muttered.

"Of course it is. Who would use a dead—" Then her eyes narrowed. "I told you not to talk like that, didn't I?"

"I didn't say anything wrong," Anakin objected.

"No. You just implied it and let my mind do the dirty work. Stop that."

Anakin held up his newly spurred thumb and looked at it.

"Don't get airs," she said. "It's not a real implant. Even I can wear one for a little while before the reaction sets in. It's not permanent. And in case you're getting any unslave-like ideas . . ." She took his wrist in a surprisingly strong grip and jabbed her palm at the sharp tip of the spur.

It immediately went flaccid.

"You might cut another slave with it," she said softly. "I've heard of such things, done for the amusement of the guards. But you will not cut a Yuuzhan Vong with such a tool."

"I would have taken your word for it."

"Good. You're learning. So, you take your spur and split the lambent casing at the top. Go ahead."

He knelt by the plants and pressed the sharp tip into the yellow bulb. It split, and a pale milky substance oozed out.

"Now cut down the side. It will be difficult."

It was. The husk was *tough*. When he had scored three sides, he managed to peel the skin away. The entire time he did this, he was acutely aware of the thing's telepathic voice, a quiet peeping somehow different from its companions, probably because of Uunu's "attunement" of it.

The big surprise was the inside. When he had cut it free, Anakin held it up, fascinated.

It looked very much like a gem of some sort.

"What is it?" he asked again.

"Later. Go, now. You will be slower at cutting them than I am at attuning them. You must work to keep up with me. Normally two or three huskers come after the attuner. When you have a rhythm, and I am certain you are not losing ground, then we will try talking. Not before."

It didn't happen that day. While Anakin eventually caught the rhythm of the work, it was only after he was far behind Uunu. The lambents distracted him. They could tickle his mind and he could touch them, but not through the Force, not in the conventional sense. He was told that Wurth Skidder had had a similar experience with a Yuuzhan Vong yammosk, the creatures that co-ordinated the actions of Yuuzhan Vong warcraft. Yammosks bonded telepathically with their daughter ships and with the crews of its fleet. It then protected them as it would its own offspring, directing their battles to minimize loss. Skidder had apparently achieved some sort of metalinkage between the Force and yammosk telepathy, at least according to his surviving companions.

Were these lambents yammosk relatives? Uunu was doing something to them; they changed as she stroked them, became more distant to Anakin. Because she was bonding them to herself? Could Anakin bond with one? Maybe if he did, he would find out what their function was. Were they what they looked like and felt like? They couldn't be exactly, of course, because they were alive, but still!

He hadn't realized how much hope he had lost until he started to get some of it back.

He slept in a dormitory for slaves, a low-roofed, creeping building with four sleeping areas carpeted in a spongy, mosslike growth. A total of eighteen slaves occupied the building, sleeping as thick as stintarils. It was nearly impossible to sleep without being in contact with someone.

To Anakin's relief, they weren't all Peace Brigade. In fact, Anakin gathered that while most of the Brigaders in the system had indeed been captured, most of those had been sacrificed to the Yuuzhan Vong gods. The slaves he shared his quarters with were from various points along the route of conquest and seemed to represent members of some sort of slave core population, one that the malcontents and firebrands had been largely eliminated from. None of them had the old style of slave implants like those Anakin had seen on Dantooine.

"They use those mostly for the ones they send into

battle," a Twi'lek named Poy told him, when he asked about it. "The thing is, if they fit you with the stuff, it takes a lot out of you. Makes you dumb. The shapers don't want dumb slaves that keep forgetting directions. The warriors just need bodies to absorb blasterfire, so it doesn't really matter there." His lekku twitched pensively. "But act up, or act stupid, and they'll fit you with it and send you to the front."

The most comforting thing about the slaves was that Anakin could feel them in the Force, but other than that, he didn't see much hope for help in them, and indeed, enormous potential for betrayal if they had any hint of who or what he might be. He gave it out that he had been captured on Duro and suggested to the more inquisitive that they didn't need to know the details.

Uunu collected him for the second morning, while it was still dark. He'd slept sporadically, trying to locate Tahiri in the Force. She was still withdrawn, difficult to find, but he was pretty sure he knew which damutek she was in.

He was a little groggy as he fell into step with the Shamed One.

"Here," she said a bit gruffly, holding out something in her hand.

"What?"

"Just watch, infidel."

A wisp of phosphorescence appeared in her palm and quickly sharpened into a substantial light. As it fleshed out, Anakin could see that it was a lambent crystal, like the ones he had been harvesting the day before.

It grew brighter until it was almost hard to look at, then faded away.

"You control the brightness with your mind," Anakin guessed.

She nodded. "Yes. We use these as portable light sources. They can also be configured with photosensitive biots to form the controls of various superorganisms, especially of the spacegoing sort." She closed her hand on the gem-like organism. "Come."

"It's still alive, though, right?" Anakin asked, as they continued toward the fields.

"Yes, of course."

"What does it eat?"

"A lambent's substance is mostly silicon and metal fixed from the soil. They transpire when gas is available, but most of their sustenance comes from the bioelectrical fields of the life around them." She stopped, staring at him. "What is that expression on your face?"

Anakin realized suddenly that he was grinning from ear to ear.

"Nothing," he said. "It's just amazing, I suppose."

"As are all gifts of the gods," Uunu replied. Anakin thought he still heard suspicion in her voice.

They worked for six hours without stopping, but Anakin had his rhythm now. He told Uunu he'd been on a freighter crew, and described Coruscant and Corellia. She was mostly disgusted by this, since it was impossible to talk about such high-tech worlds without multiple mentions of abominations. He changed the subject to lost Ithor and the moon of Endor, which were less touchy subjects.

After six hours of work, they took a short break for water and to suck a pasty pap from something Anakin knew was an organism but preferred to think of as a warm, distended bag.

"It's difficult to imagine all of those worlds, each as big or bigger than this one," Uunu said between sips. "I grew up on one of the poorest worldships. There was little room. We lived very close together. Here, there is nothing but space."

"There are plenty of uninhabited worlds," Anakin agreed. "The New Republic would have been happy to make room for you."

Uunu gave him the puzzled expression he had come to expect in their conversations. "Why should Yuuzhan Vong beg for what the gods have ordained we may have? Why should we tolerate abominations in the galaxy Yun-Yuuzhan has decreed shall be the end of our wanderings?"

"How do you know the gods have decreed this, Uunu?" Anakin asked, trying to keep the edge from his voice.

Her lips tightened. "Your mouth will be the death of you, Bail Lars. I have come to understand you are ignorant rather than stupid, but others will not be so forgiving."

"I just want to understand. From what I can tell, the Yuuzhan Vong spent centuries if not millennia in space. Why now, why our galaxy? How did the gods make their will known?"

A slight frown creased Uunu's face, but she did not berate him again. "The signs were many," she said. "The worldships began to die, and there was much unrest. Caste fought caste and domain fought domain. It was a time of testing, and many thought the gods had abandoned us. Then Lord Shimrra had a vision of a new home, of a galaxy corrupted by heresy, of a cleansing. The priests first saw his vision was true, then the shapers, then the warriors. The time of testing gave way to the time of conquest." She looked up at him. "That is all. It is how it must be. Ask no more about it, for there is nothing else to say. The people of this galaxy will accept the will of the gods, or they will die."

Anakin nodded. "And the Shamed Ones? You didn't mention them. How do they fit into this?"

Her gaze wandered away again. "We have our own prophecies. In this new galaxy, Yun-Shuno has promised us redemption."

"In what form?"

She did not answer but instead looked off at the horizon. "Look how far it goes," she said. "On and on."

Anakin thought the conversation was over, but after a long pause Uunu suddenly caught his gaze and held it. Her voice dropped almost below the range of his hearing.

"Bail Lars," she said. "Are you *Jeedai*?"

CHAPTER
TWENTY-FIVE

"What?" Anakin sputtered around the yellowish paste he was already having trouble swallowing.

"Are you *Jeedai*?" Uunu repeated. "The question is simple."

"But what makes you ask it?" Anakin said. "If I were Jedi, would I be a captive?"

"The shapers have one captive *Jeedai*. Rumor has it others are on this moon. And you—no one seems to remember you being brought here. As well, you do not act like a slave, somehow. You seem too unbent." She eyed him speculatively. "Rumor also says that *Jeedai* sometimes allow themselves to be captured."

"Well, I didn't allow myself to be captured," Anakin said. He figured that wasn't a lie, since he hadn't been captured at all.

He wouldn't be captured now, either. He was alone with Uunu, and she was no warrior. He readied himself, trying to keep his breathing normal. He didn't want to hurt Uunu. She'd treated him like more of a person than she had to. That wasn't much, but he couldn't discount it.

Then he noticed something about the set of her eyes. "You *wanted* me to be Jedi, didn't you? I've disappointed you."

Uunu sighed and touched her gaze back to the distance. "If you were *Jeedai*, you would have attacked me by now," she said.

"You believed that and you still asked me anyway? Why would you take such a risk?"

"There is no risk. Warriors are hidden near here. I voiced my fears to them." Her expression crumpled into chagrin.

The hairs on Anakin's neck prickled up. Where were the watchers? He couldn't see anyone. "Would turning in a Jedi have earned you out of the Shamed Ones?"

"Not in and of itself," she said a little wistfully. "Only the gods can change my condition. But I should like to meet one of these *Jeedai*. And the discovery of a *Jeedai might* give Yun-Shuno much leverage to intercede for me."

"You've mentioned her before. She's your superior?"

"She's a goddess, infidel. The goddess of the Shamed Ones. The only one who can make me a true Yuuzhan Vong."

"Oh."

"Return to your work."

They started again, she stroking the blossoms bald and he cutting out the lambents.

"How does one become Shamed?" Anakin asked.

"Another impolite question," Uunu said, but her tone was light, belying the chiding. "Some of us are born so. Others are cursed for misdeeds or sins."

"I've heard that some Shamed Ones do not think they deserve their status," Anakin said as casually as possible.

She barked a harsh laugh. "Deserve? What is deserve? We merely are." She looked back at him, her expression suddenly knowing. "Ah. You speak of Vua Rapuung, the one who brought you to the prefect of clearing fields."

"That might be his name. I'm not sure. But he muttered some things. Not to me—he hardly seemed to know I was there."

"He is insane, Vua Rapuung," Uunu said. "Once he was a great warrior. Now he is nothing. He cannot bear it, so he invents lies. Perhaps he even believes them."

"Lies?"

"He claims a shaper infected him with something to produce the marks of Shame, from spite."

"Why?" Anakin asked.

"Because she loved him," Uunu said, "and he spurned her."

"Love?" Somehow it had never occurred to Anakin that Yuuzhan Vong fell in love.

"Yes. But his story is impossible."

"How so?"

"More ignorance! Because the gods who govern such things—the Lovers Yun-Txiin and Yun-Q'aah—would never weave passions between a warrior and a shaper. Yun-Yuuzhan eternally punishes the twin gods for their own transgressions; they would never dare his wrath again. It is not possible, and so Rapuung's ravings are those of insanity. He is merely cursed, like the rest of us. Of late he has become even more erratic. I think the intendants will destroy him soon, if they have not already."

"Destroy him?"

"Shamed Ones must show usefulness and humility. We do the work no true caste Yuuzhan Vong may dirty their hands with. If we do not do these things, we are not worth feeding." Her head came up. "You have concern for Vua Rapuung?"

"I have concern for all living beings," Anakin said.

"And now you sound like a *Jeedai* again," she said.

How do you know so much about the Jedi philosophy? Anakin wondered. Where would a Shamed One get such information? Why would she be interested?

"Tell me," Uunu went on. "Would a *Jeedai* be concerned about the fate of a Shamed One? As concerned as he would be for a person of high caste?"

"Yes. I have known Jedi. They protect all life."

"Not Yuuzhan Vong. *Jeedai* kill Yuuzhan Vong."

"Only when they must," Anakin replied. "Jedi do not like to kill."

"They are not warriors, then?"

"Not exactly, not from what I know. They are protectors."

"Protectors. And they protect everyone?"

"Everyone they can."

She chuckled again, a bit uneasily. "An amusing lie. The sort of lie that gives hope to those who do not deserve it. A destructive lie. Some Shamed Ones even—" She broke off again, this time angrily. "How is it you make me talk so, infidel? Work, and do not speak. Ask me no more questions."

That night Anakin crept from the slave quarters. It was no great task. For most slaves, there was no escape from the camp itself. If they wanted to waste the precious hours of sleep they were allotted, the Yuuzhan Vong didn't prevent it.

Reaching the fields was more difficult, but Anakin had plenty of experience with stealth. In a few moments, by the light of the orange gas giant, he knelt in the lambent field. The plants lisped softly, like a nighttime breeze through dark treetops. Beyond the perimeter of the camp, across the river, he faintly felt the life of the jungle. Somewhere inside of it, in a bed of aches and misery, he knew Tahiri's fading touch.

He found the last of the harvested lambents and knelt beside the first of the next day's harvest, staring for a long moment at the faintly illuminated stalk. Then, hardly daring to breathe, he reached for the swollen blossom and began to stroke exactly as he had seen Uunu do hundreds of times.

The petals were as soft as silk, rubbing easily from his fingers, and Anakin felt a faint touch, like an electrical shock traveling up his arm. It was neither pleasant nor unpleasant, but more like the first taste of a food so exotic his tongue had no baseline for judging it.

As he stroked, the feeling deepened, and finally he felt not just his fingers rubbing the flower, but also the blossom being *rubbed*. He *was* the lambent, for a moment, and not only felt it wakening but felt himself awakened.

He continued until the small hum in his head was louder, more obvious than any impulse from the other plants, until the pod was smooth, then he blinked and carefully searched around him for movement. Here, in the camp, he was nearly blind and deaf. He couldn't even use the jungle moon's native life to sense what danger might be coming. If he couldn't see it and hear it, it wasn't there.

But his eyes found no shadows creeping, his ears registered no faint susurrus of motion, and so, producing his spurred thumb, he cut into the plant and stripped away the husk until he had the gem inside. He gripped it tight in his fingers, and almost without him asking it, it flared into gentle radiance.

"Yes!" he hissed.

Willing it dark, he clenched his fist tighter around it in a gesture of triumph.

Then it was back across the fields and through the houses. They were not silent at night; he passed the shrine of Yun-Shuno and heard moaning within. Whispers drifted from other doorways, and here and there someone paced in the darkness, restless.

Anakin kept going until he reached the edge of the star-shaped compound where he had exited the living boat. He slipped within.

The pool shone with a gentle phosphorescence that did not reach far below the surface. Anakin felt with the Force, hoping desperately his lightsaber was still there, where he had placed it days before.

The water was murky. He could sense it in the Force, but as if through a cloud. The crawlfish and their aquatic cousins were sensible, too, but somehow diffuse. It took longer than it should have for him to feel the play of life and current and energy in the heart of the shaper damutek. But at last he had it in his mind, wavering like a mirage, but there. The current had carried his lightsaber to fetch at the edge of the compound, against a barrier that kept the fish in. He exerted his will, and his lightsaber shifted, moved, broke the surface, and came to rest in his hand.

"Who's there?" a voice asked, from the shadows around the pool. Anakin stepped back quickly, heart running toward lightspeed, and withdrew into the darkness in the far corner of the compound.

"Your pardon," he rasped, grateful for the tizowyrm in his ear. He tried to make his voice sound as much like a Yuuzhan Vong's as possible. "I am no one, a Shamed One."

The figure in the darkness shifted, and he could suddenly see more of her silhouette. Something was strange about her head. It wriggled like a nest of snakes, like nothing he had yet seen among the Yuuzhan Vong.

"This is the compound of the shapers," the woman's voice said. "You have no business here, Shamed One."

"I beg pardon, great one," Anakin said. "I wished only—I had hoped the waters of the succession pool would inspire me to beseech Yun-Shuno persuasively."

The silence stretched. "I should report you, you know. Only those Shamed Ones with passage pheromone are allowed here. I—" He heard a little gasp of pain.

"Is anything the matter, great one?"

"No," she replied in a strained voice. "It is only my suffering. I came here to contemplate it. Go, Shamed One. I would not interrupt my reverie over you. Go, leave me in peace, and count yourself fortunate."

"Thank you, great shaper. As you will."

And with that, he withdrew. Sweat was coursing down

his brow, and his limbs trembled slightly, but triumph was a supernova inside of him. He had what he needed, now.

The supernova cooled a little as he left the damutek and padded back into the village of the Shamed Ones. He needed more than the lambent and the lightsaber. He needed time, and solitude, and even the lenient Uunu wasn't likely to give him that. But he also couldn't wait for Vua Rapuung any longer. Uunu was suspicious of him. Hul Rapuung had voiced a similar suspicion, that very first day.

And Vua Rapuung might be dead.

So he needed to hide somewhere. Where?

Puzzling over that, he ran headlong into someone. A Yuuzhan Vong cursed, and a strong hand knotted in his hair. Startled, Anakin dropped both his lightsaber and the lambent, which flared into sudden light.

In the illumination, a mutilated face stared down at him.

"Vua Rapuung!" he gasped.

"Yes," the other growled. "Quiet that lambent."

"Let go of me, then."

The Yuuzhan Vong did so, and Anakin dropped to one knee, retrieving both items. *Be still,* he thought at the lambent, picturing it dark.

The light paled and vanished.

"What are you doing with that?" Rapuung snarled.

"Never mind. I'm glad to see you. I've heard—"

"They tried to kill me," Rapuung said shortly. "We must act now. Tonight, or never."

"We can't!" Anakin said. "There's something I still have to do."

"Impossible."

"No, listen. You said one reason you wanted me was because of my lightsaber, right?"

"It would help us a great deal," Rapuung growled reluctantly. "Without it I am not certain how we will circumvent the portals and safeguards." He cocked his head. "You lied to me? You have the weapon?"

"It doesn't work. But I can fix it. With the lambent I can fix it."

"Do so, then, and hurry."

"Even if I hurry, it could take a day or two."

"Again, impossible. We cannot hide for two days here, and if we go beyond the perimeter, we will never come back in."

"I need two days," Anakin said stubbornly.

"Tomorrow they will realize I am alive," Rapuung said. "Unless you have a *Jeedai* sorcery to make us invisible . . ."

"No," Anakin said, "but—listen. The temple that was here, the one built of stone. How was it destroyed?"

"What? A damutek was landed on it. Its substance was dissolved and used to nourish the coral."

"But did they fill in the caverns below it?"

"Caverns?"

"Yes," Anakin said excitedly. "If they just flattened the temple with one of these damuteks, the caverns underneath might still be there. Didn't you say the damuteks drive down roots, or something—for water and minerals?"

Rapuung swore. "Of course," he said. "If there are indeed caverns of size below, and if the gods are with us—but of course they are. I am Vua Rapuung."

He said this last as if repeating a mantra, and Anakin felt renewed apprehension, remembering Uunu's opinion of Rapuung. If there had indeed been an official attempt on his life, he might have gone from being a solenoid short of a transformer to a fused mess of circuits.

But did it matter? Mad or not, Rapuung was the closest thing to an ally Anakin had. Right now, he would take what he could get.

Rapuung kept talking, almost to himself it seemed. "They will think we have run into the jungle again. She will search for us there, never in the very roots of her stronghold. Never below her very feet. But we will need gnullith breathers."

"You can get those, right?" Anakin asked.

"I can get them. But this is a risk," Rapuung warned him. "If we are noticed entering the roots, we will be sealed there to die very long, very ignoble deaths."

"More ignoble than dying a Shamed One?" Anakin shot back. "Besides, it never occurred to me you were worried by risk."

He couldn't see Rapuung's face, but he could imagine the glare there.

"A good thing you never thought that," Rapuung replied. "A very good thing. As I said. Wait here."

And he was gone, leaving only his putrid scent and the shadow of his anger. Anakin was once again alone.

CHAPTER TWENTY-SIX

"Adept Nen Yim?"

Nen Yim searched the darkened laboratory grotto for the sound of her name and found it coming from a young male with the forehead marks of Domain Qel—one of the smaller minor shaper domains. He lacked a shaper's hands, which placed him below her in rank.

"You have my name, Initiate," she said, letting a bit of irritation show. "*And* my attention." Her head throbbed and occasionally spiked with the pain of the Vaa-tumor thriving in it, but she embraced the growing discomfort. It would not interfere with her work, or this conversation.

The male's headdress was knotted in respect, but something about his face remained annoyingly bold, if not challenging.

"My name is Tsun," he said. "I have been assigned by Master Mezhan Kwaad to aid you today in our glorious work."

Nen Yim braided tendrils in skepticism. "The master said nothing of assistants," she noted. "She was to meet me here herself."

Again, Tsun trod the outskirts of perniciousness in the studied ease of his answer. "Mezhan Kwaad sent me, Adept, to explain that she will meditate today rather than labor. Her Vaa-tumor is to be removed next cycle, and she wishes these last periods to contemplate her pain."

"I see. Your message is delivered then. But how am I to recognize her authority in it?"

Tsun's eyes flashed with a certain mischievous light. "I must say," he purred, "I am honored. I have much wished to meet you, Adept Nen Yim."

That had a strange effect. She felt a slight warmth creep up her neck. Was this another side effect of her Vaa-tumor? She commanded her headdress to remain quiescent. "Oh?" she replied.

"Yes. I was once a companion to a friend of yours. Yakun."

This time she had to clench her tendrils to keep her emotions hidden. This was suddenly a very dangerous and painful nestling of history and words to be a part of.

"Yakun?" she said, as if just remembering that there was such a name. "He was a Domain Kwaad initiate in Baanu Kor?"

Tsun nodded. "Yes. He introduced me to you once, when you tended the mernip breeding pools together."

"That was before his heresy," Nen Yim said.

"Yes," Tsun agreed. "Before they took him."

"We shall not speak of him, then, shall we?" Nen Yim replied. "For he is a heretic and not to be spoken of. I will forgive this mention of him. Once."

Tsun genuflected. "I knew him well, Adept Nen Yim, in the days after your reassignment. He spoke of you often. He often wished to hear from you, especially near the end."

She kept her tongue and tentacles as still as unliving stone, but she remembered. Remembered hearing the news of Yakun's accusation and sacrifice. She remembered private, forbidden moments with him before, and her vain prayers to Yun-Txiin and Yun-Q'aah to protect him.

How she had tried not to think of him at all.

Perhaps Tsun understood her posture, or her headdress betrayed her, for through the sudden renewal of pain behind her eyes, she saw he *knew*.

"I do not mean to sadden you," he said. "It is only that Master Mezhan Kwaad asked me to tell you I knew him, that we were confidants."

The flash of agony released as suddenly as it had come. *Mezhan Kwaad did send him,* Nen Yim thought, her growing panic taking a step back. *This is her message I am to trust him. Yakun was a heretic. My master is a heretic. So is Tsun.*

"Initiate Tsun," she said firmly. "I said we should not speak of that person. I mean it. Now let me show you our work."

The *Jeedai*'s eyes had lost much of their focus; she no longer glared like a predatory beast. Instead she stared for long hours at nothing, a look of puzzlement on her face.

"She seems stunned," Tsun noticed.

Nen Yim signaled the vivarium to become opaque to sound. "She can hear us, and she knows the tongue of the gods. Even in that state she might remember anything we say. Or nothing."

"She is being drugged?"

"Not precisely. We are altering her memories."

"Ah," Tsun said knowingly. "The protocol of Qah."

"No," Nen Yim corrected, "not exactly. That protocol was ineffective on her human brain."

"How can that be?"

"It is a simple biotic protocol in which clumps of memory neurons are introduced into a Yuuzhan Vong brain. The *Jeedai*'s brain is too different."

"And yet you *are* modifying her memory."

"A bit at a time. Soon we will be able to do so much more efficiently."

"You have prayed for a new protocol?" Tsun asked slyly.

"No," Nen Yim replied. "Our approach has followed two axes. We have mapped and remapped her nervous system. We have identified her memory networks and are using the provoker spineray to discourage their use."

"You mean her old memories trigger pain?"

"Yes. Accessing her long-term memory extracts a pain sacrifice. The more connected memories she tries to bring to conscious thought, the greater her suffering."

"Why not simply wipe clean the centers of memory and begin again?"

"Because she retains the knowledge of her *Jeedai* powers. A day will come—after we've shaped her—when we'll want her to remember how to use them."

Tsun studied the human. "I see you have scarred her forehead with the Domain Kwaad sign."

"We will do more, in time. We will alter her face, especially that strange nose of hers. But that is superficial. Attend."

Nen Yim squatted near the vivarium membrane, opened it again to sound, and spoke to the *Jeedai*. "What is your name?" she asked.

The *Jeedai* didn't react. With a sigh, Nen Yim stimulated a minor pain center and cortical nerve with the provoker spineray.

What would have once made the young *Jeedai* shriek in agony only cycles before now merely made her flutter her eyes and frown.

"Yes, Adept?" the *Jeedai* said, as if waking reluctantly from a dream.

"What is your name?" Nen Yim asked.

"My name?"

"Yes."

"It is—" She frowned, then suddenly her eyes bulged and she gripped her head. "My name is—" Her teeth clenched and her face went white. Then, as if in sudden remembrance, the *Jeedai*'s face cleared.

"My name is Riina Kwaad," she said.

"Very good, Riina," Nen Yim said. "You have learned. And today you will learn more."

"I see now," Tsun said. "You trellis her thoughts. Unwanted responses bring pain. Desired ones do not."

"No," Nen Yim replied. "That name came from an implanted memory."

"But you just said that the protocol of Qah was ineffective."

"Yes. But we can build a kind of Qah cell using her own, human brain cells."

A look of sheer delight crossed the initiate's face. "So it *is* true," he whispered. "Here, you pursue our dream, the superprotocol—the methods of finding new knowledge without asking the gods."

Nen Yim felt infected by his joy, but she drew her tentacles into a mild admonishment. "Here, in these chambers of the master, such things may be spoken in security," she cautioned. "But outside of this room, have a care."

"Yes, of course. I know what happens to heretics as well as you. But what am I to do? Command me, Adept Nen Yim. Make me a part of this!"

He was very like Yakun, Nen Yim reflected. How had she not seen it immediately, the passion in his eyes? It was almost as if her lover had been reborn.

Keep to the task at hand, she counseled herself. "The modified memory cells are weak," she told Tsun. "Most are rejected within a matter of hours and have to be reimplanted. My task is to understand why; it is not a biochemical matter, as I see it—difficult to explain, and perhaps connected to her *Jeedai* powers. Your task, Initiate Tsun, is to grow new memories for her. We are in the process of transferring a complete set of false memories developed in the Qah protocol to a human-cell equivalent. We can then bud them as many times as we wish. When I have found a way to condition her to accept implanted memories permanently, we will then have a complete set to transfer. Meanwhile, we modify the cells, try them out, and see how long they last. We might stumble

on a biological solution in the process, or at the very least
learn more about how her memory works."

"I hear and obey," Tsun said eagerly. "But since there
is no protocol to follow . . ."

"I will demonstrate. The trials were rigorous and required much testing—"

"Testing," Tsun breathed. "A word I never thought to
hear spoken aloud in this context."

"Are you listening, Initiate, or will you comment on
my every word?" Nen Yim remonstrated, trying to keep
her voice stern.

"Apologies, Adept," he said. "I am all attention."

"Good. I was saying, *Initiate*, that developing the process was difficult, but the resulting protocol is simple,
and as easy to follow as any of the god-given ones. If you
come here, I will describe it to you."

He genuflected and followed her eagerly, but did not
interrupt her again except with necessary questions.

Riina watched the two Yuuzhan Vong go about their
work in confusion. Who were they? Why was she here?

Discontinuity. She came to, trembling, her thoughts
drifting in angry swarms, unwilling to associate with one
another. She remembered the female asking her name,
and answering "Riina." That hadn't hurt.

But somehow it was *wrong*.

There were things she could see from the corner of her
eye she could never see looking straight on. Her real
name was like that, lurking just out of sight. When she
tried to stare straight at it, it bit her with hot needle teeth.

That was true of a lot of things. The face that kept appearing in the dark of her mind, the voice that sometimes
rang in her head, the memory that kept trying to surface
of how she had gotten here—all were shifting trails in the
sand, all led to agony.

But she couldn't give up. She wasn't supposed to
be here.

Or was she? Brief flashes of color and sound came, now, of a world turned inside out, with no sky but only land that curved up to meet itself. A crèche-mother with a sloped forehead and nearly noseless face. The prickly sweet scent of fuming omipal during the ritual of appellation. The spicy, slightly rotten taste of von'u, a rare treat given her by her naming-father.

Riina they called her. *Riina Kwaad.*

She felt as if she were drifting down a stream of soothing water, surrounded by comforting voices. She rubbed her forehead and felt the marks of her domain, and even the raw pain of them felt good, in its own way.

Tahiri!

The voice again. Memories of her past splintered like crystal and cut into her brain. Other images flashed, names. One name.

Anakin.

The stream became a river, raging, sucking her under, and Anakin was in it with her. She held to the image, though paroxysms shook her body.

This was real. This happened! We were little, at the academy, we were following dreams that drew us together—

She screamed, leapt, and slammed into the barrier that separated her from the Yuuzhan Vong. She reached out in the Force to try to choke them, but they weren't there, somehow. There was nothing real behind their startled faces.

"My name is Tahiri!" she screamed at them. "I am Jedi! Tahiri!"

Then a tidal wave of dazzling anguish crawled up every single nerve, centipedes with legs of fire, and she lost consciousness.

"What did it say?" Tsun asked.

"That was Basic, the language of the infidels," Nen Yim told him.

"Should she be able to access that?"

"No. She still resists. We found that she somehow re-routes to nerve clusters we have not mined. However, the provoker spineray follows the reroutes and stimulates them, as well. In time, she will have no way into or out of those memories save through the embrace of pain. By that time it will not matter. She will be infidel no longer, and will welcome the challenge."

"Thank you for explaining," he said.

Nen Yim acknowledged him with a twist of her head-dress, returning to her work.

CHAPTER
TWENTY-SEVEN

The damutek root was a hollow tube, and when Anakin and Vua Rapuung entered it, it was almost a meter in diameter. Close, but not claustrophobic.

As soon as it sensed their presence, it constricted, hugging the contours of their bodies with insistent strength. Anakin had to straighten his arms in front of him and drag himself downward with the strength of his fingers.

He felt as if he was suffocating. He couldn't go backwards, not with Vua Rapuung behind him. To make matters worse, he was moving against a gentle but unrelenting current. When the pressure against him grew too great he would curl his body into a fetal position, something that took almost every bit of strength he had. When he released and straightened his body, it took several seconds for the root walls to contract and conform to his body again. It felt like trying to crawl up the esophagus of a snake intent on swallowing. The only problem with that analogy was that if he were doing that, he would be assured of light at the end of the mucilaginous tunnel. Here he was crawling toward darkness, maybe nothingness. What if the root ended in a sealed aquifer? How long would the breather shoved down his windpipe continue to work? Until he starved, probably.

If he ever got off Yavin 4, he promised himself, he would visit his uncle's homeworld, Tatooine, or some other similarly desiccated place. He had had more than enough of water and other fluids on this trip to last him decades.

Fighting a nattering little panic, Anakin continued dragging himself forward. Minutes piled into hours.

He thought of sunlight, wind, infinite space.

He thought of Tahiri. Was he wrong to try to rebuild his lightsaber? Should he have gone on charging after her without it? The strong, early contacts in the Force had faded to occasional brushes, most powerfully when she was in agony. Anakin had the clear impression that Tahiri was actually avoiding contact, shoving him away.

Despite this, an image of her prison had assembled itself in his mind—a small chamber divided from a larger one by a thin but unbreakable membrane. Her jailers were Yuuzhan Vong like the one he had seen by the succession pool, the one with the tentacled headdress. Several other cells like the one she was in were visible, but these were empty and dark, presumably waiting for more young Jedi captives.

The other thing he was certain of was that Tahiri was in a great deal of confusion. Not only did she not respond to his touch, she sometimes didn't even recognize it.

If he thought he could save her without his lightsaber . . .

But he couldn't. Even the insanely reckless Vua Rapuung thought so, or they would never be squeezing themselves down a kilometer of small intestine.

Tahiri could hang in there for another two days. She had to. And to save her, he could crawl through anything.

Muscles trembling, even when he freshened them with the Force, he moved on.

When he finally emerged into a space large enough that he could float free and touch nothing, he silently celebrated it by stretching, bending, kicking his arms, and waving his feet. It was the most delicious feeling he could imagine at that moment. For perhaps a minute he thought of nothing but this simple jubilation, but then the darkness lurking in his mind reminded him he would have to crawl right back up the Sith-spawned thing if this cavern didn't go anywhere. He took out his lambent crystal and willed it to life.

Rapuung appeared, floating facing him, looking like a reptilian water monster. Beyond him Anakin saw the tube opening extruding from a stone surface that bent to envelop them in a cavern of indeterminate size. Anakin found gravity's direction and started following the surface up, trailing one hand on it. At the same time he stretched out with the Force, sensing water drumming slowly through stone, searching for the sounding boards, the hollow places where air held court.

Anakin thought he'd been happy to leave the tube. Pulling himself onto damp stone, yanking the gnullith from his mouth, was infinitely better. He sat there, gasping and wet, as Vua Rapuung climbed out of the water behind him.

"I hope this was worth it," Rapuung growled.

"It will be."

"Heal your weapon so we can leave this skulking pit."

"I'll start in a moment," Anakin said. "But first, Vua Rapuung, tell me something. Do you really believe that the marks of your shame were inflicted upon you by a shaper? That she did this to you for rejecting her love?"

"Who have you been talking to?"

"The other Shamed Ones talk. They saw me with you."

Rapuung's face contorted as if he had swallowed the foulest thing in the world, but his head chopped affirmatively.

"Our love was forbidden. We both knew it. For a time neither of us cared. We believed that Yun-Txiin and Yun-Q'aah had taken pity on us, dared the wrath of Yun-

Yuuzhan, and given us a special dispensation. Such things have happened before, no matter what ignorant things you may have heard." His lip curled. "It did not happen with us. We were wrong."

"And you broke it off."

"Yes. Love is a madness. When my sanity began to return, I knew that I could not violate the will of the gods. I told her so."

"And she didn't like that."

Rapuung snorted. "She blasphemed. She said there *were* no gods, that belief in them was superstition, that we are free to do whatever we dare so long as we are strong." His eyes turned away from Anakin. "Despite her heresy, I would never have told anyone her words. She did not believe that. She feared I would denounce her, or that one day our forbidden trysting would come to the attention of her superiors. She is ambitious, Mezhan Kwaad. She is spiteful. She made me appear Shamed because she knew no one would credit my words then, that anything I said would be taken as the ravings of a lunatic."

"Why didn't she just kill you?" Anakin asked. "Give you some poison or fatal disease?"

"She is more cruel than that," Rapuung snarled. "She would never give me the release of death when she could debase me instead."

Rapuung's eyes focused on the lambent. "What else did the other Shamed Ones say? They called me insane, yes?"

"Yes, as a matter of fact."

"I am not."

Anakin measured his words out carefully. "I don't care if you are," he said. "I don't care about your revenge any more than you care about Tahiri. But I need to know how far you will go. You say you're reconciled to me using my lightsaber."

"I have said so."

"I'm going to rebuild it, as I told you. What I didn't mention is that I'm going to rebuild it using this." He held up the lambent.

The Yuuzhan Vong's eyes widened. "You would graft a living servant to your machine?"

"A lightsaber isn't exactly a machine."

"It isn't alive."

"In a way it is," Anakin said.

"In a way dung is the same as food, at the molecular level, perhaps. Speak plainly."

"To do that, I have to tell you about the Force, and you have to listen."

"The Force is what you *Jeedai* kill with," Rapuung said.

"It's much more than that."

"Why do you wish to explain this to me?"

"Because when I use my lightsaber, I don't want any surprises from you like I got when I lit the fire. I want to have this out here and now."

"Very well. Explain your heresy to me."

"You've seen me use the Force. You have to admit it is real."

"I've seen things. They may have been tricks. Talk."

"The Force is generated by life. It binds all things together. It's in everything—the water, the stone, the trees in the forest. I am a Jedi Knight. We're born with an aptitude for the Force, an ability to sense it, to control it—to guard its balance."

"Balance?"

Anakin hesitated. How to explain sight to a blind man? "The Force is light and life, but it is also darkness. Both are necessary, but they have to be kept balanced. In harmony."

"Putting aside the stupidity of that whole idea," Rapuung said, "you're telling me you *Jeedai* Knights keep this 'balance'? How? By rescuing your comrades? By killing Yuuzhan Vong? Does fighting my people bring balance in this Force? How can it, when you admit we do not *exist* in it? You can move a rock, but you cannot move me."

"That's sometimes true," Anakin admitted.

"Very well. If your superstition demands you seek to balance this mysterious power, why are the Yuuzhan Vong your concern? Why bother with us at all?"

"Because you've invaded our galaxy, killed our people, stolen our worlds. You don't expect us to fight back?"

"I expect warriors to fight, to embrace pain and death, to sing the song of slaughter with bloody lips. That is what Yuuzhan Vong do, and we do it not to bring balance, but *truth*. What you describe makes no sense. Tell me—are the Yuuzhan Vong part of this 'dark side' you speak of?"

Anakin looked at him frankly. "I think so."

"Does your magical Force tell you this?"

"No. Because—"

"Because we do not exist in it. It is not a part of us or we a part of it. So again, how do you judge us a part of your dark side?"

"By your actions," Anakin said.

"Actions? We kill in battle. You kill in battle. We kill in stealth. You kill in stealth. You fight for your people. I fight for mine."

"It's *our* galaxy!"

"The gods have given it to us. They have commanded we bring you the truth. This Force of yours is for lesser beings, those who do not know the gods."

"I do not accept that," Anakin said.

"And yet you would have me accept something I cannot see or smell? Something you merely tell me exists? Do you believe in the gods?"

Anakin hesitated, then tried again. "You've seen me use the Force."

"I've seen you do amazing things. I haven't seen you

do anything that we Yuuzhan Vong could not accomplish. Our dovin basals can move planets. Our yammosks and even the lowly lambent you hold there can speak mind to mind. I admit what I see—that you have powers I do not have. I need not believe your superstitions as to where these powers come from."

"Then don't," Anakin said hotly.

"And what does all of this have to do with building your abominable weapon?"

"A lightsaber is more than just an ordinary weapon. Each Jedi builds his or her own. The pieces are bound together by the Force and by the Jedi's will and make something greater than the sum of its parts. It becomes a thing alive in the Force."

"It is made of inanimate parts. It cannot be alive."

"All living things are made of inanimate parts, if you look small enough," Anakin pointed out. "Nothing is really inanimate. As I said, the Force is in everything. There will be something of me in my lightsaber, and something of this lambent in me."

Vua Rapuung nodded thoughtfully. "I begin to see the roots of your foul heresy, now. You make use of abominations because you somehow think them alive?"

Anakin stood abruptly. "I've explained what I'm going to do. Will you oppose me? Are you going to snap when I start fighting your people with my lightsaber?"

Vua Rapuung glared at him in the dim light of the lambent. Anakin could hear his teeth clicking together.

"The gods led me to you," he said at last. "Not Yun-Shuno, that many-eyed mother of snivelers, but Yun-Yuuzhan himself. He told me in a vision that the *Jeedai* infidel with his blade of light would lead me to my revenge and vindication. That is why I followed you down here, when my instincts screamed against it. It is why I did not kill you when you used the first abomination. Everything you say sounds to me as a lie. The reasons

you give for me to accept your weapon make no sense.
But Yun-Yuuzhan has spoken to me."

"Then you accept what I told you about the Force?"

"Of course not. As I said before, I can admit that what
my senses tell me is true without believing your delirious
justification of it. Your weapon may be acceptable to the
gods; your heresy is not. Build your blade."

With that, Rapuung stalked off into the darkness.

"And you say *I* don't make any sense," Anakin sighed.

Disappointment edged at Anakin, but he fought it back.

He could feel the lambent, but not in the Force, not the
way he could feel everything else about his weapon.
Everything was in place, fitted, ready to work. But what
he had told Rapuung was the truth; the real moment a
lightsaber became a Jedi's weapon was when the first
amperes of power trickled through it, when each piece
became a part of the other and a part of the Jedi building it.

But the lambent was resisting that. Well, not resisting
actually, but not going along with the whole scheme,
either.

And time was passing, each moment bringing Tahiri
closer to something terrible.

Concentrate, he thought. *There is no try.*

But there was failure, especially here. Master Yoda's
words, his entire philosophy, required the presence of the
Force in everything.

But the Force wasn't in the Yuuzhan Vong. It wasn't in
their biotech. They could be fought only indirectly, with
things that *could* be sensed in the Force.

Something slapped him, then, something that had
been cocking its hand back for a long time.

Master Yoda was wrong.

The Jedi were wrong, and Vua Rapuung was right. If
the Jedi stood for nothing but seeking balance in the
Force, then he *did* have no business fighting the Yuuzhan

Vong. Oh, he could rescue Tahiri; after all, preventing her from becoming a dark Jedi was at the core of the philosophy. But were actions—however bad or evil they seemed—were the actions of the Yuuzhan Vong in and of themselves worth opposing if they had no effect on the Force?

To be sure, the aliens were killing people, which always disturbed the Force. But did it unbalance it? The Yuuzhan Vong weren't gathering dark energy about themselves. If anyone ran the risk of doing that, it was Jedi like Kyp and maybe even himself. Seen like that, fighting the Yuuzhan Vong was more likely to unbalance the Force than any action they themselves might take.

Sure, that all made sense. It almost sounded like something Jacen or Uncle Luke would say. But that was all predicated on the certainty that the Force was in everything.

And it wasn't. And while the facts of the matter were staring them all in the face, no Jedi had had the guts to confront the new reality. Instead they were acting like spoiled children, complaining that the Yuuzhan Vong didn't play fair, weren't following those black-and-white rules. So Kyp went out to shoot them, to try to make the problem go away by killing it. Jacen huddled away in indecision. Maybe he was right.

No. It wasn't right for the Yuuzhan Vong to kill whole planets. It wasn't right for them to enslave people. Those actions were evil, they were wrong, and they had to be fought. If the Force did not draw that line and set great dark-side alarms wailing, then maybe Anakin didn't serve the Force. Or to put it more precisely, he served something more fundamental than the Force, something of which the Force was a manifestation, an emanation—a tool. Not Rapuung's gods, or any god, but some fundamental truth built into the universe at a subatomic level. In his galaxy, the Force was the servant of that truth. Wherever the Yuuzhan Vong were from, some other manifestation must prevail. But light remained light, and dark, dark. And whatever had happened to the Yuuzhan Vong, they had turned to the dark side long ago. If the Empire of Palpatine had prevailed and traveled to another galaxy on an errand of conquest, a galaxy where the Force was not known, what evidence would the people there have of the light side of the Force? Could they know that the Empire was an aberration of what ought to be? No. Similarly, Anakin didn't know—couldn't know—what manifestation of the light the Yuuzhan Vong had left behind them. But they *had* left it behind.

Maybe this was even the result of a whole people turning entirely to the dark side. Maybe the Force simply rejected them, or they it.

That didn't make them all evil, any more than everyone who served the Empire was evil. But it made them worth opposing. Without anger or hatred, yes. But they had to be stopped, and Anakin Solo would never turn his eyes from that.

With a sudden surge of confidence, he reached for the parts of his lightsaber in the Force and then pressed deeper.

So he had to work indirectly with the Yuuzhan Vong and their things. Fine. But behind the seeming disunity, there must be unity.

And in a flash of epiphany he had it. The link between the rest of his lightsaber and the lambent was Anakin Solo. It was in *him* the changes had to happen.

Power surged and crackled, and the cavern echoed with a *snap-hiss*, and somewhere Vua Rapuung snarled.

Anakin opened his eyes to the purple glow of his lightsaber and felt a grin slash his face in half.

"I am Jedi again," he said quietly.

Perhaps a new kind of Jedi altogether.

"Two cycles have come and gone," Vua Rapuung growled, a few moments later. His features were hollow in the violet glow. "Your abominable weapon works, it seems. Are we done with skulking? May we at last embrace our foes?"

"*You* embrace them," Anakin said. "I'm going to knock them down. Your shapers want Jedi? One is coming to them."

PART THREE

CONQUEST

CHAPTER TWENTY-EIGHT

Mezhan Kwaad curled her headdress in recognition at Nen Yim as she entered the laboratory.

"Detail your progress, Adept," the master said. Her tone was curt and her tendrils suggested irritation.

"We made good progress in your absence, Master," Nen Yim said cautiously. "I think with only minor genetic adjustments, the memory implants will be permanent. She resists them less than she did when last you were here."

"Yes," Mezhan Kwaad replied, anger twitching her tendrils. "Valuable days, missed." She turned to Nen Yim. "But at least you were here, my adept, and competent to carry on."

Nen Yim watched Mezhan Kwaad cross to the vivarium. The *Jeedai* still had a blank look most of the time, but now and then Nen Yim thought she saw something working behind those alien green eyes. Something more Yuuzhan Vong than human.

"Can you tell me your name?" Mezhan Kwaad asked the *Jeedai*.

Only a slight hesitation, this time. "Riina," the *Jeedai* said. "My name is Riina."

"Very good, Riina. Did Nen Yim explain what has been done to you?"

"A little."

"Tell me what you remember."

"The infidels captured me as a child, at the rim of their

galaxy. They made me look like one of them and gave me false memories with their *Jeedai* powers."

"This seems right to you?"

"Not always. Sometimes I think I am—" She gasped and clenched her hands. "—someone else."

"The infidel conditioning was excellent. Before we rescued you, they tried to wipe your mind clean. There was much damage."

"I feel that," the *Jeedai* answered.

"There is something I need to know," Mezhan Kwaad replied. "You were born with certain powers. You were taught lies about these powers, but we are attending to that. What I fear, Riina, is that your injuries may have crippled those powers."

"I cannot even think of them," the *Jeedai* said. Small droplets of water formed in the corners of her eyes and ran down her face.

"I'm going to help you with that," the master said. She gestured to make the vivarium opaque to sound and spoke to Nen Yim. "Quiet the provoker spineray."

Nen Yim started. "Master, that might not be wise. She still has moments when she asserts her real identity. We have closed most of those neural paths, but if we remove the promise of pain—"

"The new memories are in place for now, yes? They seem to be working quite well. They will keep her in check. This will not take long."

"This will confuse her," Nen Yim argued. "It might set us back."

"Who is master here, Adept?" Mezhan Kwaad asked brusquely. "Are you seriously questioning my expertise?"

Nen Yim quickly genuflected. "I am pitiable, Master. Of course I shall do as you say. I merely wished to voice my concerns."

"They are noted. Now, silence the spineray."

Nen Yim did so, and Mezhan Kwaad once again made the membrane permeable to sound. She produced a small stone from her oozhith's pouch and placed it on the chamber floor.

"Once you could lift a stone like this with your will," she told the *Jeedai*. "I wish to see you do so now."

"I will have to call upon false memories," the *Jeedai* moaned. "Painful ones."

"We embrace pain," Mezhan Kwaad said. "Your resistance to it is a human weakness implanted in you. Do as I say."

"Yes, Master," the *Jeedai* replied. She fixed her gaze on the stone and closed her eyes. She winced, but then her face smoothed, and the stone lifted from the floor as if grasped in an invisible hand.

Mezhan Kwaad barked a brief, victorious laugh. "Nen Yim," she commanded, "map the brain areas showing the most activity."

"Yes, Master."

"Riina, you may lower the stone, now."

Obediently, the stone sank back to the floor.

"It didn't hurt," the *Jeedai* said. "I thought it would hurt."

"You see? Your cure is progressing well. Soon you will remember everything about your life as a Yuuzhan Vong."

"I wish . . ." The *Jeedai* trailed off wistfully.

"What?"

"I feel like I'm two halves of two different people, glued together," she said. "I wish I were whole again."

"You will be," Mezhan Kwaad answered. "Before you know it, you will be. Now, if you could lift the stone again, please."

"Clearly these abilities aren't located in a single brain center any more than they are generated by an organ," Mezhan Kwaad said later, as they looked over the results of their experimentation.

"Her *Jeedai* powers are distributed in the neural net somehow, nonlocalized. The commands come from this lobe in the front of her brain, obviously, which is where most of her coherent thought occurs, as well. And yet there is also considerable activity in the hindbrain."

"Perhaps her control emanates from modified muscular systems," Nen Yim suggested.

"I see no evidence that this young female has been modified in any way, and the infidels have shown only the most rudimentary knowledge of biology."

"I meant modified by selection from generation to generation."

"Selective breeding? Interesting. We know from our infidel sources that this 'Force' runs more strongly in some families than others, and that *Jeedai* often mate with *Jeedai*." Her tentacles knotted in frustration. "We need more *Jeedai*, a larger sample. The incompetence of warriors—" She suddenly tremored and reached her eight-fingered hand to her head. "It is time. I must have the Vaa-tumor removed. Yet another despicable delay."

Nen Yim gave her master a puzzled look. "I thought that's where you've been, having the Vaa-tumor removed."

Mezhan Kwaad's eyes went to slits. "What? Why did you think that?"

"You were gone for two cycles, Master."

"Indeed, engaged in meaningless political exercises with Master Yal Phaath. He called via villip for a formal convocation of masters on the matter of delegating responsibilities on the new worldship. I was forced into a ritual seclusion, and at a quite inconvenient time."

"But the assistant you sent said nothing of that. He did say you were having your Vaa-tumor removed."

That had a remarkable effect on Mezhan Kwaad. Her tendrils fell limp, and her tone went colder than frozen nitrogen. "What assistant?"

"Tsun."

"I know no one by that name," Mezhan Kwaad said.

"But he told me you sent him."

"And that I was having my Vaa-tumor removed?"

"Yes. But he knew things about me. About what we do here."

Mezhan Kwaad folded down to a sitting mat and rubbed her head.

"No," she sighed. "He guessed that we were engaged in heresy, and you confirmed it. The convocation was a ruse to keep me busy. Yal Phaath now has his evidence, thanks to you."

"No!"

"Oh, I'm afraid so," a voice from the doorway boomed. Nen Yim spun to see Commander Tsaak Vootuh standing in the doorway, an escort of his personal guard just behind him.

Mezhan Kwaad drew herself to her full height.

"This is a shaper damutek. You do not have my permission to enter it."

"I do not need it," the commander replied. "I have the authority of Master Yal Phaath. I'm also afraid I must take both of you captive and search your chambers for evidence."

"Evidence of what? Accuse us!" Mezhan Kwaad snapped. "Do not insult us with captivity without challenging!"

"The accusation is heresy, of course," Tsaak Vootuh replied. "An accusation readily born out by the evidence, I feel certain."

CHAPTER
TWENTY-NINE

Going back up the root was much easier than coming down it; the current was with them. It was not one micron more pleasant.

They emerged in the succession pool under orange Yavin light.

On the way up, Anakin had noticed an interesting thing.

Vua Rapuung existed for him now.

Not in the Force, not with the clarity that the Force offered, but he was there, a shadow of fury cast from the lambent to Anakin's mind.

That wasn't all. He also felt the confused, staticky hum of the hundreds of Yuuzhan Vong around him. The noise cut in and out, like a bad comm transmission, but it was undeniably there.

It wasn't the Force, but it was something, and he could see their works with new eyes. His gaze was drawn to details in the living structures around him he hadn't noticed—or cared to notice—before.

With Rapuung, Anakin slipped into the shadows.

"Your *Jeedai* is still in this damutek?" Rapuung asked.

Anakin concentrated. Tahiri was there, but every day she became . . . fuzzier, harder to pinpoint. Now he barely heard her at all.

"She hasn't moved," Anakin replied. "She's that way." He pointed.

Rapuung grimaced. "That's not the core laboratories of the shaping compound."

"It's where I feel her."

Rapuung rubbed his flat nose. "It makes sense. It's where *her* quarters are, her personal chambers. If she keeps the work on the *Jeedai* close to her, and hopes it will go unseen, she would do it there."

"Why would she want that?" Anakin asked.

"I don't know. I don't understand the way of shapers. And yet she was always secretive in what she did. She was always nervous." His voice softened slightly. "Always doing things she shouldn't."

"Like having an affair with you."

Rapuung's nostrils contracted until they were nearly closed, but he chopped his head once. "Yes. Speak no more of it. Come, infidel."

"Lead on. I know the direction, but not the way."

Without another word, Rapuung padded off. An opening in the wall parted for him.

The shaper compound was an eight-armed star with the pool in the center. The corridor they entered took them up one of the arms. Within, the compound was illuminated by phosphorescence punctuated by the occasional lambent that sparked to life when Rapuung came near. A faint smell of seaweed and lizard permeated the corridors, which were at turns quite regular and wildly asymmetric. The pool was not the crosswalks of the place; a torus of connecting corridors joined the rays of the star and served that purpose.

Anakin tensed as they met their first Yuuzhan Vong. A cluster of them stood together, discussing something he couldn't quite catch. When they saw Rapuung and Anakin they stopped and stared, but didn't say anything.

"This is easier than I thought it would be," Anakin said, after they were past the group.

Rapuung grunted. "I would have killed them if I

thought it would help, but they sent the signal the instant they saw us."

"What are you talking about?"

"A Shamed One and a slave in a shaper compound? Unlikely."

"But they didn't—"

"Scream? Run? Shapers they may be, but they are Yuuzhan Vong. If we came to kill them, they would be dead. They know that."

"So what do we expect now?"

But Rapuung didn't have to answer. Ahead of them, the walls, floor, and ceiling of the corridor suddenly met one another.

"Whoops," Anakin managed. A quick look behind him showed the same thing.

"We have seconds," Rapuung said. "Do not inhale."

Anakin nodded and ignited his lightsaber. The fierce purple light highlighted the mist emerging from the corridor walls. Anakin approached the obstruction and cut into it with broad strokes.

Vonduun crab armor it wasn't. After the first cut, the stuff actually flinched away from his blade. In moments he had carved a hole large enough to step through.

Beyond, the corridor continued another four meters and ended in another dilation. This section was already full of mist.

Anakin cut through that, too, but his lungs were starting to hurt now, and black spots danced before his eyes, so rather than attacking the inevitable barrier that had closed beyond the second one, he cut through the wall to his right.

That spilled the pair into a large chamber where two startled Yuuzhan Vong looked up from examining something that resembled a twined bundle of black vines as big around as Anakin's thigh. He couldn't tell if it was animal or vegetable, and he didn't care.

"Which way now?" Anakin asked.

Rapuung stabbed a finger at the two shapers. "One of you. Take me to the personal laboratories of Master Mezhan Kwaad."

The shorter of the two frowned. "You're a Shamed One."

Rapuung reached him in two strides and struck him high in the chest, lifting the shaper from his feet and slamming him into the wall. He slumped to the floor, blood spilling from his lips.

"You," Rapuung said to the other. "Lead us to Mezhan Kwaad."

The second shaper looked at his unconscious companion.

"Come with me," he said.

"Can they fill this chamber with gas?" Anakin asked Rapuung.

"Of course. However, now that we've exited the corridor they think we're in they'll have to consult with the damutek brain to find us. That will take time. By then, the warriors will be here."

"I was wondering why there weren't any guards."

"This is a shaper place. Warriors must be invited here, and then only in times of duress. Normally there is no need for guards. It's been centuries since anyone invaded a shaper damutek. Who would wish to but an infidel?"

"Vua Rapuung, apparently," Anakin replied.

The shaper took them through a quick series of turns and then into a long, straight corridor that ended in one of the membranes that normally served as doors.

"Through there," their captive said, "is the master's personal chambers. But the threshold will not open itself to any of us."

"That is why I have a *Jeedai* with me," Rapuung told him, as Anakin thumbed the blade on and cut through the door. In doing so he nearly bisected the warrior just on the other side. The Yuuzhan Vong blinked at him in astonishment, then jerked his amphistaff to an attack position.

Rapuung charged past Anakin, lunged beneath the warrior's not-quite-ready guard, and struck him under the chin with the deteriorating talon on his elbow. The implant jammed in the being's mandible and tore out. Rapuung hardly seemed to notice, turning his attention instead to the roomful of warriors beyond.

Anakin leapt in behind him and turned aside an amphistaff slashing toward Rapuung with the blade of his lightsaber. Rapuung's attacker, recognizing the new danger, twisted the amphistaff and let it go limp. Then he whipped it underhand toward Anakin's throat. Anakin did a quick circular parry, wrapping the limp staff around his blade, and did a jumping front kick. The Yuuzhan Vong blocked that with his free hand, but some of the blow's force got through. Anakin cut his blade, dropped in at close quarters, jammed the blade emitter under the warrior's armpit, and flicked it back on.

The warrior jerked and fell away, exhaling a cloud of steam.

Anakin sensed a blow from behind, and without thinking he ducked, did a behind-the-back block, and felt the sharp rap of an amphistaff. He dropped, swept his unseen attacker's feet, and tumbled away from yet a third attacker.

Only when he was back in the clear, preparing to meet the two, did he realize what had happened. He had sensed the Yuuzhan Vong behind him. Not as clearly as he might in the Force, but it had been good enough to save his life.

They came at him with a certain caution, which gave Anakin time to notice that Vua Rapuung had downed another warrior and was busily engaged with three more. That seemed to complete the count of warriors in the chamber, though others might run in from the large opening at the other end of the room.

One problem at a time.

One of the Yuuzhan Vong slashed at Anakin's left leg,

while another did a whip-over toward his right shoulder. He leapt over the low attack and sliced his blade down the semirigid side of the high one. His blade hit the Yuuzhan Vong's fingers, and two of them came off. From there Anakin lunged toward his second foe's eye. The fellow jerked his head back and yanked his amphistaff up to parry. Anakin disengaged, avoiding the parry, and finished his blow right where a human sternum would be. The vonduun crab armor scorched but did not split, but the blow was strong. The Yuuzhan Vong was already off balance from avoiding the thrust to his eye, and now he sprawled heavily to the ground.

In those two or three seconds, Anakin's other opponent whipped the amphistaff in such a way that it coiled around Anakin's head and blade, the latter of which he had just drawn to an inner guard at his shoulder. Only turning the blade off kept him from being cut by his own weapon, but then there was nothing to prevent the amphistaff from closing around his neck like a garrote. Anakin reached reflexively for his throat, dropping his weapon. With a cry, the Yuuzhan Vong warrior turned his back, clearly intending to heave Anakin in a hard shoulder throw and snap his neck in the process. Anakin went with the throw and came down face-to-face with the warrior, his neck still intact.

Of course, he couldn't draw the tiniest sip of air. Almost contemptuously, the warrior lifted him from the floor, both hands still gripping the ends of the amphistaff.

The Yuuzhan Vong didn't see the lightsaber lift from the floor behind him, but he did notice when the purple blade appeared in his neck. He dropped Anakin, then.

Unfortunately, the amphistaff continued with the business of choking Anakin, and his second foe had found his feet. Anakin managed to get his blade in hand in time to block a dozen blows from the warrior's staff, before he felt his lights going out. His blood screamed for air and his legs felt like they were made of wood.

He fell away from the attack, dropped like a rag doll, and in the minute pause when his enemy thought he had really collapsed, he turned the fall into a roll that took him past the Yuuzhan Vong, where he cut both legs behind the knee.

Then Anakin saw space.

"How long was I out?" Anakin asked Vua Rapuung. The Yuuzhan Vong dropped the amphistaff that had been coiled around Anakin's neck.

"Only heartbeats."

Anakin pushed himself up. "Are there more warriors?"

"None capable of fighting, not in this chamber. There may be more nearby."

Anakin gingerly massaged his neck. "I thought you said there wouldn't be warriors in here."

"I was wrong. But they must be here for some purpose."

"Maybe they knew we were coming."

"Perhaps. I do not think so. These are the commander's personal troops."

"Wonderful. We'd better hurry this up, then."

"Our guide fled, but we need him no longer. We must be near now."

Anakin looked around at the fallen warriors. "Not that you seem to need it," he said, "but why not take one of these amphistaffs?"

"I have sworn an oath to the gods," Rapuung said. "Until I am redeemed before my people, I will not lift the weapon of a warrior."

"Oh. That makes sense." Anakin took a few steps and windmilled his arms, making sure everything worked.

"I don't like the warriors being here," Rapuung said.

"I'm not fond of it myself."

"That's not what I meant. If they are here without the permission of the shapers, it could mean they've come to arrest a shaper or to take something from them."

"Can they do that?"

Vua Rapuung rasped a laugh. "You know too little of our ways, infidel, and too little about Mezhan Kwaad."

"But what—" Anakin began, but then he got it. "Tahiri!"

"Come," Vua Rapuung said. "There is still time."

"This is the place," Anakin said. "This is where they had her." His gaze searched wildly about the room. It didn't resemble a laboratory so much as a vivisectorium, each surface covered with internal organs—except some of these pulsed and mewled the way severed body parts didn't. Usually. A quarter of the chamber was walled off by a transparent membrane. "She was in there," he clarified.

"Of course."

"Where would they have gone?"

"I don't see any other way out," Rapuung replied.

"Well, then—" But as before, he sensed something at his back. Another section of the wall had just gone transparent and permeable. Yuuzhan Vong warriors were pouring through it. Behind them Anakin could make out the yellow of Tahiri's hair.

"Tahiri!" he shouted, and threw himself at the wave of enemies.

CHAPTER THIRTY

Vua Rapuung howled. Anakin fought in grim silence. Their initial charges carried them into the midst of the warriors, but unlike the group they had just bested, these weren't scattered around a room, unprepared for a fight. Anakin and his companion were soon forced back toward the first vivarium by the six warriors who had engaged them. The other six—one of whom was vastly more scarred than the rest, probably a leader—led Tahiri and what appeared to be two female shapers back out the door Anakin and Rapuung had entered through.

"No!" Anakin exploded. He tried to leap over the warriors blocking his way, but one snagged his ankle with the amphistaff and used the momentum of his leap to slam him into the floor. Anakin cushioned the fall with the Force, but his enemy was still between him and the door, and his foot was still caught. That is, until Rapuung hit the fellow on the back of the head so hard that teeth flew out. Rapuung stood over Anakin, and for a moment, they weren't under attack. The warriors merely stood there, watching the Shamed One and Anakin warily.

"Vua Rapuung," one of them snarled finally. "What are you doing here with this infidel? You should be in the Shamed One's village, pursuing your redemption."

"I have nothing to be redeemed for," Rapuung said. "I have been wronged. You all know it."

"We know your claims."

"You, Tolok Naap. You fought beside me only a few tens of cycles ago. You believe me cursed by the gods?"

The warrior he had addressed flared his nostrils, but did not reply. The one who had spoken before, however, lowered his voice. "Whatever you were, whether you are cursed or not, you have clearly gone mad. You fight with an infidel against your own kind."

"I seek my vengeance," Rapuung said. "Mezhan Kwaad. Where is she going?"

"The shaper master has been taken up for her trials. The accusation is heresy."

"They're taking her outsystem?"

"I do not know."

"I cannot let her be taken, not until she admits she has wronged me. Any who stand in the way of that will leave this life on wings of blood."

"We will stop you," Tolok Naap said. "But we will fight you as the warrior you once were." He threw Rapuung his amphistaff. "Take up a weapon. Do not make us kill a bare-handed man."

"Thus far I have triumphed without weapons," Rapuung said. "If the gods hated me, would this be so?"

"You have this *Jeedai* as your amphistaff," one of them sneered. "Lay him aside, and we will lay down our weapons. Then we shall see how the gods love you."

Rapuung turned a glaring eye on Anakin. "Stand away, *Jeedai*."

"Rapuung, I have no time for games. Tahiri—"

"Is with the object of my vengeance. If we lose the one, we lose the other. I will make it swift."

Anakin stared at Rapuung, then nodded curtly. He stepped back and switched off the weapon.

Eighty seconds later, stepping over the corpses, Anakin glanced sidewise at Rapuung.

"What was it you needed me for?" he asked. "I'm forgetting."

They jogged down the corridor, gazes cutting right and left, alert for ambush from side corridors.

"When we have Mezhan Kwaad," Rapuung said, "you must keep death from my back until I have forced her to speak. That is why I need you."

"I can do that."

"Swear it. Swear it by this Force you worship. Keep death from my back until she speaks—for no less a time and no longer."

"I swear it," Anakin replied. "If we ever get that close, that is. How long before reinforcements arrive?"

"Not long."

"Well. Then we're going about this all wrong. We're just going to run into whatever ambush they have planned."

"And we will walk through them."

"Neither of us is made of neutronium," Anakin observed.

"I will hide no more."

"Hiding isn't what I had in mind," Anakin said. "Just a little change in tactics."

"Explain."

For answer, Anakin raised his lightsaber and sliced a hole in the low ceiling. "Do you need a boost up?" he asked.

Moments later, from the roof of the star-shaped compound, Anakin and Vua Rapuung watched warriors station themselves at the ground-level exits and entrances. Yavin was half-set, and it was darker now than it had been when they emerged from the succession pool, but Anakin knew the sun would be up soon.

"They will find our escape route quickly," Rapuung said.

"I know. I don't need long." Once again, he reached out through the Force, searching for Tahiri. She was there, but her presence was still fitful, hard to pinpoint.

Tahiri. Hear me. I must find you.

The response was rejection.

Tahiri. You know me. You're my best friend. Please.

This time he caught a faint hesitation and then something like a step in his direction. He saw a brief vision of coralskippers and larger Yuuzhan Vong ships he had no name for.

"Sithspawn!" he exclaimed. "They're going to board a ship."

Rapuung growled, deep in his throat. "No, they are *not*," he said. "This way."

They leapt down to the outside of the compound between the rays, far from any entrances, and slipped past the most lightly guarded exit, apparently without being noticed. Another hundred meters brought them to the ship compound.

Like its cousin, this damutek was a sprawling star with entrances and exits at the tips of the rays. Unlike it, its succession pool was covered, surfaced with something alien to provide parking space for Yuuzhan Vong ships. Tahiri and the group of warriors with her were walking up the ramp—or tongue, or whatever it was—of one of the larger ships. Perhaps fifty other Yuuzhan Vong went about various tasks in the compound. Most looked like Shamed Ones, though a few intendants were also at hand. Stifling a shout, Anakin threw himself into a run, Rapuung a silent shadow beside him.

When they were yet twenty meters from the ship, a cry went up. Three warriors guarding the ramp dropped to their knees and hurled thud bugs. Time slowed for Anakin as he ignited his blade and brought it up to deflect them.

Three snapped against the bright blade and arced off on divergent tangents as embers. None of them hit Anakin, but Rapuung grunted.

He didn't slow, however. They hit the three guards like a thunder front and sprang up the landing ramp into another hail of thud bugs.

This time Anakin was not as fortunate. One of the things went through his thigh, and he dropped to one knee, blocking two more that would have opened his chest in unpleasant places. Rapuung yowled, twisted, and hit the ramp with a damp, meaty thud.

Anakin struggled to rise.

"Stop, *Jeedai*," a cold voice said.

It was the commander. He stood next to Tahiri, with an amphistaff curled around her neck. His remaining three warriors gathered in front of him.

"Tahiri!" Anakin said.

"That isn't my name," Tahiri told him. "I am Riina Kwaad."

"You're Tahiri, my best friend," Anakin said. "Whatever they've done to you, I know you remember me."

"You may be a part of the infidel lies implanted in her," one of the female shapers—the older one—said. "But you are no more than that."

"Enough," the commander snapped. "This is to no purpose. You, *Jeedai*. If you have come to rescue this one, you have failed. I will kill her where she stands if you continue to struggle."

"Is this the vaunted courage of the Yuuzhan Vong?" Anakin asked. "Hiding behind a hostage?"

"You misunderstand. I know who you are. You are Anakin Solo, brother to Jacen Solo, he who is so much desired by Warmaster Tsavong Lah. I wish to have your surrender. I wish to have you alive. If I do not get my wish—if you take another step in attack—then the female will die. After that, I will cripple you if I can. Since the latter approach might lead to your accidental death, I prefer the former."

"I'll go in her place," Anakin said. "Of my own will. But you have to release her."

"How ridiculous," the commander said. "I will do nothing of the kind. Your decision will decide whether she lives or dies, nothing more. She is ours."

"*Jeedai,*" Vua Rapuung croaked, rising shakily to his feet. "Remember your oath to me." Anakin saw with dismay that Rapuung had one hand stuffed into a gaping hole in his belly.

What could he do? The commander would kill Tahiri. He was sure of that, and in his present condition he would never be able to stop it. But if he surrendered, he betrayed Vua Rapuung.

But Rapuung was probably dying. How would regaining his honor now do anyone any good?

Anakin put his hand on Rapuung's shoulder. "I remember my oath," he said. "Which one is she?"

"The female with the eight-fingered hand."

Anakin looked back up at the commander. "All right, this one thing, then, if you want me alive. It will cost you nothing."

"I doubt that. Speak."

"Compel the shaper named Mezhan Kwaad to speak the truth."

"About what?"

"The questions Vua Rapuung will put to her."

"I see no 'Vua Rapuung,'" the commander said stiffly. "Only a Shamed One who does not know his place."

"It is not I who am shamed," Rapuung said. "Do as the infidel says, and know the truth."

"There is no sense in listening to any demented lies from this one," Mezhan Kwaad said. "He fights by the side of a *Jeedai* infidel. What more need be said?"

Behind them, the square was gradually filling with warriors and onlookers. A shout came from below.

"Do you fear the truth, Mezhan Kwaad? If he is mad, then compelling you to speak will do you no harm."

Anakin looked over his shoulder and saw the warrior who had stopped them the first day—Hul Rapuung, Vua's brother.

A general murmur of approval went around with that.

"How many of you fought with him?" Hul continued.

"Who ever questioned the courage of Vua Rapuung? Who ever doubted the gods loved him?"

"Mezhan Kwaad is correct, however," the commander said dryly. "He is self-evidently pronounced mad by his behavior." He glanced at the shaper. "However, having found one treachery in Mezhan Kwaad—the treachery of heresy—I see no reason to doubt she is capable of others." He turned to the shaper master. "Master Mezhan Kwaad, I compel you to answer truthfully whatever questions the Shamed One once known in Domain Rapuung puts to you. Your truthfulness will not rest on your honor, but on the truthhearer I procured for your questioning in the other matter."

"I will not submit to any such indignity," Mezhan Kwaad replied.

"You do not have the right to refuse, and your domain will pay the full price if you attempt to. Answer his questions and let us end this."

Mezhan Kwaad's eyes glittered curiously, and she lifted her chin. She bared her teeth contemptuously at Vua Rapuung.

"Ask your questions, Shamed One."

"I have but one," Vua Rapuung said. "Mezhan Kwaad. Did you intentionally rob me of my implants, ruin my scars, give me the appearance of being Shamed? Did you do these things to me, or did the gods?"

Mezhan Kwaad stared at him with an unreadable expression, then lifted her chin even higher.

"There are no gods," she said. "This miserable thing you are is what *I* made of you."

The crowd erupted in frenzy.

Mezhan Kwaad spread her eight fingers, as if waving. Faster than the eyes could catch, those fingers elongated, spearing out. Before the commander could even blink, one went through his eye and out the back of his skull. The warriors around all dropped without a sound, similarly murdered. Anakin lurched forward, but a flick of the shaper's wrist, and one of the finger-spears pierced his forearm and wrapped around it. Torment contracted every muscle in Anakin's body, and his lightsaber went clattering down the landing ramp. Vua Rapuung, a blur of motion, fell from a similar wound in the leg. His face flopped next to Anakin's, eyes fluttering open and shut, a confused expression on his face. His lips were wet with blood.

"*Jeedai . . . ,*" he croaked, but his words drowned in a fit of hacking.

Anakin's pain lessened, but he found he could move little more than his eyes. He could see Mezhan Kwaad held something in her other hand that resembled some sort of nut.

"This is huun," Mezhan Kwaad shouted to the crowd. "It releases a nerve toxin sufficient to kill each and every one of you. I am immune to its effects. Your deaths will be useless; they will not serve the Yuuzhan Vong. Commander Vootuh and these others are the real traitors. I am Mezhan Kwaad, and I answer only to Supreme Overlord Shimrra. When he hears of these incidents, he will set things right. In the meantime, I will take this ship, to better defend myself. I do not wish to harm my fellow Yuuzhan Vong. I will do so only if I must."

The crowd, led by Hul Rapuung, had started up the ramp. Now they stopped.

Mezhan Kwaad turned to her assistant. "Nen Yim. Drag those two on board." She motioned toward Anakin and the fading Vua Rapuung.

The younger shaper hesitated, then started toward Anakin. She stopped when she saw Anakin's lightsaber floating up from behind him.

Mezhan Kwaad saw it, too. She sent a jolt of pain coursing through Anakin's body that scrambled his thoughts into random impulses.

But the lightsaber continued on. Mezhan Kwaad redoubled her torture of Anakin.

Tahiri plucked the blade from the air and ignited it with a *snap-hiss*. Mezhan Kwaad's expression froze halfway between puzzlement and the sudden, fatal understanding that it hadn't been Anakin levitating the weapon at all.

Then Tahiri decapitated her.

Tahiri stood for a moment, looking at what she had done, and smiled. Like heat lightning, Anakin's vision struck back into him, the older Tahiri, the dark Force around her, her pitiless, glacial laughter.

"Tahiri!" he managed.

She looked at him, then, and took a hesitant step toward him, then another. She let the point of the blade drop so it was almost stroking his cheek.

"My friend," she said, her voice low and weird. "My best friend. You left me." Her eyes were wrong. They were the same color they had always been, but they had once been warm, full of laughter. Now they were chlorine ice.

"I've been trying to find you," Anakin said. "This whole time . . ."

"You aren't real," Tahiri said. "None of this is. You are a lie."

He held her gaze and saw the bleakness there, the confusion. He could sense her turmoil. "It's not a lie, Tahiri. You are my best friend. I love you."

The blade stroked off a lock of his hair, but he didn't flinch.

"I love you," he repeated, the seeds of his vision beginning to take root.

Tahiri closed her eyes, and when she opened them again, they became the green eyes he knew—or almost. "Anakin? Are you really—?" She looked around, as if noticing the crowd for the first time. "Well, this doesn't look good," she observed.

Anakin saw what she meant. With Mezhan Kwaad down, the warriors in the crowd had come to the forefront. Armed to the teeth, they stood watching the strange spectacle only meters away.

They wouldn't just watch for long.

"We have to get out of here," Anakin said.

"And this is your plan?" Tahiri asked, in something like her old voice.

"Hey, I'm doing my best. I'll hold 'em off and you run into the ship."

"No. I don't care about dying, Anakin. Not after what they did to me. Let's just take as many of them with us as we can." She lifted the lightsaber. Her eyes were cooling again.

"Can I have that back?" Anakin asked softly.

She looked as if she would say no, but then shrugged and handed it to him. "Sure. It's your blade. I lost mine."

Anakin took the weapon, stood shakily, and faced the gathered warriors.

CHAPTER THIRTY-ONE

Hul Rapuung raised his amphistaff to guard. "*Jeedai*, you have proven yourself a great warrior. It will be my honor to kill you."

"No," a voice from behind Anakin grated.

Impossibly, Vua Rapuung rose to his feet. He took an amphistaff from one of the dead guards. "No. While I live, none of you shall fight the *Jeedai*."

"Vua Rapuung," his brother said, "we all heard what Mezhan Kwaad said. You are Shamed no longer."

"I was never Shamed. But now you *know* it is a warrior you face."

"Vua Rapuung, no," Anakin said. "This is over for you."

Rapuung turned to him. "I will die soon," he said. "I am able to give you only a small chance. Take it. Now." He turned back to the crowd.

"A salute to the *Jeedai*!" he shouted. "A salute of blood!"

With that he leapt at the front rank of warriors, amphistaff spinning. His first blow struck his brother, knocking him to the ground unconscious, but still alive. The others he attacked with much more lethal precision.

"Anakin?" Tahiri asked.

"Into the ship," he shouted. If he could get her safe, maybe he could come back for Rapuung.

No. His first duty was to Tahiri. If he tried to help Rapuung, they would all die.

"Can you fly it?" Tahiri asked.

"We'll worry about that once we figure out how to get the boarding ramp up."

They ducked inside the hatch and started searching frantically for some sort of control.

"What are we looking for?" Tahiri asked.

"A knob, a smooth place—a cluster of nerves. I don't know."

"I don't see anything like that! This is hopeless!" Tahiri said.

Anakin ran his hands over the spongy interior of the ship. Tahiri was right. If they couldn't even get the ramp up, what chance did he have of flying the stupid thing?

Next to none, probably, but he had to try. He couldn't have come this far just to fail.

He saw Vua Rapuung die. Already surrounded by a pile of corpses, his feet were trapped, forcing him to fight without footwork. An amphistaff struck Rapuung a downward blow in the neck and came out the small of his back. He dropped his own amphistaff down like a blaster bolt and crushed the skull of the one who had wounded him before collapsing. Then the other warriors were on him, amphistaffs slashing, surging past him up the ramp.

"Sithspawn," Anakin snarled, planting himself in the doorway, lightsaber blazing, determined to go out at least as well as Rapuung had.

"Oh!" Tahiri exclaimed. "*Tsii dau poonsi.*"

The tizowyrm translated it as *the mouth, cause to close*.

The ramp sucked in, out from under the feet of the charging warriors, and the hatch shut.

"You have to know how to talk to it, I guess," Tahiri said. She'd tried to say it lightly, but it was almost a parody of her old self. She knew it, too. Tears brimmed in her eyes. "They put things in my head, Anakin. I don't know what's real anymore."

He reached for her shoulder. "I'm real. And I'm going to get you out of this. Believe me."

She folded into him, suddenly, and his arms went around her without him even telling them to. She felt warm, and small, and good against him.

Then his wounded leg refused to support him any longer.

They cut part of Tahiri's garment to make a tourniquet. The living fabric worked even better than anticipated, because after the shock of being severed, it contracted, perhaps dying. Anakin wished he had some of Rapuung's healing swatches. Maybe they could find some on the ship.

They found the controls just as the craft rocked to a tremendous blast.

"Boy, that didn't take long," Anakin said. "I wonder why they didn't just open the hatch."

"I sealed it," Tahiri said "It won't listen to anyone outside."

"How do you know?"

"I just do. I mean, I'm sure they have *someone* who can open it, but not before we get off the ground."

"Assuming we can get off the ground," Anakin said, looking at the controls and fighting a feeling of helplessness. He recognized a villip and an acceleration couch, and that was all. A wide array of not-quite-geometrical shapes extruded from the "console," along with a variety of patches of differing color and texture. Nothing about any of them spoke to him. There seemed to be no writing or numerals either, no gauges or readouts. The walls of the room were opaque, as well. He couldn't even see what the Yuuzhan Vong outside were doing, though it was obvious they had dragged up some sort of big gun or explosives.

The ship rocked again, and several of the patches emitted a dull phosphorescence, which probably indicated damage to something-or-other.

"Okay," Anakin said. "Maybe I *can't* fly anything."

Tahiri lifted a sort of loose bag from the acceleration couch. A thin creeper attached it to the console.

"Put this on your head," she suggested.

"That's right!" Anakin said, remembering. "Uncle Luke tried one of those on. It's some sort of direct brain interface." He looked at the thing dubiously, then tried it on. Immediately he heard a distant voice, murmuring something he couldn't understand.

"The tyzowyrm isn't translating," he said. "I guess it's being bypassed by the hood."

He tried a few mental commands, with no result.

"This could be bad," he muttered. "It must be like the lambent. Without attunement, our brains won't interface directly with Vong technology."

"Yuuzhan Vong," Tahiri corrected absently.

"Right. Maybe it's just the language barrier. Maybe . . . Tahiri, you try it."

"Me? I'm no pilot."

"I know. Try it anyway."

Tahiri shrugged and placed the sack over her head.

It squirmed and shrank to fit.

"Oh!" she said. "Wait."

The walls became transparent as another concussion set the ship quivering. Anakin could now see what was causing this; another ship, also grounded, was firing on them with one of its plasma weapons. The Yuuzhan Vong had cleared out a safe lane for the shots. Anakin reflected that they probably hoped to break through the hull— skin?—without seriously damaging the ship.

"Okay," Tahiri murmured, her fingers caressing the various nerve nodes. "Let's see what—yow!"

The ship jumped off the ground like a fleek eel from a hot pan. Anakin gasped and then whooped, slapping Tahiri on the back.

"We'll do this yet!" he shouted. "Let's burn out of here."

"Which way?"

"Any way! Just go!"

"You're the captain," she said. The damutek suddenly blurred away beneath them.

"Not bad," Anakin said. "Now, if you can figure out how the weapons work—"

Tahiri shrieked suddenly, clawing off the headgear.

"What's wrong?" Anakin asked.

"It's in my head! Telling me to turn back! In another second it would have had me!"

"This isn't good," Anakin said, watching the ground rush up. It seemed to him he had seen altogether too much of that lately. Gravity was highly overrated.

By the time they found the hatch and crawled out, Anakin could hear the drone of another Yuuzhan Vong ship approaching.

"Tahiri," he said, "run for it. I'll just slow you down with this leg."

"No," Tahiri said simply.

"Please. I came all this way to rescue you. It can't have been for nothing."

Tahiri brushed his cheek with her hand. "It wasn't for nothing," she said.

"You know what I mean."

"I know we used to be in everything together. I know if this is the end, there's nobody I would rather be standing with. I know that we can still make them sorry they ever tried to mess with the two of us." She took his hand.

Anakin gripped it back. "Okay," he conceded. "Together."

It didn't take the ship long to find them; they hadn't made it more than a kilometer beyond the river. This was no speeder analog, either, but something more corvette-sized.

Tahiri touched Anakin in the Force, tentatively, and for the first time he really felt what they had done to her—the pain and confusion, the sickening nightmare sense of unreality. He poured his sympathy and strength back into her, and the bond strengthened. And as she gripped his fingers tighter, as he finally surrendered the last of his barriers against her—against *them*—the Force blew through him like a hurricane.

Tahiri laughed. It was not a child's laugh.

Together you are stronger than the sum of your parts, Ikrit had said.

Together.

They wrenched a thousand-year-old Massassi tree out of the ground and launched it straight up. By the time it struck the Yuuzhan Vong ship it was traveling as fast as a speeder. It smacked into the dovin basal and splintered, twisting the ship half-around. Another tree jerked out of the ground, and another. The ship listed, firing gobs of molten plasma into the trees, not understanding exactly what was happening. One of the trees rammed into the cannon structure, and flame burst out all along one side of the ship.

In theory, a Jedi could use the Force effortlessly, without tiring. In practice, it seldom went that way.

Anakin and Tahiri had gone beyond their limits, and now their strength was ebbing.

The ship wobbled and molten fire dripped from its ruined weapon, but it was still there, and there were plenty more where it came from.

Still, Anakin gripped Tahiri's hand. "Together," he said.

The air above them shrieked and strobed, and sharp lines of red light carved into the Yuuzhan Vong ship as if it were a root vegetable. A too-bright-to-watch ball of flame followed close after, striking the craft in its already bleeding wound, and then the Yuuzhan Vong ship was a corpse hurtling to the ground. Anakin looked up, mouth open.

Another ship was descending, a ship made of metal and ceramic, not living coral.

It was Remis Vehn's battered transport, and it was the most beautiful thing Anakin had ever seen.

It dropped on repulsorlifts, and the hatch swung open.

Qorl stuck his head out. "What are you waiting for?" the old man shouted. "Come aboard."

CHAPTER THIRTY-TWO

Talon Karrde followed the pinpoint on the long-range scanner with a raptor gaze.

Still, he was fully aware when Kam Solusar came silently up behind him.

"What is it?" the Jedi asked.

"Long-range sensors tell us some sort of transport just broke the atmosphere of Yavin Four," Karrde told him.

"Only moments ago, I felt an incredible surge in the Force," Solusar said. "I'm sure Anakin was involved, and I think Tahiri, as well."

"Can you feel them now? Are they on that transport?"

"I think they must be," Solusar replied.

Karrde shook his head. "Not good enough. If I commit that deeply into Yuuzhan Vong territory, there is every chance not a single ship in my fleet will come back out. I need to *know*. What if it's just a Peace Brigader or two who've been hiding on the far side of Yavin?"

"It's Anakin," Solusar replied.

Karrde let his shoulders relax. "Well. That's better. As long as you *sound* certain," he said. "Fine."

He turned to his crew. "This looks like what we've been waiting for, people. Our mission has changed. Up until now we've just been surviving, picking off strays. From what I gather, the Yuuzhan Vong have been using us for target practice and to thin the stupid from their gene pool.

"They'll behave differently when we push to intercept the ship out there. They'll probably hit us with everything they've got, and we'll be in a position to get hit. We can forget backup from the New Republic; we're on our own. If there are any doubts about this course of action, I need to hear them now."

Silence, as he swept his gaze around the bridge and the screens depicting the captains of his other ships.

"When have we ever not been with you, Captain?" Shada asked from the *Idiot's Array*.

A chorus of cheers punctuated Shada's remark.

Karrde's chest tightened with pride. "All right, people," he said. "Let's go to work."

A series of bleeps and whistles greeted Anakin as he came aboard the transport.

"Hey, Fiver," he said. "I'm glad to see you, too."

"Get back to work, you lazy little droid," Vehn snapped over his shoulder from the pilot's seat. "And you, hotshot, pick a cannon. Let's see if we can shake this crud."

"I'd feel better at the controls," Anakin said, watching Yavin 4 dwindle to starboard.

"After what you did to her last time?" Vehn said. "No, thanks. No vapin' thanks at all."

"Your ship," Anakin said.

"Ramming right it is."

Anakin looked over the pilot's shoulder at the screen. "Nice lead," he remarked.

"Yeah. Those Vong ships take longer to pull out of an atmosphere. Out here they're gaining, though."

"What's the plan?"

"Fly real fast until we get away."

"That's it?"

"Hey, I'm improvising. You gonna complain about me saving your butt?"

"No," Anakin said, "I was thinking about thanking you. Now I'm not so sure."

"Stop it. You'll make me cry. If you have a plan, let me hear it."

Anakin looked at the starfield. He was weak, very weak, but he thought he felt something.

"Give me long-range sensors," Anakin said.

"Sorry, no can do. We were working on those when the creepy twins back there told me they 'felt' you needed help. We cut the repairs short and hot-jetted it."

"Sannah, Valin," Anakin said, gesturing them forward. "Concentrate. Do you feel something out there?"

"Sure," Valin said, after a minute. "Kam Solusar is out there, somewhere."

"Yes," Sannah said. "I feel him, too."

"I'm too weak to be sure, and so is Tahiri. Tell Vehn where."

Valin studied the space around him for a moment, then pointed at around ninety degrees to starboard. "There."

" 'There'?" Vehn asked. "That's supposed to be a direction?"

"Do we have hyperdrive?" Anakin asked.

"No."

"Then I suggest you set course where Valin tells you. Otherwise, we're going to end up as star food."

"It's better than being captured again," Tahiri said.

"Well, fine," Vehn said. "The little creeps have been right so far, today."

Anakin started to take the copilot's seat, but Vehn placed his hand in it. "That's Qorl's," he said.

"I'll give it up," Qorl said. "Every Solo I've ever known was a better pilot than me."

"Don't be silly," Anakin said. "Even if that were true, you're in better shape than I am to fly. Sorry to presume. You two seem to make a good team."

The two men glanced at each other.

"Qorl gave me a certain . . . perspective on things," Vehn said.

"With my boot, more often than not," the old man said. But he was smiling, too.

"Well," Anakin said awkwardly. "Thank you both. You came through for Tahiri and me when you could have just run."

"Are you kidding? And have the little creeps back there slag my brain?" Vehn said.

"Anyway," Qorl reminded them, "we're not out of this yet. Twice I've been shot down on Yavin Four. My luck's not so good when it comes to getting out of this system."

"True," Anakin said, "but we're a lot nearer than we were."

"Speaking of which, we're gonna have words with some Vong in about half an hour," Vehn said.

"They're catching up that fast?"

"No. These are already out here."

"I'll take the turret gun," Anakin said.

"Right. Give 'em an argument at least," Vehn said.

"The transport has been engaged by Yuuzhan Vong, sir," H'sishi reported. "They've taken a few hits, but they're still coming, right for us."

"How soon?" Karrde asked.

"If we plot a straight course, less than twenty minutes. But if we do that, we'll be perfect targets for the blockade that's forming up down there."

"Yes, but if we go around, we'll never reach them before that destroyer analog. Dankin, plot it straight in, and have the *Idiot's Array*, the *Demise*, and the *Etherway* escort us."

"Sir, they're hardly our best-armed ships."

"But they're the only ones who can keep up with us, aren't they? Keep her steady."

"Very good, sir. We'll be in their range in ten minutes. Unless they have something we don't know about, which seems to be almost a given with the Vong."

* * *

Anakin watched the third coralskipper spin off to port. He hadn't destroyed it—his first two shots had been sucked in by the gravitic anomalies its dovin basal projected and the third had only tapped it—but the smaller craft didn't have the speed to stay with the transport. They were more than nuisances, but not much more at this point.

It was the destroyer analog coming in from above starboard that bothered him, that and the fact that they couldn't see much beyond it. For all they knew, there could be an entire fleet between him and Talon Karrde. If Karrde was there at all. He tried once again to reach out for Kam Solusar's familiar presence and thought, briefly, that he had found it. But Kam might be light-years in that direction—or it might be wishful thinking. He couldn't be sure.

What *was* sure was that very soon the destroyer was going to catch them. He hoped Vehn had a few tricks up his sleeve.

"Direct hit on the *Idiot's Array*, sir," H'sishi reported.

"Shada, are you there?" Karrde asked, over the comm.

"Still here, boss. They tickled us, but we can still keep up."

"One more hit like that and you're ions," Karrde disagreed. "Peel off. You've done enough."

"Sorry, boss. Can't hear you. Something wrong with my comm unit. Hang tight, we'll get you there."

The power on the *Wild Karrde* suddenly dimmed and reasserted itself, and a distant vibration shivered the hull. The two ships still running escort weren't keeping everything off of them; the *Demise* had flamed out in the first exchange, probably with all hands.

Good people. He would mourn them later, when he had time.

He saw the *Idiot's Array* take her final hit, right

through the engines. Plumes of plasma streamed from her, and atomic devils danced in the ruined aft section.

"Get out of there, Shada!" he shouted into the comm. No answer came.

"The *Idiot's Array* is still keeping pace with that destroyer, sir," H'sishi reported. "I don't understand it. Her engines are gone, and their reactor is building to critical."

Karrde blinked. "Shada!" he snarled. Then he snapped at Dankin. "Alter course two degrees to starboard and brace."

"What's she doing, sir?"

"She's got a tractor lock on them. She must have diverted all of her power to that. Everything."

An instant later the *Idiot's Array* vanished in a sphere of pure white light, taking most of the Yuuzhan Vong destroyer with it.

"Shada," Karrde murmured again, feeling very tired. He'd lost more friends than enemies through the years. He'd faced death himself enough times that he had no illusions; one day the game would go against him and he would die. But somehow, of all the people he knew, he'd imagined that Shada would outlive him.

"One destroyer down," he gritted, "and one to go."

"We've just lost the *Etherway*, sir," H'sishi said.

"Destroyed?"

"No. Her power grid is down."

"Then it's just us."

"Yes."

"Against all that."

"Unless you want to wait for everyone else, sir, I—sir, behind us!"

Karrde saw the ship appear on the screen; sheer conditioning kept his heart from jumping up into his throat.

The ship that had appeared, almost on top of them, was an Imperial Star Destroyer.

A *red* Imperial Star Destroyer.

"Message, sir," Dankin said.

"Put it on."

A bearded human face appeared. "Well, Karrde," he growled. "I suppose I'll be pulling you out of this mess, as well. I hope you have something appropriate to compensate me with."

"Booster Terrik!"

"None other."

"I'm sure I can dig something out of my warehouses."

"Never mind that. Where's my grandson?"

"We think he's on the transport that big Yuuzhan Vong ship's about to swallow."

"That's all I wanted to know. See you on the other side, Karrde."

"The other side of what?"

"The nebula I'm about to make."

The screen went dark.

"All right, everyone," Karrde said. "We've got a new game here. Let's play it well."

Anakin kept the turbolaser pumping steadily, causing plumes of molten yorik coral to spew from the destroyer analog. It didn't seem to notice, even at extreme close range, which was where they were—a few tens of meters from its surface.

He had to admit Vehn wasn't doing a bad job of flying—dropping in close to avoid the big guns, playing an elaborate spiral dance around the ship's axis, dodging out from the gravitic embrace of the dovin basal. If they cleared the big ship by much, their luck would change. One good hit by one of those big plasma cannons would be the end of them.

"Heads up, back there," Vehn's voice crackled. "They're launching coralskippers."

Anakin saw. The Yuuzhan Vong didn't localize their fighters in bays, but kept them attached all over the outside of the ship. Anakin had nailed a few of the inactive ones already. Now they were detaching in swarms.

"You'll have to keep them off, Solo," Vehn said, his voice tinged with desperation. "If I try to outrun 'em, we'll be sitting pretty for the destroyer."

"Understood," Anakin replied. He didn't have time to talk after that; everything in him focused on the weaving, organic forms of the enemy. He couldn't begin to count them.

They came, and he shot them. He fell into a one-two-three rhythm—first shot to draw out a gravitic anomaly, second shot just outside its event horizon. It would move to intercept, and he would fire even wider on the other side. Sometimes it managed to swallow all three shots, but often the coherent light blazed just far enough outside the singularity to merely bend around it. Once he got the timing right, he could land that crooked third shot where he wanted it.

But he couldn't shoot them all. The transport bucked and complained as molten plasma did its damage. Ignoring the tremors, Anakin fought on in grim silence.

Vehn, too, kept his silence—the occasional curse aside. They were all beyond talking now.

An enemy shot got through Anakin's barrage, glancing from the turret cockpit, leaving a molten streak on the transparisteel. Anakin traced after the offender, but it was gone. He whirled back to take one of three crisscrossing his field of vision and hit it solidly. It spun, then straightened.

Toward him. With quiet calm Anakin fired at it, watching it come closer. A singularity gulped his first shot, and the second bent wide. The third beam hit dead center. The skip flared out of existence, but the debris came on, smacking into the cockpit in a hundred meteoric shards.

Hairline fractures spidered everywhere.

One more hit, and I'm breathing vacuum, Anakin thought.

But he certainly couldn't leave the turret. He checked to make certain the lock behind him was sealed, closed off from the rest of the ship. There was no need to take everyone with him.

He took out two more skips, but then three dropped into a wedge headed straight for him. He took a deep, calming breath and began firing, but he knew he wasn't going to get them all.

In fact, he had fired only two shots before the damaged laser overheated and went into temporary shutdown. Anakin watched impassively as the skips approached. He reached out in the Force, hoping to find debris to throw at them.

He wondered what it was going to feel like when his blood started boiling.

He felt them in the Force at the same time the coral-skippers vanished in a searing white haze, and two X-wings whipped around the expanding cloud of gas and molten coral. His comm crackled.

"Need a hand, little brother?"

"Jaina!"

"This is some mess you've gotten us into, Anakin," a masculine voice replied.

"Jacen! Where . . . how . . ."

"Explanations later," Jaina said. "Who's flying that crate?"

"That's me," Vehn cut in.

"Get out of there, fast," Jaina said. "We'll keep these pups off you. Corran Horn's out here, too. I almost pity the Vong."

"But if I clear . . ."

"Believe me," Jaina said, "you'll *want* to be clear."

Anakin breathed a sigh of relief as the turbolaser came back on-line. "I've got the back door," he told his siblings. "You just clear a path. Vehn, better do what they want."

"Whatever you say," Vehn said sarcastically. And then he just gasped. Anakin didn't see why until they were on the other side of the *Errant Venture*. By that time, the Yuuzhan Vong ship was blazing like a newborn star.

Anakin stared through the transparisteel and grinned wide enough to swallow a crescent moon.

Karrde wasn't grinning, a standard day later, when the Yuuzhan Vong ships finally packed it in and jumped to hyperspace. He was watching the drifting ruins of ships, Yuuzhan Vong and otherwise, and grimly tallying his losses.

Yes, he was getting too old for this nonsense.

"Captain. Message for you, sir," H'sishi said.

He considered ignoring it, but at this point—so soon after the battle—it could be something critical.

"Put it on, H'sishi," he said.

A few seconds later a lean, middle-aged face appeared.

"Corran Horn," Karrde said. "It's good to see you. I assume you were on your father-in-law's Star Destroyer?"

"When Jacen and Jaina found us, yes. I was one of the X-wings out there. I . . . ." His face contorted very briefly, then returned to a neutral expression. "Karrde, I want to thank you for saving my son and the other children. I know what it cost you."

No, you don't, Karrde thought. "You're welcome," he told Horn. "When I make promises, I do my best to keep them."

"We're alike in that," Horn replied. "And I also pay my debts. I owe you a big one."

Karrde received the sentiment with a nod of his head. "I'm glad your son is well. Is there anything else I can do for you? I'm sorry to be short, but I'm not much in the mood for conversation right now."

"I'll let you go in a second. This doesn't even come close to squaring us up, but I do have something for you."

"What's that?"

"Someone, I should say." Horn moved aside and was replaced by Shada D'ukal's wry features.

"Shada!"

"Come on, Karrde," Shada said. "You didn't think I was stupid enough to *stay* on a flaming ship, did you? Once I got the lock, we went for the escape pods. Horn ran across us in his X-wing, doing a slow spiral toward the gas giant." She squinted at the screen. "Hey, boss, what's wrong with your eye?"

"The air unit has been blowing dust in from somewhere," Karrde said, blinking away the suspicious moisture. "Get your tail back over here, so we can discuss how long it will take you to pay me back for the *Idiot's Array*."

Shada rolled her eyes. "See you soon, boss."

Then, despite his losses, Talon Karrde did allow himself a small, quiet smile. Why not? They'd won.

EPILOGUE

"We never thought we'd find Booster," Jaina confessed, around a mouthful of food. "I was ready to hijack the *Jade Shadow* and fly straight to Yavin. When Booster doesn't want to be found, he can really disappear."

"What was he doing?" Anakin asked.

"Running weapons to the Hutt underground, actually," Jaina replied. "I just asked myself where Booster would go if he wanted to help the war effort and still turn a profit without feeling bad about it."

"You're kidding."

"It didn't hurt that Corran was with him," Jacen said. "We got hints of him in the Force."

"Still."

"Jacen's being modest," Jaina said. "He spent a lot of time in deep meditation, *trying* to find Corran. It was no accident."

"That's pretty impressive," Anakin allowed.

"Thank you, Anakin," Jacen said, as if surprised. His brow wrinkled in such a way that made him look briefly very much like their father. "Are you okay, Anakin?"

Anakin nodded. "Yes, actually. I mean, my leg still hurts, even with the bacta patch, but otherwise, I think I'm fine. In fact, better than fine."

"What do you mean?" Jacen asked, perhaps a little suspiciously.

Anakin chewed thoughtfully for a moment. "Up until

now," he said, "I had no way to think of the Yuuzhan Vong except as enemies."

"They *are* enemies," Jaina said.

"Yes," Anakin replied. "So was the Empire. But Palpatine aside, it must have been possible for Mom and Dad and Uncle Luke to at least conceive of the people they were fighting as possible friends. In fact, that's how Uncle Luke destroyed the Emperor, right? He was able to imagine Darth Vader as his father, as a friend. The Yuuzhan Vong—well, to be frank, I didn't even *want* to conceive of them that way."

"They don't make it easy," Jaina said. "Look what happened to Elegos when he tried to understand them."

"So you think you succeeded where Elegos failed?" Jacen asked.

"Do I understand them? No, not completely. But I have a deeper understanding than I did. I can think of them as people now, and that makes a difference."

Jacen nodded. "You're right, of course. Does that mean you've decided not to fight them anymore? Are you going to work for peace?"

Anakin blinked. "Are you kidding? We *have* to fight them, Jacen. *I* have to fight them. I just know more about how to do it now."

Jacen's frown was fully developed now. "Are you sure that's the right lesson to take away from all this?" he asked.

"No offense, Jacen, but I think I'll leave off worrying about what lesson I *might* have learned if I had been someone else. Because frankly, if I had been someone else, I don't think I would have survived to learn *any* lesson."

"Tell Booster we're going to have to evacuate the ship," Jaina said. "The way Anakin's head is expanding, it'll split through the hull in no time."

"Believe it or not," Anakin replied, "I don't say what I just said with pride. I'm just stating a fact."

"Pride is pretty sneaky," Jacen warned. "It disguises it-self pretty well. I hope you'll have a long talk with Uncle Luke at some point. Unless you don't think even *he* has anything to teach you."

"Don't put words in my mouth, Jacen," Anakin said.

"And don't you forget who pulled your butt out of the fire there at the end," Jaina replied.

Anakin let a grin creep across his face. "But that's what I meant, don't you see? When I said that no one but me could have survived what I did. Because no one else in the galaxy has you two for his brother and sister."

He picked up his tray, trying not to laugh at their gaping mouths.

"Now, if you'll excuse me," he said, "I have someone I need to go see."

Anakin found Tahiri's stateroom door open a crack. Through it he saw her lying on her bed, bare feet propped up on the wall. Her gaze was fastened on the transpari-steel window and the distant spray of the core beyond.

Anakin rapped the door frame. "Hi," he said.

"Hi. Come in if you want."

"Okay." He took a seat on the edge of the bed.

"You didn't show up for dinner," he said. "I thought I would bring you some." He placed a food container on the bed. "Corran made it. Seems he's been doing a lot of cooking these days."

"Thanks," Tahiri said. She turned her head and for the first time met his gaze.

"What happened to it?" she asked. "The shaper base?"

"You sure you want to hear about it? Every time someone brings up the subject—"

"I wasn't ready to talk about it then. Now I am."

"Okay. Well, Booster pretty much slagged it. Karrde and his people evacuated the slaves. We're going to drop them off someplace soon. Of course, the Yuuzhan Vong can come back, I guess, since we left the system pretty much without defenses, but there's nothing we can do about that."

"No," Tahiri said. "There isn't. I guess that's the end of the academy.

"Of course it isn't. The academy was never a *place*. It's a thing, an idea. We're just taking it on jets. Booster's going to let the academy kids stay on the *Errant Venture*. He'll make random jumps around the galaxy until it's safe to settle the kids down someplace."

"Safe?" Tahiri hissed. "How can it ever be *safe*? How can *anything* ever be—" Her words seemed to clot up in her throat, and she turned back to the view of space.

"Tahiri, I know how you feel," Anakin said.

She closed her eyes, and two small tears squeezed from the corners. "If anyone does, I guess you do," she said after a moment.

"What they did to you was horrible, I know, and—"

"What they did to *me*? Anakin, I cut Mezhan Kwaad's *head* off."

"You had to."

"I wanted to. I liked it. I *loved* it."

"She tortured you. She tried to destroy everything you are. You can't be blamed for a moment of anger."

"I think she *did* destroy everything I am," Tahiri said. "When I killed her, it was the end of *me*."

"No," Anakin said, "that's not true. And I should know, shouldn't I? The best of you is still there, Tahiri." He reached his hand out. It hung there in space for a long time before she reached back, taking it without looking.

"It was all my fault," she said. "Master Ikrit died because of me. Karrde's people died because of me."

"Now *this* I'm pretty good at," Anakin said. "Blaming myself for things. I can really teach you to do that right. In fact, if we think really hard about it, I bet we can find some way to blame you for the Yuuzhan Vong finding this galaxy in the first place." He cocked his head. "No—I think *I* want the blame for that. We can blame Palpatine on you, though. How's that?"

Tahiri frowned at him. "When did you start talking so much?" she asked.

"I don't know. When did you start coughing up one word at a time as if three or four were going to break your mouth?"

The corners of her lips twitched up, not quite forming a smile. "Just shut up, will you? I liked you better the other way."

"Me, too."

They watched the stars in silence for a while.

"Where will you go now?" Tahiri asked, when the silence was too thin. "Back out to fight the Yuuzhan Vong?"

"Eventually."

"I want to go with you."

"That's why I said *eventually*. I'm staying on here for a while. Until you've healed. Until *I've* healed. Then if you still want to go, we go. Together."

She didn't say anything, but for the first time since they'd left Yavin, he felt something like hope in her.

"Adept Nen Yim. Step forth."

Nen Yim genuflected and then stood before the warmaster, Tsavong Lah.

"First I want your account of the fall of the shaper compound. After that I have other questions."

"Yes, Warmaster. At your command."

"My command is given. Speak."

"Of the space battle I know nothing, Warmaster. Many of our ships died on the ground or struggling through the atmosphere. Then the damuteks were attacked from above, and damaged beyond healing."

"So much is obvious. Go on."

"Then the bombardment ceased, and the infidels commenced landing. We did not understand why, at first. A more thorough bombardment would have killed us all with no risk to the infidels. As it was, some of them were slain by our surviving warriors."

"You do not know these infidels as well as you might, Shaper. Their attachment to their own kind leads them into pointless maneuvers."

"Agreed, Warmaster. In retrospect, it is clear that their intent was to recover the slaves."

"And where were you during this?"

"I hid among the Shamed Ones, Warmaster. I thought they would take true castes captive."

"A cowardly thing to do, Shaper."

"I beg your indulgence, Warmaster, but I had more than selfish reasons for doing so."

"Explain them. Be brief."

"My master, Mezhan Kwaad, was slain by the *Jeedai* we were shaping."

"You did not shape the *Jeedai* well, I think."

"On the contrary, Warmaster, given a few more cycles, she would have been ours. If not for the interference of the other *Jeedai*."

"Yes," the warmaster snarled. "The other. Solo. Another Solo." He paced violently away from her, then turned back. "Master Yal Phaath disagrees with you, Adept. He claims that your master conspired in heresy, and that any results you obtained were stained by ungodliness."

"Master Yal Phaath is a respected shaper. So was Mezhan Kwaad. She was never able to answer these charges, and I may not speak for her. But I tell you this, Warmaster. What we learned from the *Jeedai* was valuable. It has worth to the Yuuzhan Vong. The records in the damutek were destroyed, and my master is dead. Only I remain to remember. That is why I secreted myself among the Shamed Ones, to protect that information."

"You did so for no reason. The infidels took no captives."

"No, Warmaster. But I could not know that at the time."

"Agreed. They are a strange breed. They keep no slaves and make no sacrifices. They do not appreciate captives. They do not make war to obtain them. They consider them burdens or currency for the return of their own worthless kind. An ugly and godless motley of species."

"If I may ask your opinion, Warmaster—why then did they not slay us once they had what they wanted? Corpses are no burden."

"They are weak. They do not understand life and death." He waved the whole issue aside with the back of his hand, then returned his stare to Nen Yim.

"This was badly bungled by shapers and warriors alike," he said. "If Tsaak Vootuh were not dead, I would kill him myself. And I should have you sacrificed."

"If death is my lot, Warmaster, if that is what the gods desire, I embrace it. But I repeat—what we learned of the *Jeedai* here ought not to perish with me. Give me at least a chance to record what I know in a worldship qahsa."

The warmaster's cruel eyes did not waver. "You will have that chance. It has been given you. Do not squander it as your master did here."

"And if more *Jeedai* are captured? Will our work shaping them resume?"

"Your domain has failed. They will not be given a second chance with the *Jeedai*. Domain Phaath will continue the work on the *Jeedai* problem."

Then it will never be solved, Nen Yim thought to herself. She did not dare say this to the warmaster, of course. "And Domain Kwaad?" she asked instead.

"The worldships are failing. They must be maintained."

Nen Yim nodded solemnly, but in her belly she was sick. Back to the worldships, to closed skies and rotting maw luur, to masters so mired in the old ways they would let the Yuuzhan Vong perish rather than contemplate change.

So be it. But in her heart, Nen Yim still considered Mezhan Kwaad her master. Nen Yim would continue the work they had begun, somehow. It was too important. And if Nen Yim must die for this, she must. The glorious heresy would live on.

"I submit to your will, Warmaster," Nen Yim lied.

"One other thing before you go," Tsavong Lah said. "You spent some time among the Shamed Ones before the reoccupation force arrived. Have you heard of a new heresy amongst them, one concerning the *Jeedai*?"

"I have, Warmaster."

"Explain it to me."

"There is a certain admiration for them, Warmaster. Many feel that Vua Rapuung was redeemed from Shamed status by the *Jeedai* Solo. Many feel their own redemption lies not in prayer to Yun-Shuno, but in the *Jeedai*."

"Can you name any who espouse this heresy?"

"A few, Warmaster."

"Name them. This heresy will die on this moon. If every Shamed One here must perish in glorious sacrifice, it will end here."

Nen Yim nodded affirmation, but in her bones she knew the truth.

Repression was the favored food of heresy.